The Cartel 5:
La Bella Mafia

The Cartel 5:
La Bella Mafia

Ashley & JaQuavis

www.urbanbooks.net

Urban Books, LLC
300 Farmingdale Road, NY-Route 109
Farmingdale, NY 11735

The Cartel 5: La Bella Mafia

ISBN 13: 978-1-62286-736-3
ISBN 10: 1-62286-736-X

First Mass Market Printing January 2017
First Trade Paperback Printing December 2014
Printed in the United States of America

10 9 8 7 6

Distributed by Kensington Publishing Corp.
Submit orders to:
Customer Service
400 Hahn Road
Westminster, MD 21157-4627
Phone: 1-800-733-3000
Fax: 1-800-659-2436

Dedication to the Fans

Thank you to all of you who have watched us grow both individually and as a couple through our writing. You have turned two kids from Flint, MI into New York Times best selling authors. We love y'all for that and are forever grateful for your support. As you pick up this next chapter of The Cartel we hope you enjoy. It doesn't end with this book. As we move into the next phase of our careers we plan to bring you *Cartel 6*, a fresh spin-off called Zyir: *son of the Cartel*, and who knows maybe even a book called, *Ethic*, if you're lucky. You guys have held us down from the very beginning and it is because of you that we are inspired to continue this journey. We are fortunate to be able to live our dream every day. We are blessed to have literary fans like you! There is no limit to what the future holds for our readers and us. Much love.

Mr. and Mrs. Coleman

Previously in: The Cartel 4

Final Chapters
"No Guns. No Goons. Just me and you."
—Carter

Carter looked in his rearview mirror and noticed that the same two cars had been following him for blocks. At that moment, he knew that the Feds were on him. The white boys who were driving the cars that were tailing him were a dead giveaway. Carter immediately put the pedal to the metal and bent a couple corners to shake them. With his foreign car and world-class speed, there was no competition. Carter checked his rearview mirrors after a couple corners and brief stretches and just as he expected, he was in the clear. He headed toward the hospital for Zyir. It was a must that they shook out of town until things died down. The heat from the authorities was too much to bear. As Carter made his way toward the hospital, his phone began to ring. He looked down at his caller ID and noticed that the call originated from Los Angeles, California. He picked it up, only to hear another person breathing on the phone.

"Hello," he said again and still received no answer. He then knew that the call was coming from Polo. It was a discreet way of telling Carter that the Feds were about to move in on him. Carter hung up his phone and shook his head in frustration. He knew that if he stayed around, it was only a matter of time before he went down. First and foremost, he had to get his li'l man out of the city too. Zyir was his right-hand man from day one and he refused to flee the city and leave Zyir hanging out to dry.

Carter arrived at the hospital and immediately knew that he would be walking into a trap. He could spot unmarked cars from a mile away and the entrances were swarmed with them.

"Fuck!" he said as he hit his steering wheel with force and aggression. He picked up his phone and called Zyir.

"Hello," Zyir answered in a low, raspy tone.

"Listen, who is in there with you?" Carter asked, cutting straight to the point.

"Just me and Fly Boogie," Zyir said as he slowly sat up in the bed while grimacing.

"Listen closely, because we don't have a lot of time. The Feds are coming in. Do me a favor. Tell Boogie to look outside the door and see if there are any agents outside your door," Carter said as he pulled off and looked at the cop cars filing into the hospital through his rearview mirror. Zyir immediately told Fly Boogie to check and he poked his head outside of the door and came back.

"It looks clear. Just a couple of nurses," he said as he stood there wide-eyed trying to figure out what was about to go down.

"Shit looks normal," Zyir said to Carter.

"Okay good, good. That means that they are on their way to you right now. Listen, you have to get the fuck out of there, Zyir. Like right now," Carter said.

"Damn. Okay cool. Where are you at?" Zyir answered.

"Meet me at the take-off spot. You already know what it is," Carter said, not wanting to tip off anyone, just in case he had wiretaps on his phone.

"On my way," Zyir said as he began to snatch the wires off of him that were monitoring his heart rate.

"Yo, Zyir," Carter said as his tone dropped.

"What up, big homie?" Zyir replied.

"I'm not leaving without you, so make sure you get there," Carter said with all sincerity in his voice.

"I'll be there," Zyir confirmed just before he hung up the phone.

Carter headed in the direction of Monroe's condominium. He had unfinished business with his brother that needed to be handled. Carter made sure that there wasn't anyone trailing him before he turned into Monroe's place. Carter took his gun from his waist and exited the car. He threw the gun in the seat, not wanting to even have it on him when approaching Monroe. He didn't want to go that route with Monroe. Carter just had to tie up loose ends. He walked to the doorstep and knocked. He didn't know what to expect on the opposite end but he was prepared for whatever God had in store for him. As Carter waited for someone to answer, he got a bad feeling in the pit of his stomach. He took a deep breath and then exhaled trying to calm his nerves.

The sounds of locks being unclicked sounded and Carter stood strong as he waited for the face of his brother to appear. Once the door was open he realized that it wasn't a face that he was staring at, but it was the barrel of a double pump shotgun that Monroe was holding about five inches from his nose.

"I come in peace," Carter said as he put both his hands up. Carter walked toward the gun, pressing his chest against the barrel and slowly walking Monroe backward. "I don't want no smoke, bro. Just want to talk," Carter pleaded as he spoke softly, slowly, and collected. There was no hostility showing in his voice or mannerisms. He knew that he was playing Russian roulette at that point but he knew it had to be resolved.

"You come to my house after you sent ya li'l mans to get me? You must be out of your mind," Monroe said as he stopped and dug the barrel into Carter's chest even deeper.

"You're right. But if I recall right, you sent Buttons' niggas to kill me in Rio. Remember that? Look, we both have been at each other, but this shit has to stop," Carter said with no malice in his heart. Monroe was at a loss for words.

"I'm tired of the killings. I just want this shit to end. Honestly, I would prefer if you get this gun out of my chest. If you want, I'll shoot you a fair one and we can handle it like men," Carter said, referring to a one-on-one fight. "No guns, no goons. Just me and you," Carter suggested.

Monroe paused as if he was in deep contemplation and released a small smile, gladly wanting to take Carter up on his offer. Monroe slowly lowered the gun and then tossed it on his couch.

Carter stepped completely in the house and closed the door behind him. He then took off his shirt, exposing his chiseled body and ripped abs.

"I thought you would never ask, playboy," Monroe said as he snatched off his shirt and put up his hands. They were both the direct bloodline of the most fearless man who ever walked the earth: Carter Diamond. So there was no fear in either one of their hearts.

Carter also put his hands up and the men began to circle each other in the middle of Monroe's living room.

"This ass whooping has been a long time coming," Carter said as he began to inch closer to his brother. Monroe threw the first punch. Carter side-stepped to the left, just barely missing get hit by Monroe's punch. Almost simultaneously, Carter snapped a quick jab to Monroe's kidney.

"Too slow, li'l nigga," Carter said as he smiled and swiped his nose taunting him. This enraged Monroe. Monroe began to throw haymakers at Carter, trying to knock his head off. Carter caught a couple of them but the majority of them he dodged artistically. Carter saw that Monroe was getting tired and he knew it was time for him to put in work. He went after Monroe relentlessly. Left hook, right hook, jab . . . sending Monroe flying onto his back. Carter then pounced on Monroe, straddling him while wrapping both hands around his neck, trying to choke the life out of him. Monroe fought for air as Carter gripped his neck tightly. Monroe felt that Carter was much stronger than him and knew that he needed help getting Carter off of him. He reached for the lamp and grabbed it. He then smashed it against Carter's head, making the lamp shatter into pieces and temporarily got Carter off of him. Carter flew to the ground as the world began to spin. He temporarily saw stars and tried to get up, but couldn't keep his balance. Monroe on the other hand was panting on the ground trying to catch his breath. Blood leaked from Monroe's swollen lip and Carter had a huge gash on the right side of his head. It was an awkward moment of silence as both of them leaned their backs against the wall and tried to regain their composure.

"We could have been a dynasty. We . . . could . . ." Monroe tried to say in between breaths as he steadily held his throbbing neck.

"That was the plan," Carter said as he sweated profusely and sucked air trying to get his wind.

"You let that nigga Zyir take my place," Monroe admitted as he expressed his true feelings. He was envious of the place that Zyir held in his brother's life. They were close and Monroe felt as if he had missed out by being away from life for so long.

"Zyir is my nigga. He's been there with me from the start. He wasn't taking anyone place because he always had a place of his own. So this what this is all about, huh?"

"I just believe in blood over everything. I was raised in this drug game and what I learned is that anybody will cross you for the right price. But family, family doesn't have a price. Family is forever. Diamonds are forever."

"Diamonds are forever. We have to end this, Money. We have to," Carter said as he looked over at Monroe. Neither of them wanted the beef to go any further. It was as if them saying that Diamonds were forever released the tension out of the room. "I've lost everybody from this game. This game has no love for anyone. I don't want to lose the only brother I have left behind this," Carter admitted.

"I want this shit to be over too, bro. I swear to God I do. It seems like it's at a point of no return," Monroe replied.

"It's never too late, my nigga. All we have to do is let it end here," Carter said as he slowly stood up, sneering at his aching headache. He reached down his hand to Monroe and looked at his brother in the eyes. Monroe paused and took a long, hard thought about what he was about to do. He took a deep breath and reached out his hand, letting his older brother help him up. They embraced and rocked back and forth, both of their souls being cleansed in the process.

"Now we have to go. The Feds are coming," Carter said, as he went to the window and looked down over the street cautiously. "We have to go. They will be here any minute."

"What?" Monroe asked, trying to grasp what was going on.

"They're on to Estes, which means they're on to all of us. Just come on! I don't have time to explain, but I have a jet waiting to take us to Bermuda. All we have to do is make it to the airstrip. We have to go!" Carter said as he fled out of the door. Monroe followed closely behind and just like that they were gone out of the door.

Zyir looked at the dashboard and saw Fly Boogie pushing over 120 miles per hour. Zyir then looked in his rearview mirror and saw the trail of police cars and flashing lights. They were on a high-speed chase and Zyir knew that it wasn't looking good. He looked at Fly Boogie and noticed a grin on his face. He was actually enjoying the high-stakes car chase. A helicopter was hovering above them, keeping up with their every move. Zyir shook his head and had no choice but to smile. He gripped his wounded stomach and felt his phone vibrate. It was Carter.

"I'm on my way. But I have a couple friends with me," Zyir said, knowing that it didn't look good for him.

"I'm waiting for you, homie. You have to get here. I am not leaving without you, Zyir. Make a way," Carter said confidently. He heard the sirens in the background and knew that Zyir wasn't looking too good. Carter hung up the phone and took a deep breath. He and Monroe were sitting on the jet waiting to go. Carter looked at his watch and took a deep breath. "He'll be here," he assured Monroe as he looked out of the window. "Come on, Zy," he whispered to himself.

Fly Boogie jumped off the highway, pushing almost 150 miles per hour. He had created about a thirty-second lead on the cops and he had an idea. He saw a tunnel and knew that that was their only chance. With the helicopter still on their tail, Fly Boogie raced into the tunnel and stopped about halfway through it.

"Look, big homie. You go that way and I'm going to shoot out this way, taking all them Feds away from you."

"Damn, Boogie. I'm not going to let you go out like that. Fuck it. I'm rolling with you. Let's get it," Zyir said bravely as he steadily clutched his stomach and frowned.

"Naw, I got you, big homie. They want you not me. I have zero strikes and they have nothing on me. This shit going to make me a legend in the hood," Fly Boogie said as he kept a childish grin on his face. Zyir shook his head and returned the smile.

"You a crazy li'l nigga. You know that?" Zyir said as he held out his hand and gave Boogie a pound.

"And you know this!' he said playfully as he dapped up his mentor. Zyir got out of the car and began to walk the opposite way. Fly Boogie put the pedal to the metal and shot out of the tunnel like a bat out of hell. He shot out of the tunnel and the helicopter got right back on his tail. The federal agent in the helicopter called in Fly Boogie's location and a mile down the road the cops were back on him; this time it was double the amount of marked cars chasing him. Fly Boogie was about to go down like a G.

Zyir casually walked into a gas station that was nearby and used the payphone to call a cab. Within thirty minutes he was pulling up at the jet strip where Carter was waiting for him. Carter helped him into the jet and Zyir was startled when he reached the door and saw a hand reaching to help him in ... It was Monroe. Zyir got onto the aircraft and Carter immediately shut the door. "Okay, let's go!" he yelled to the pilot as they took off. Carter looked at Zyir and then Monroe. He was determined to bring his family back together and he was not taking no for an answer. Before they would kill each other, Carter would kill them both. He wanted the war to end for good. They had other problems ahead of them, problems that they could have never foreseen. The three biggest gangsters in history were on their ass: The F . . . . . . B . . . . . . I.

The jet lifted into the air and disappeared into the clouds as three of the realest niggas in Miami flew off into the sunset. Carter directed the pilot to head directly toward the Bermuda triangle; a no-fly zone where many aircrafts have vanished in American history. He instructed Zyir and Monroe to sit back and relax until they reached their destination. He had a plan ... a master plan.

Carter sat back in the luxury chair and stared out of the window. Just before they entered the Bermuda triangle, he smiled and whispered, "Diamonds are forever."

Weeks Later

Leena lay in bed, holding her son to her chest as she cried her eyes out over Monroe. She had lost him once before and now she was reliving the horror of his death all over again. *How can a plane just fall out of the sky without anyone noticing? God please keep them. Bless their souls,* she prayed silently. The minutes on the clock ticked by, torturously slow as she waited for the sun to break through the dark sky. She needed to speak with Breeze and Miamor. They were all that she had left. Leena felt more vulnerable than ever and they were the only women in the world who could relate to her pain. Widows of The Cartel they had more in common now than they ever had before. Through circumstance they had been made sisters and everything that their men had left behind was now in their hands. Power, paper, prestige . . . an entire empire now lay at their feet. Leena kissed her son's head, grabbed her cell phone off the nightstand, and rose from the bed. Putting on her silk kimono robe she walked out onto the balcony that overlooked the entire estate. Monroe had her living in the lap of luxury. Their mansion rested on a ten-acre compound on the outskirts of the city limits. He provided her with the best of everything. From labels to diamonds she was afforded her heart's desires, but the material things seemed so pointless now. None of it mattered. She would burn the multi-million dollar walls she dwelled in to the ground if it meant Money could live again. What she wanted most was time; time with the man she loved. It seemed as though life always tore them apart and for a second time she was mourning his loss. Her mind was so full and her heart so heavy that she could barely breathe. She felt weighted with emotion and she needed to get some of it off her chest. Leena dialed Miamor's number. Full of tension she didn't even realize that she was holding her breath.

"Leena, why are you awake? It's so late," Miamor answered.

Leena exhaled loudly and chuckled slightly. "I could ask you the same thing. Doesn't sound like you're getting much sleep either."

"The baby is restless. To be honest so am I. I miss him. I can't believe he's gone," Miamor admitted. "He was all I had left. So what the hell do I do now?"

Leena's heart went out to Miamor. To see Carter and her together was to see true love. Leena knew that not even her own relationship with Monroe could rival the one she witnessed whenever she was around them. "Have you spoken to Breeze?" Leena asked.

The sound of sirens broke through the silent night and Leena looked around in confusion and then she looked at her security cameras.

"The police are here," Leena announced. Unmarked black cars were pulling onto her property. "They must've found the plane," Leena whispered as she rushed back into the house, tightening the belt on her kimono as she raced through the massive mansion. "I'll call you back," Leena said.

"Lee . . . wait . . ." Miamor began to protest, but Leena ended the call. Her feet slapped the cold tile floor as she headed toward the front door, frantically, as hope began to rise in her broken heart. She flung open the door and ran out into the yard, meeting the officers in front of her home before they even got out of their vehicles. She was taken aback when she saw how many had come. By the time she realized something was wrong it was too late. Twenty federal agents exited their vehicles swiftly with automatic weapons aimed toward her face. Red beams appeared all over her upper torso and as Leena looked down she realized that all it took was an itchy trigger finger to end her life.

"Let me see your hands! On the ground now!"

Leena went deaf as the thunderous hum of a helicopter roared above her head. The windstorm that it created as it circled above her, shining a bright spotlight on her, caused her hair to blow wildly.

"What? What is going on?" she shouted frantically.

"Hands up! On the ground now!"

Leena was manhandled to the cement as she resisted their demands. She watched as the Feds swarmed her home. "Wait! My son is inside! My son is in the house!" she screamed as she tried to stand.

One of the men put a forceful knee in her back causing her to grimace in pain as he cuffed her wrists tightly. The metal bit into her skin and her wrist snapped from the agent's brute force. They held no sympathy for her as they made their arrest.

"You can't do this! I've done nothing wrong! My son! If you touch one hair on his head I will have your fucking head!" she screamed as she resisted arrest. She lunged, kicking and screaming as she tried to break free. All she could think of was her son. Leena had no idea why she was even under arrest, but the Feds had come at her so heavy that she could only assume the worst.

Leena's heart broke in half as they forced her into the car. She looked out of the rearview window and saw her son crying hysterically in the arms of one of the men. She broke down instantly. She had no clue of what would become of her and her child.

"Please, just tell me what is going on? What will happen to my son?" she asked, as snot and tears wrecked her pretty face. There was no keeping her composure. Leena was distraught. She knew that the tides of life were changing. With the death of the men the Feds had grown balls of steel. They would have never come at The Cartel with such arrogance and disrespect otherwise.

"Your son will be placed in temporary custody of the state," one of the Feds said as he drove away from her home.

"No, please! You can't," she said with a gasp.

"We can and we will, unless you can tell us something that will make us change our minds and set you free. Your cooperation will make all of this go away. So do yourself a favor and tell us what you know about the murders, the cocaine, the dirty money laundering that The Cartel is involved in. It's in your best interest to start talking."

***

"I'm not telling you anything," Breeze stated as she sat with her hands behind her back, handcuffed to the hard chair.

"We have evidence against you and everyone affiliated with The Cartel. We've got you for drug trafficking, running a criminal enterprise, fraud, tax evasion, the list goes on and on."

Breeze kept her eyes on the wall in front of her, barely blinking as she blocked out the voice of the federal agent. The olive-skinned man leaned in menacingly over Breeze, using intimidation tactics to get her to break. Zyir had trained her well. Breeze knew better than to volunteer any information. They couldn't even get her prints on a coffee cup, she was so seasoned. Growing up in the folds of the largest organization in the South had prepared her for this moment. "We found pieces of an aircraft, scattered throughout the Atlantic Ocean, about 150 miles off the coast of Bermuda. Too bad the cowards left their ladies to take the fall for their bad deeds."

Breeze's eyes turned dark at the insult and her heart wrenched.

"You don't have anything on me," Breeze said.

"We have everything on you. You recognize this face?" The agent tossed a photo of Estes onto the table in front of her and Breeze turned green as her stomach turned.

"Let's just say family doesn't mean much these days. He's singing like a canary and has implicated not only your husband and brothers, but you and over a hundred other mid- and low-level dealers across the state," the agent said. He noticed that Breeze's demeanor had changed.

"Not so cocky now huh, princess?" he mocked. "We picked up over thirty people directly affiliated with The Cartel. You're standing tall, but do you honestly think all of them will too? Now the way this works is who ever talks first gets the deal. There is only one way out of this."

"Magdalena!" Miamor yelled in urgency as she quickly dressed. The Spanish housekeeper appeared in the doorway. "I need you to watch the baby. Do not let anyone into this house under any circumstances. I don't care if God himself knocks on the door, you don't let anyone in. *Comprende?*"

"*Sí, sí,*" Magdalena replied.

Miamor placed a call to Carter's attorney and within minutes she was headed to the federal building. She knew the game and now that the Feds felt The Cartel was weakened, they were coming in for the kill. There was no way that Miamor was letting all that Carter had built be destroyed. She had watched him closely, studied the way that he reigned and just as she had in life, she would now hold him down in death. She already knew that Leena had been arrested and when she couldn't reach Breeze she had a gut feeling that she was being held too. Surely they had intended to come for her next, but Miamor moved to her own beat. She wasn't being taken into custody without representation.

She rode in the back of the plush interior of the Maybach as her driver guided through the city's streets. Miamor's chest heaved as anxiety crept into her bones. Today her worst fear was coming true. She was about to go up against the law. Most who did it had no wins, but with the team of sharks that Carter had left her with she was confident that she could come out of things unscathed. The car arrived at her destination and Miamor saw that Carter's legal team was waiting at the top of the steps. Steve Rosenberg, the best esquire in the city, was already on retainer. Standing confident and dapper as ever in a Brooks Brothers suit, he waited with a briefcase in hand. Miamor waited for her driver to open her door, then she emerged from the vehicle.

"Ms. Matthews, I'm glad you were smart enough to call me," he said as she shook his hand.

"Thank you for coming, Mr. Rosenberg," she replied anxiously.

"Looks like they're reaching a bit. They do have extensive evidence on Carter, Zyir, and Monroe, but seeing as though they are now deceased that pigeonholes their investigation. They're using scare tactics to try and get an informant out of you ladies. The Cartel has been responsible for drugs and crime in this city. They need a kingpin to tie it to, but in this case they are willing to settle for a queen pin. Since they can't get your men, they now are gunning for the three of you."

"They have Leena and Breeze. Have they turned them?" Miamor asked, as she bit her inner jaw, hoping that the ladies could stand tall under pressure.

"Not yet, but let's go get them out of there before one of them do. The DEA has been known to flip the most hardened of criminals."

Just seeing the face of such a prestigious defense attorney turned the tables in the girls' favor. Within an hour Breeze and Leena were released, but the struggle was far from over.

"They'll keep coming for you. As long as they have Estes's cooperation, it's only a matter of time before they bring indictments down on anyone he's naming. I'll do more research in the morning to find out what we're up against. I'll be in touch," Rosenberg said.

"What about my son?" Leena asked urgently.

"I've already made arrangements to have him returned to you. As soon as they process the paperwork a caseworker will drop him off to your home. Shouldn't take more than a few hours."

He bid adieu to the ladies and they each watched him pull away.

"They found the plane," Breeze informed sadly as tears flooded her eyes. "It crashed in the middle of the ocean. Divers are still looking for their bodies."

"What are we going to do? Everything is falling apart," Leena whispered. The three women formed a small circle and put their arms around one another, creating a circle of power … street royalty. They were the queens who would inherit the throne.

"We do what we have to do. We take over The Cartel," Miamor replied. "And the first thing on the agenda is to clear our names." She turned sympathetically toward Breeze. "I know that Estes is your grandfather, but—"

Breeze put her hand up and interrupted. "Do what needs to be done. If he's talking it'll be well deserved anyway. I'm numb to the death around me by now. It doesn't even matter."

"Do you guys know what this means? We can't just step in their shoes. I just sat back and spent the money. I'm not in the streets. I don't know the first thing about running anything . . . I can't do this," Leena protested.

"You can and you will. For years we've sat back and watched the throne. It's time we inherited it. It is our time now, ladies, and we either do this together or watch the entire Cartel fall. The vultures will pick everything our men established apart until there's nothing left if we don't assume our roles," Miamor schooled. She knew the streets. She had come up in the trenches and her murder game was official. There was nothing in her that was scared of this opportunity. She was reveling at the chance to continue Carter's legacy.

"We have no muscle," Breeze said.

"Some will stay loyal, others will test us. Niggas gonna learn a hard lesson when they buck, but they not knocking us off," Miamor assured.

"First we memorialize our men. Give them a home going that the streets will never forget," Leena whispered.

Breeze nodded and added, "Then the takeover begins."

Prologue

*"There is a price to pay for breaking my heart.
I'm going to ruin you nigga."*

—Miamor

"Dig deeper," Miamor stated coldly as she stood over the two burly men that were unearthing the desert soil. Their shovels clanged loudly against the earth as their grunts filled the air. "It can't be shallow. We don't want any mangy coyotes coming along and digging the body up." Miamor was livid and her heart pumped pure ice as it violently beat in her chest. Her emotions went haywire and her mind was everywhere at once. Any chance of her turning back now and stopping this madness went out the window every time she thought of how she had been betrayed. Reason was non-existent at the moment, she was acting off of raw rage. Her Cavalli sunglasses masked her watery eyes as she thought of the motivation behind her actions. She had murdered many times before. Fuck it. It was nothing for her to go boom on a nigga. She was in the business of extinction, but when business became personal it always played a tug of war with her mental.

Her judgment hadn't been this clouded since she had lost her sister at the hands of Mecca. She had promised herself that she would never let her emotions get so tangled again, but yet here she was years later . . . devastated . . . heartbroken . . . confused all over again. She should have been taking her aggression out on the root of the problem. Her man. Carter 'muthafuckin' Jones. He was the perpetrator of the crimes that had been committed against her heart. It was he who deserved to be buried in this shallow grave but instead it was his pretty little mistress who was in her crosshairs. Miamor saw red when the blacked out SUV pulled up a few yards away, because she knew who was hidden inside. They were in the middle of nowhere . . . thirty miles into the Mojave on uncharted land to be exact. No one came out this far unless they were looking to add to the secrets of the land. It was an unofficial graveyard. Many a mobster had held court in these deserted deserts. There was no telling how many bones were buried beneath the hot sands. Miamor was about to host a funeral and the guest of honor was a Persian bitch named Yasmine.

The most dangerous thing in the world was a woman scorned, but a Miamor scorned was deadly. No one had seen the kind of damage that Miamor could do. She hadn't had to deal with groupies in Miami. Carter had always walked a straight line. Their love story had been so complicated that he hadn't found the time to entertain anyone but her. Even during her absence from his life he had remained true, but Yasmine . . . Yasmine had distracted him. She had seduced Miamor's man and there was a price to pay for that. *The bitch clearly doesn't know who she's fucking with,* Miamor thought, her temperature rising as she stalked across the desert. She was heated . . . not from the sun that blazed down on her, but from the hatred that burned in her heart. As an unsuspecting Yasmine climbed from the backseat of the car, Miamor approached.

"What the hell is the meaning of this?" Yasmine asked as she held up a note. "Where's Carter? I'm supposed to be meeting him here? He sent this car for me."

Miamor was as feminine as ever in designer clothes and five-inch heels. She hadn't anticipated getting too dirty. She had men who followed orders at her discretion now. She barely had to lift a glass to her lips these days because her men waited on her hand and foot. They were young wolves and she was the leader of the pack. They attacked at her command. So there was truly no reason for her to break a sweat today. When she wanted someone to bleed, it never dripped on her shoes now. But this bitch Yasmine was a bit too pretty for her tastes. The way Carter's name dripped off of Yasmine's lips made Miamor shake with disgust. The smug, entitled, expression she wore irked Miamor to the point where she couldn't stop herself from slapping the taste out of her mouth. Miamor struck her violently.

"Agh!" Yasmine yelled as Miamor muscled her to the ground. Miamor's vice grip on Yasmine's jet black hair caused the girl to scream in alarm as she tried to pry Miamor's hand from her scalp. Sweat started to form on Miamor's forehead as she spoke through gritted teeth. "I sent a hearse for your bitch. There are plenty of men in Vegas. You should have chosen somebody else's," she said. She didn't even care about getting her hands dirty anymore. When her temper flared it took nothing less than murder to calm her down. She was on ten, it was too late to be rational now.

She pulled Yasmine through the desert, destroying along the way, the all white dress that the girl wore.

"No!!" she screamed as she clawed at Miamor's wrist while kicking her legs violently as she tried to break free.

Miamor mustered strength that she didn't even know she had and she didn't stop until she had pulled her from the car to the hole that was now complete. Her men stood around, unflinching as they watched revenge be served. Fuck cold, Miamor was serving revenge frozen. She hadn't even let it thaw out first.

As soon as Yasmine laid eyes on the ditch, terror filled her. She turned to Miamor, scrambling on her knees. "Do you know who I am? You can not get away with this!"

Miamor smirked as she shook her head incredulously. "I know exactly who you are. You're nobody. You live off of your daddy's name to get by. You think because you're a pampered little bitch from Saudi Arabia that you can do whatever you want, but you made one mistake. You didn't know who you were offending. You didn't check my resume. You see me in the casino in my fancy clothes, prancing around as Carter's arm accessory and you got me confused. You thought I was just a wife . . . just a mother perhaps? You didn't do your homework. Should have checked my background mama."

"Please! You can have Carter . . ." the girl began to plead.

"Bitch I *already* have Carter. There ain't a woman alive that can take Carter away from me. I own that nigga. That's my dick, my houses, my cars, my everything. Everything dope about him belongs to me. You're just a whim, but one that annoys the fuck out of me."

"Okay, okay. I won't even look at him. I swear to you," Yasmine stated as she held her hands out in front of her. "Just let me go. This isn't necessary."

"You fucked my nigga. This is very necessary. I hope it was good. Was it to die for?" Miamor asked. Suddenly she snatched one of the shovels from her bodyguard's hands and swung it full force, hitting Yasmine in the side of the face. She fell to the ground as blood poured from her ear. Miamor's rampage exploded as she hit her repeatedly, again and again. The sound of metal cracking human bone wasn't enough to make her stop. She showed no mercy as she took her frustrations out. She didn't care that she was literally beating the life out of the girl. Yasmine's efforts to block the blows were futile. There was no protecting herself from this ruthless assault and as the excruciating beating continued she could do nothing but pray. Miamor's chest heaved as she felt her clothes begin to stick to her skin. She held the shovel high above her head as she prepared to bring it down once more, but the sniffling, bloody, mess of a woman before her was no longer worth the effort. This beating wasn't making her feel any better. It didn't dull the pain that plagued her. She was still aching inside. The unbearable emotion haunted her, making it hard for her to breathe. Tears clouded her vision as she tossed the shovel to the ground. "Should have never crossed me," she said. She turned to her men. "Put the bitch in a box and bury her while she's still breathing. Leave a little air hole for her. I want it to be slow. Let her feel every single moment of what's left of her miserable life." Miamor left two of her men behind to clean up her mess as she headed back to the car with her driver. She had a meeting to attend. Yasmine was only the first to be punished. Carter would feel her wrath as well. As she climbed into the back of the car she knew that no matter what fate she delivered to him . . . she would always suffer behind his betrayal. Nothing she could do to him would ever make this right because even when she hated him . . . she loved him.

***

Carter was a man of little patience and as he checked the presidential that occupied his wrist he had to contain his anger. Tardiness was a sign of disrespect and Carter clenched his jaw as he folded his hands, placing them on the conference table in front of him. He was all business as he sat with a stern expression. The tailored Tom Ford suit he wore proved that he had graduated from the streets. He was no longer chasing hood fame; he was chasing them M's . . . the legal way. Owner of The Davinci, Las Vegas' newest resort and casino, he was a man with little free time. He had no hours in the day to waste. Miamor knew that. She had been by his side for so long that he already knew that her late arrival to their meeting was intentional. She was purposefully showing him that no matter how large he became, she would always run the show. He had given her the throne beside his. She was his queen and because of that he was on her time, like it or not. Carter leaned into the attorney that sat to his right. "We need to wrap this up."

Einstein looked across the table at the opposing counsel. "Mr. Levie, if your client doesn't show up in the next five minutes, we will have to reschedule this mediation session," he spoke. "Clearly she isn't taking this situation very seriously. Mr. Jones has asked her numerous times what she wants. We have yet to receive a response and today she doesn't even show up . . ."

Davison Levie drummed his fingers on the oak table as he leaned back in his chair with one hand placed underneath his chin. "She will be here"

"I am here."

Miamor's voice caused all three men to turn their attention toward the door. Standing in a Carolina Herrera bodycon slip dress and five-inch heels, each of them were mesmerized by her beauty. Her hair fell in an asymmetrical bob around her face. Beautiful wasn't quite the right word to describe Miamor. She was dangerous, enticing, and alluring. Miamor was simply a bad bitch. The curves of her body were so sharp that they were deadly. Even with her battle scars her face was still so pretty that it was deceptive. She was like a black widow. It was easy to get caught up in her web and very few escaped it. She took a seat beside her lawyer, sitting directly across from Carter. Her heart thundered in her chest. Seeing him made her blood boil, but oddly she loved him so much all at the same time. She could not believe that she was sitting across from him, when her place had been next to him for so long. Once lovers, they were now adversaries and it was still so hard for Miamor to believe.

As she sat silently, soul bleeding, love dying, she wished that she could turn back the hands of time. Her eyes were cold, dark, and distant as she sat stiffly, trying to remain strong. There was no way she would give Carter the satisfaction of seeing her break, not over him, not over his infidelity and lies. She had thought he was so different. Carter had promised her a unique love, but in the end he had turned out to be just another nigga. He had broken her heart and now there was no turning back. They had survived many things, but his one mistake had brought their love to a screeching halt. Now they sat, at the divorce table, enemies as they each watched their love slip away.

"Glad you could make it," Carter said sarcastically.

Miamor nodded her head but didn't respond with words. She had nothing to say to him. She knew that if she opened her mouth to speak that nothing but tears and sobs would fall out. No, it was best if she remained composed and let her attorney do the speaking. She and Carter were beyond words at this point. She leaned into her lawyer and whispered, "Lay out my demands."

Levie cleared his throat. "Mrs. Jones wants everything. She wants to keep the fifty percent stake that they currently share in ownership of The Davinci Resort and Casino, she wants the house in Summerlin, and she wants the $10,000,000 that is in the joint savings. According to our records, Mr. Jones has another savings account that he opened last year. In that account is $50,000,000 that he had hidden from Mrs. Jones. She wants that as well. She wants to keep all vehicles that are currently parked at the home in Summerlin. She also wants all stocks and bonds that they have purchased since being married. The estate in Miami, he can have and the home in Flint, MI she has no interest in."

Miamor didn't even need to mention the real money . . . the street money held more worth than all of their legal assets combined. It was hidden in safety deposit boxes across the country. She had already cleared out half of them and he didn't even know it.

Carter scoffed as if he had just heard a joke.

"This should not be amusing Mr. Jones. Mrs. Jones is very serious about her demands. Considering that there was no prenuptial agreement . . ."

"She's not getting my casino," Carter interrupted coolly, with a calm but serious tone.

"That is my casino," Miamor said. "While your ass was hiding out from a Fed case in Saudi, I was here with Breeze, with Leena, establishing The Davinci."

Carter stood to his feet and Einstein followed his cue. "Let us know when you have a serious offer. Mr. Jones is willing to offer a generous settlement. He has no intention of putting Mrs. Jones out in the streets. He wants to ensure that she is comfortable. But these demands are ludicrous. No judge will grant them," Einstein stated.

"A judge won't have to," Miamor replied. "I've got more than enough dirt on you Carter. It's in your best interest to give me what I want." Miamor spoke these words because she knew that if her attorney ever came out the mouth at Carter in such a way it would be the beginning of his end.

"Mr. Jones because you are felon, you don't have any real ownership at the Da Vinci," Levie informed.

"We signed a separate agreement," Carter spoke. "A private agreement."

Levie pulled the contract out of a briefcase and placed it on the table. "Of which I am aware, but this won't hold up in a court of law. The Casino is rightfully Mrs. Jones'."

"You're being ridiculous," Carter stated directly to Miamor. "You can have this fit at home ma. You're not going nowhere so let's stop racking up the billing hours and send the suits home."

He could see the hurt in her eyes. No matter how hard of a front Miamor put on, Carter knew her. He could feel the disappointment and resentment radiating from her heart. He turned to Einstein. "Take Levie and step out of the room."

Levie objected. "I don't advise my client to speak with you without me."

Carter's eyes turned dark as he turned his attention to Miamor's attorney. "Leave the room," he demanded, his shoulders squared in authority as his baritone banished both men from the room.

He turned toward Miamor when they were alone. It was the first time he had seen her in weeks. She had accepted no phone calls from him and hadn't been home since she had found him cheating. Carter had no idea where she was even staying. "Can we talk?" he asked.

"No," she replied, stubbornly.

"It's not what it looks like. If you let me explain . . ." Carter started.

"I caught a bitch half naked in your bed, it's exactly what it looks like. There's nothing more to say," Miamor spat. Her words were so sharp that they cut Carter to the core. He could hear the contempt lacing her words. She was scorned, dejected, and scarred by all of the promises that he had broken. So many apologies sat on the edge of his tongue, waiting to leap out of his mouth, but he held them back. She was too full of anger to hear anything that he had to say at the moment and he wasn't into wasting time.

"I want it all," she continued. "Every dollar, every business, every asset."

"You're pushing me Miamor," Carter warned. "I'm trying to be patient with you because I know that I hurt you. I fucked up," he said through gritted teeth. "But don't take that as weakness ma. You out of everybody know what it is. You *know* exactly what I'm capable of."

Miamor cut her eyes low in disgust. "Yes I do know Carter, but clearly you have forgotten what I'm capable of. You'll soon find out. There is a price to pay for breaking my heart. I'm going to ruin you nigga."

Miamor stormed out of the conference room, bypassing both Levie and Einstein as she made her exit. Heat pulsed through her as she made her way to her chauffeured vehicle. She was so full of emotion that it felt like she would combust. The history that she shared with Carter made it so hard to let him go. She had made him her everything and now that he had let her down, she was left with nothing but resentment. She looked at the world through a bitter lens as she slid into the plush interior of the Cadillac

truck. The driver closed the door and Miamor
leaned her elbow against the windowsill. Rest.
Contentment. Peace of mind. She wondered if
she would ever feel those things again. Turmoil
had taken over her world and a sick knot was
ever present in her gut. She was sick from grief
as she mourned the loss of the greatest love she
had ever known. She let her head fall to the side
as her chin rested against her balled fist. Tears
came to her eyes. *How did I let another woman
sneak into his bed?* she pondered, miserably.
She tried to think of where she had gone wrong.
What had she done to deserve the disloyalty that
Carter had shown her? She hadn't even seen
the signs or had she seen them and just ignored
them. She had trusted Carter and he had burned
her. Miamor was lost. She was once a woman
who needed no one until Carter had changed
that. He had convinced her to trust him, had
gotten her dependent on his affection. Now
that they were at odds all she felt was pain. Her
pain made her want to cause pain and she had
her cross hairs focused on the man whom had
wronged her. Killing his little jump off wasn't
enough. Miamor wanted Carter to pay for making her feel like just another lovesick girl. Taking
his empire was the only way to make him feel as
small as she did right now. Despite her hate for

Carter, she couldn't bury her love. It had been too strong. It would take years for her to get over Carter Jones. He was undoubtedly the great love of her life. Miamor knew that the type of bond that they had shared would never exist again. As her mind drifted down memory lane she looked for someone, something to blame. She couldn't help but think back to Miami, where The Cartel reigned, and all of the drama began . . .

Chapter 1

"I've been to a funeral where there was a body but no death."

—Miamor

Miami
5 years prior

Lost in the morning sky, Carter was silent as he stared out of the window, his mind full of a million thoughts and his heart conflicted. The billows of white clouds gave him a sense of serenity. At 30,000 feet in the air he felt as if nothing could touch him. Fuck a fed, he was flying high. No case could bring him crashing to the ground, or so he hoped. Running from a fight wasn't really Carter's style, but things had happened so quickly that he didn't have a choice. If he and his brothers had stayed in Miami, they would be in federal custody right now. He needed time to make these problems disappear. His mind drifted to Miamor and his newborn son. Guilt-ridden by his sudden departure, he tortured himself with the fact that he wouldn't be around to take care of the ones he loved. He didn't know how long he would have to stay away and it killed him that he wouldn't be around to get to know the life that he had created. He wouldn't be there to see Miamor transform into the woman she was born to be. He had confidence that she would be a great mother, but to see her playing the role that every woman was made for would have made his heart loyal to her forever. He was missing all of that and it left him with a disgruntled soul. They were half way across the Atlantic, as the private jet ate away at the distance between the States and Bermuda. They were out of U.S. airspace so they were safe. Their escape had been executed flawlessly. He just hated that they had left their families behind. He was confident that Miamor could handle herself in his absence. Unlike Breeze and Leena, she knew the game. Miamor would be just fine until he returned . . . of that much he was certain. Carter looked over at Monroe and Zyir, grateful for his right and left hand. Although they had been at odds, there was nothing like a common enemy to make men come together. The federal case against them was enough to make them put their differences aside for the time being. Carter only prayed that the peace lasted because if he had to choose between the two of them, even he couldn't call how it would turn out.

"Everything good?" Zyir asked, noticing the wrinkled brow of his mentor. He knew that whenever Carter grew silent and his eyes distant that there was something in the air.

Carter pinched his chin as he rested his elbow against the armrest. He rubbed his five o'clock shadow as he nodded his head.

"We left something undone," Zyir stated, knowingly. Carter didn't have to disclose his thoughts in order for Zyir to know what was wrong. "The women."

Carter confirmed with a nod, still deep in thought. Zyir sat up in the leather seat and rested his elbows on his knees as he rubbed his hands together. "They don't know anything, they can't be touched."

Monroe interjected, "That don't mean shit. The Feds will catch em' up with RICO. Just from spending the money they can build a case against all of them. Then what? Li'l Money ends up where? Li'l Carter goes to who? There is no more family left. We are all we got."

"If the Feds go after the ladies the case won't stick," Carter said. "I know Miamor. She'll handle it and I left a bank account full of money with the lawyers. Nothing will happen to them, they're protected."

"I hope you're sure," Monroe said.

"I am brother," Carter confirmed.

Zyir raised his head. "Is there a chance we could go back?" He had left without a good-bye, without warning. One moment he was with Breeze, the next he was not. He had done so many things that he had yet to apologize for and still had so many I love yous that he wanted to express to her. He felt as if he had left his home unstable. He could only imagine how she felt at the moment.

"I don't know," Carter admitted. "Right now, this brotherhood here . . ." He pointed between the three of them. "This is all we have. This is the family that we can rely on. We left Leena, Breeze, and Miamor with enough money to last a few lifetimes. The Feds took some of it, but there is so much more that they will never trace. Our families are set. They will survive. Miamor is a shooter with a reputation behind her. Niggas won't run up on her without thinking twice. She can hold down The Cartel. They are safe. The question is are we?"

"The Fed case is solid," Monroe said dismally. "If we get caught . . ."

"We can't get caught," Carter said with finality.

He stood and walked up to the captain's cabin. The middle-aged white man had large headphones on his head and aviator shades covering his eyes. He focused intently on the sky before him. The serene look on his face was understandable. As Carter looked out of the front window he realized that the pilot had the best view. Nothing but white clouds filled his vision. It was easy to get lost in the sky and Carter stood mesmerized for a moment at the incredible sight. It was one that not many people got to see. He placed a hand on the captain's shoulder. "It's time," he announced. "Turn off all communication. As far as the government is concerned this plane should drop out of the sky. We're all dead to the world from this moment forward. You do understand that you can never go back to the States?" he grilled.

"I understand. A million dollars is enough to make a new life somewhere else," the pilot responded.

"Good," Carter said. He gave the pilot a pat on the back and then watched as the man made the flight disappear from airspace.

***

The ocean below them sparkled many shades of blue and turquoise as the plane descended out of the sky. They arrived in paradise as the plane's wheels touched the ground with a gentle thud. The cabin rocked slightly as the pilot slowed and taxied to a stop on the private clear port. The three men emerged, suited, and unscathed as if escaping federal custody was a simple feat. When the federal scope fell upon most empires it fell instantly, but The Cartel would survive. Carter was smart. He had prepared himself for the scrutiny. It was his ability to foresee the government's attack that had allowed him to elude it. Carter shrugged on his suit jacket as he frowned from the bright sun that shined into his eyes. A titanium briefcase was gripped tightly in his hand. The three men stood at the bottom of the steps and waited for the pilot to exit.

"Safe and sound in Bermuda! Just like I promised you boys. Now where's my million dollars," he said as his face pulled outward in a wide, gap filled, smile. He was already spending the money in his head. His greedy palms couldn't wait to feel the tax-free dollars flipping through his fingers.

Carter passed the man the briefcase and shook his hand firmly. "Stay out of the states. Go anywhere but there," Carter instructed.

"You've got it, you're the boss," the pilot replied. Carter nodded at the warehouse that sat adjacent to the airstrip. "There's a mechanic waiting inside there. He will get you refueled and make sure you're good before you take off."

"Take-off? I though Bermuda was the final destination?" he asked.

"It is our final destination, you will be going elsewhere," Carter answered sternly. The pilot nodded in reluctant understanding as Carter, Zyir, and Monroe walked away.

They looked like Mafioso as they strutted powerfully across the clear port in their expensive Italian suits.

"You know he is going to go right back to Miami right?" Monroe stated. "There is no telling who he's going to run his mouth to. We need to dead that nigga."

"He'll never make it. The mechanic is going to make sure of it. The Feds will find the plane at the bottom of the ocean, assuming that we were on it," Carter replied. He swiped his nose arrogantly, feeling no remorse for double-crossing the pilot. He knew that the man would not be able to resist returning to Miami. He had just come into a million dollars. He wouldn't want to be rich alone; he would want to share it with the people who knew him. There was no point in getting money if you couldn't floss in front of the people that you were once broke in front of. He would disobey Carter's orders and surely attempt to return to Miami. Unfortunately for him Carter had anticipated this. The man would be half way across the Atlantic ocean when the engines on his plane gave out. It was cold blooded, but the men couldn't afford any slip-ups. The pilot was a casualty to the game. No one, not one witness to their escape could remain alive. No one needed to live to tell the story of how they had evaded the law. A black, tinted, Escalade pulled up directly in front of them with two Arab men in dark suits inside.

Zyir instantly reached in his waistline, but Carter grabbed his wrist, halting him. "They're allies," he informed. "Polo arranged for us to hideout in Saudi Arabia. We'll be safe there."

"The Middle East? That's not an easy move bro. We don't have friends there. We don't speak the language. This is the plan?" Monroe protested unsurely.

"Your father," Carter paused. "Our father, had friends there. He put in work that is protecting us today. We will be well taken care of. It's our only play right now, unless you have a better idea. We can't stay in Bermuda. The Caribbean will be the first place that the Feds look. Its too predictable."

"The way you're talking we ain't never going back," Zyir interjected solemnly. "My lady is in Miami. You have a new baby in Miami? Li'l nephew is there . . ."

"What about family?" Monroe finished for Zyir. Zyir shook his head unsurely.

"I'm not going to leave her unprotected fam. You talking about letting them think we're dead," Zyir stated. The thought of never seeing Breeze's face again, or hearing the sweet tone of her voice sickened him. He knew what his "death" would do to her. She would crumble.

Carter sighed in frustration. "Look. I would like to move as a unit but we're all grown men. I'm going to Saudi, but if this is where the road separates for the three of us I understand. I'm not worried about Miamor. I know her. She is more than capable of holding things down while I'm away. Until I can get word to her that we are safe the girls will just have to go through the pain of our loss. Eyes are on them right now anyway. Their grief will make it look real."

If Zyir could think of any other solution he would have offered it. The situation was just bad from all angles. Zyir may not like the plan but he trusted Carter with his life. It was time for loyalty to kick in. Everybody in the crew couldn't be chief. It was Zyir's turn to take the back seat so that anarchy didn't divide them.

"I'm with you my nigga," Zyir conceded.

Carter turned to Monroe. "What about you? We've got another flight to catch. What's it going to be?"

Since Monroe's return he had been the rebellious soul. Carter half expected him to buck against him once again. Instead Monroe nodded. "I'm with you bro."

Good. Carter opened the back door of the truck and climbed inside. Zyir and Monroe piled in behind him. "By this time tomorrow we will be half way around the world."

Breeze's heart felt frozen. A plane crash. The moment she had heard those words her heart had stopped beating inside of her chest. It was like the blood refused to flow through her veins. Her fingertips were ice cold, her eyes void of emotion, and her mind blank. How could this have happened? Zyir, Carter, and Monroe were three of Miami's most powerful men and they had been killed. Not by a bullet, a war, a rival or even a cop . . . but by a mechanical error on a private plane. She sat still, staring out of the window as the chauffeured Benz truck pulled up to the church. It was the same church that her father's funeral had been held in. Now here she was years later, burying not only the love of her life, but her brothers as well. She rode alone. It was how she preferred it. Since hearing of the tragedy she had wanted no one around her. She needed time. Space. Silence. She and Zyir had been beefing before he fled town. Their last words had been hostile ones and it was a regret that she would live with for the rest of her life. What had once felt like not enough time, now felt like too much. With Zyir by her side it seemed like life was not long enough to love him, to be with him. She had wanted a couple of forevers to bask in the joy he gave her. Now with him gone, she didn't want to go on another day, another year . . . let alone a lifetime without him. She was beginning to think that her family was cursed. No one she knew, no one with whom she shared blood had ever lived without looking over their shoulders. She was the last one standing. The only Diamond left of her generation. A heavy burden had been placed on her shoulders and she could feel it weighing her down already. As the driver sat silently in the front seat, waiting for her command to open her door she sighed deeply. Once she stepped out of the car all eyes would be trained on her. News cameras, the ghetto grapevine, friends, foes . . . they would all be awaiting her reaction. She had been young when her father had been murdered. She hadn't known the rules. Now she was well versed in the ways of the underworld. She remembered how strong her mother had been during her father's funeral and she vowed to be that strong today. If she was going to do that however, she needed to get it all out now because there was no way she was going to let the world see her cry. She cleared her throat. "Please lift the partition," she instructed. The driver nodded and as soon as Breeze saw the dark glass slide up her soul bled through as a gut wrenching cry came over her.

Leena held Carter Junior in her arms as Monroe's heir rested his curly head in her lap. Her red-rimmed eyes cloudy as she sniffled slightly. She wasn't ready for this day. Burying Monroe. It was too soon. Life was not supposed to come to this. She had done this routine before and he had promised her that she would never have to see him lying in a casket again. She couldn't help but be mad that he had broken their pact. She hadn't bothered to put on make-up. She knew that her sorrows would do nothing but wash the charade of happiness away. She was shaken to her core. Her baby, their baby was left without a father and Leena didn't know if she could do this alone.

She had gone through a lot being first Mecca's, then Monroe's girl but nothing had ever made her feel more alone than this. "Where is daddy?"

When her son asked the question her entire body quaked. He was old enough to realize that Monroe wasn't around. He missed his father and Leena's lip quivered as she searched for a response. "Daddy's . . ." she paused, unsure of what to say. She gripped her son's hand and took a deep breath. *Get it together. You have to keep your shit together for your baby. You're all he's got now. Do not break down in front of him,* she told herself. "Remember when I told you about God and how he has angels by his side baby?"

Her son nodded innocently. "Well God loved daddy so much that he needed him by his side baby. Daddy is resting now. He lives with God and we won't be able to see him anymore. More he's always with you. He's your guardian angel and if you close your eyes and listen to your heart you'll feel him. He is always watching over you baby. Do you understand?"

Monroe Jr. nodded and smiled as he closed his eyes, squeezing them tight as he said, "I feel him mommy! I feel him!" He opened his eyes excitedly. "Close your eyes too mommy! Hurry, hurry!"

When Leena closed her eyes she felt the tears drop out of the sides of them but she didn't make a sound. Her heartbeat increased and she sobbed silently, not wanting her child to hear her grief. "Keep them closed baby. Just be with daddy for a little while," she said. She opened her eyes and saw her driver extending a handkerchief to her. She mouthed the words, *thank you,* and wiped away her tears. Taking a deep breath she said, "Okay baby. Its time to go inside now. I love you."

"I love you too."

The smile of her child put the strength in her legs that she needed to stand on her own two. She reached into her bag and pulled out the Xanax she had been prescribed. She needed to take the edge off a bit. She placed it inside of her mouth and took a swig of her son's apple juice before she readied herself to face the world or rather the underworld of Miami.

Miamor sat behind the windows of the tinted Maybach. She was last in the procession of fancy escorted cars. The fleet had cost them almost $50,000 but she had spared no expense. Bulletproof everything was not a luxury it was a necessity and she took an extra measure of security by putting Leena in a car with the kids because she knew that no one would target her. They saw her as a grieving widow not a member of the Cartel.

Leena would be the last to be hit if anything did go down.

Miamor hadn't actually gotten time to process the plane crash just yet. She was in shock. So many things had fallen apart simultaneously that the only thing she could do was go into autopilot. She was handling the Feds, the organization of the memorial, a newborn baby. It was all so overwhelming and time consuming that the fact that Carter was never coming home to her had not yet hit her. She would never see his face again and still no emotion had materialized within her . . . not just yet. Miamor knew that once she allowed herself to feel that she would feel it all and falling apart was not an option at the moment. She would mourn him in private, after the memorial was over, but right now she had to protect his legacy. She had to protect his seed, his sister, and what was left of their family. She clicked her gun off safety and placed it inside of her Chanel bag. She wanted to wear it on her body, but the black Herve Leger dress left no room for her to tuck it inconspicuously. Miamor hoped she wouldn't have to use it but in any case she would be prepared to pop off. She herself had once walked into a Cartel funeral with the intent of murder so she didn't put it past anyone.

The Cartel was weakened by the death of their men, it was the perfect time for infiltration. She looked out of the window at the massive crowd that was filtering out of the church. Even the mega church wasn't big enough to accommodate the amount of people that had come out to pay their respects. Everybody was there, but not all that attended came out of love. She was sure a few enemies lingered in the crowd to confirm the deaths. The Feds were lurking. She could sniff out the pig bastards from a mile away. They were so obvious that she almost wanted to go and say hello. But the majority of the attendees were Cartel affiliates. Wives, girlfriends, hustlers, runners, muscle, groupies. Everybody was out and dressed to impress. If the mood wasn't so somber it would have been a hell of a party. Even in death Carter commanded respect. It was one of the many things she had loved about her man. She climbed out of the car and watched as Leena, Breeze, and the kids did the same. The bodyguard that Miamor had assigned to Leena and the younger ones escorted them in first as Breeze and Miamor trailed behind. Concealed behind designer shades they all made their way into the church and with heavy hearts they said good-bye to the men that had ruled not only the streets of Miami, but their hearts like no other before them.

"It didn't feel like a funeral," Leena said. "Their bodies. Where are they? Am I the only one that feels like maybe this is a mistake? Maybe they're alive?"

"They're not alive," Breeze said. "No one could have survived that wreckage."

"And I've been to a funeral where there was a body but no death," Miamor said, reminding them of Monroe's fake funeral years prior. "We just have to accept what is. The kids are asleep. I'm going to bed. You're more than welcome to stay the night if you want. Choose a room," she said, motioning to her massive mansion. She secretly hoped they would stay. With Carter gone it felt ominously empty . . . void of color . . . of life . . . of hope. She used to dream of filling every room with Carter's bobble head babies. She imagined that their girls would have long, curly coils, and big brown eyes. Their boys would be dark and strong with serious temperaments like their father. Now, she saw nothing. She couldn't even imagine what tomorrow would be like let alone foresee far into the future. Time stood still. Death would do that to you. She remembered the healing process when her sister was murdered. It had taken years for her to get over the loss. Feeling hurt every moment of everyday made days feel like weeks and weeks like months. It was all just so unbearable. It was worse than any physical torture that she had ever encountered. She would need something to help her sleep through the night and a bottle of wine was the only remedy. She walked into the finished basement and then down another set of stairs where Carter had insisted on building a wine cellar. She would have preferred a gun chamber but his incessant passion for fine wine had quickly rubbed off on her. She grabbed a vintage bottle. It was one that he would have never allowed her to open had he been alive. She pulled it down as she thought, *you shouldn't have died on me.* A tear fell down her face as she carried it up to the basement. She couldn't wait until she got upstairs. She sat at the basement bar and frantically uncorked the bottle as she poured herself a full glass. As the bitter redness entered her mouth she felt her emotional dam breaking. She lowered her head as she gripped her wine and let her tears flow. Finally, it hit her. Carter wasn't there to chastise her over his expensive bottle of wine. He wasn't there to hold her. To love her. To help her find her way as a new mother. She was by herself. It was how she had started out. She almost wished she had never loved Carter because losing him was worse than never having him at all. She wished that she had a fast forward button to push her past this part. When she felt pain she liked to inflict pain, but as a new mother she could no longer follow that pattern. Miamor was in unchartered territory. She didn't know how to be this girl. She didn't know how to live this life without Carter there to guide her. She had become the type of woman he could trust, but now that he was gone she didn't trust herself. She had loved him so hard that she had lived her life in accord to his liking but he was gone now. *Where does this leave me?* She thought sadly.

Before she knew it the entire bottle of wine was empty and she had cried so many tears that her eyes burned. She hated being so weak, it didn't suit her. She walked upstairs, bumping the walls along the way from her drunken state. She wasn't for this sulking shit. Her emotions were getting the best of her and she didn't like it. She located her Chanel bag and pulled out her pistol. She was glad that the memorial had gone peacefully but the pop off queen in her needed a release. She found Breeze sniffling quietly on her living room sofa.

"You're still awake?" Miamor asked.

"Can't sleep," Breeze responded with a shrug. The evidence of her loss was written all over her face.

"Come on," Miamor said. She went into the hall closet and pulled down a case that held a 9 mm inside. She passed it to Breeze.

"What are you doing?" Breeze asked, confused.

"Showing you the perfect stress reliever. Follow me," she answered. Miamor led Breeze out of the back of the house and out into the vast yard.

"Where the hell are we going?" Breeze asked.

"Whenever I feel overwhelmed I come out here," Miamor said. The amount of land that they had was unbelievable. Huge lots weren't common in Miami, but Miamor had acres. Carter had wanted a large yard and a big house to raise his family in but today it hurt to even breathe the air inside. When they were far enough away from the house Miamor stopped walking and pointed to a ledge that held bottles on top.

"Pulling a trigger is a stress reliever for me," she admitted.

"Figures," Breeze shot back with a smirk. "Let's go ahead and test your theory." Breeze aimed.

BOOM!

She hit nothing.

Miamor chuckled. "We need to work on your aim. I thought Zyir taught you how to shoot."

"Not in the middle of the night," Breeze said. "Give me a break. You're drunk. You probably can't do any better."

Miamor aimed.

BOOM!

The glass broke as Miamor hit her mark effortlessly.

Breeze threw up her hands incredulously causing Miamor to laugh out loud. Her laughter turned into cries as Breeze's eyes watered. The two women embraced, leaning on each other. They were sisters, not by blood but by street law and at this moment all they had was each other.

Chapter 2

"D.E.A is all over us. The workers are snitching, they have photos, and evidence . . ."
—Breeze

Four Weeks Later

Miamor sat in her son's nursery as she swayed gently in the wooden rocker. Her emotions were all over the place. Here she was holding the newborn child of the man that she was supposed to spend the rest of her days with, yet he was gone. It seemed as if they had just reunited. They hadn't had enough time together before Carter was taken away. "A plane crash," she whispered still in disbelief. She was still getting used to being a mother. Her body, her emotions, her view on the world . . . it had all changed the moment she gave birth. She had prepared herself for her life to alter drastically, but not in this way. She would never get used to raising her child alone. All she wanted was forever with Carter but it seemed that forever was elusive. Miamor wanted to break down, but everything seemed to land on her shoulders. With the absence of the male heads of The Cartel, the empire was in need of leadership. Breeze had come up around the game, but she had never been a player in it. She was a pampered princess. All she knew was the money and the reputation that she got from being affiliated. She knew nothing of the stripes that it took to lead an army of street niggas. Then there was Leena. A pretty face who had stood on the arms of made men for years. She had been around, but Miamor was almost sure that she was just like the average hustler's wife, she knew no details. Leena wasn't street, but could still prove valuable because she was sharp, and she seemed to be loyal. Still, she lacked the raw courage that it took to run things. In an organization as infamous as The Cartel, there couldn't be weakness. Miamor was used to running with a pack of thoroughbreds. Leena and Breeze were a far cry from The Murder Mamas. Miamor had trusted them with her life, she wasn't sure if Breeze and Leena could compare.

The doorbell rang causing Miamor's body to tense. Her son was so in tune with her body that he erupted with cries simultaneously. "Shh!!" she whispered as she stood to her feet, her maternal instincts to protect kicking in. "Shh, its okay." She ran into the panic room that was attached to the nursery and put in a code quickly, her hands shaking violently. Miamor was normally so rational, so meticulous, but having another life to look out for besides her own made her emotional. Just the ring of a doorbell scared her. Normally the security cameras would have announced the identity of whoever was ringing her bell, but the Feds had disarmed all of her cameras when they had hit her with the warrant. The streets knew that Carter was gone. There was no telling who would come to her door trying to usurp her kingdom. Miamor was on edge. She placed her baby in the bassinet inside of the panic room and then rushed to the safe. With her hands free she calmed herself slightly as she punched in the combination. She grabbed the loaded .357 out of the safe and rushed out, locking her crying child securely inside. It was two o'clock in the morning. Nothing good could possibly come to her at that hour and whoever was at the door was about to feel her wrath. Miamor rushed to the door and pulled it open swiftly, ready to pop off, her gun aimed, arm steady.

"Whoa!! Whoa!"

Miamor popped off, shooting past the kid's ear only missing his head by an inch.

"Who the fuck are you?" she asked.

The kid grimaced as his mouth fell open from the deafening ringing in his ear. "Whoa ma, chill out. Fuck! You gon' blow my fucking eardrum! Who are you? Femme Nikita or some shit! You busting at niggas," the guy responded with his hands still raised to show he had come in peace.

"You've got five seconds to tell me who you are and why you at my doorstep in the middle of the night," she demanded, voice cold, finger wrapped securely around the trigger.

"I'm a friend. My name is Fly Boogie. I was with Zyir the day that he ran from the Feds. I distracted the cops so that Zyir could go meet Carter and Monroe. I swear on everything I'm a friend. I ran one of the trap spots," Fly Boogie said. The words flew from his mouth so quickly that Miamor knew they had to be true. He was fearful of his life. He wanted to give her no reason to pull the trigger. "Can I put my hands down now?"

Miamor eyed him suspiciously and then grabbed his collar and put him against the brick wall. Her pistol kissed the back of his skull. She felt his waistline for a gun. He wasn't carrying.

"I don't got shit on me. I just got out of county. They locked me up for the high-speed chase I took them on the day it all went down. Look, I know it's late and I shouldn't have come but I came straight here as soon as they let a nigga go. I received this post card in prison. Your address was the return address but there was no message written on it. I know the game. Seems like I was supposed to deliver this to you."

Miamor lowered her gun and Fly Boogie lowered his hands while breathing a sigh of relief. She snatched the post card out of his hand. She knew that he was right; this was no incident. She hadn't sent the post card and there was only one other person who could have. *He's alive,* she thought. She looked down at it and saw a Desert Oasis printed on the front of it. Her hand shot to her mouth, covering it in disbelief. *Are they in Saudi Arabia? Could this be for real?* she thought as she read the wording on the front. Her worry transformed to relief as the ball of tension that her body had become melted. She looked up at Fly Boogie, unable to stop the tears from glistening in her eyes. "Thank you," she said.

"Thank you for not blowing my brains out," he replied with a sense of humor before walking off of the porch. Miamor closed the door, locking it securely behind him. She rushed upstairs, heart pounding, eyes clouding with tears of uncertainty. *Oh my God please let him be alive. Let this postcard mean what I think it does,* she thought as hope flared in her chest. She rushed up the stairs to retrieve her son and then picked up her phone to call Breeze. She paced back and forth, child in one hand, as she held the cell to her ear.

"Miamor?" the rasp in Breeze's voice cracked in the late night hour and she cleared her throat.

"I can't speak to you over the phone. Call Leena. Come now. It's important," Miamor said. She hung up the phone before she could receive protest. She wouldn't have taken no for an answer. She was used to leading and if Leena and Breeze wanted the legacy of the Cartel to continue they had to get used to following.

Within the hour Breeze and Leena arrived with little Monroe in tow. Miamor took the sleeping toddler from Leena's arms. "I'll put him upstairs in my bed," she whispered. After ensuring that he was comfortable she joined the ladies in the kitchen. The smell of mocha thickened the air as Breeze grinded fresh coffee beans. "We'll need it," Breeze said when Miamor entered the room. "Seems like it's going to be a long night."

Leena leaned over the island that sat in the middle of the room. She folded her hands atop of the counter as she looked up at Miamor anxiously. "What's going on Miamor?"

Miamor pulled the post card out of the pocket of her Ralph Lauren plaid pajama pants. She slid it across the counter.

Leena picked it up and turned it over, surveying the front and back. Frowning in confusion she said, "You made me pull my son out of his bed at two in the morning to look at a postcard. What we doing? Taking a vacation?"

Breeze crossed the room and took the postcard out of Leena's hands. "Saudi Arabia," she read. Her brow furrowed.

"A li'l nigga named Fly Boogie dropped it off here," Miamor started . . .

Breezed nodded. "I've heard Zyir mention the name before . . ."

Miamor continued, "He said it was sent to him anonymously. I think Carter is in Saudi Arabia with Monroe . . . and Zyir."

The entire room seemed to freeze as Leena and Breeze looked up at her, eyes wide, mouths open in shock from the possibility.

Leena shook her head in denial. "They found a plane in the middle of the ocean Miamor," she whispered. "They couldn't have survived a plane crash."

"What if they were never on it? They didn't recover any bodies," Breeze said hopefully.

"I know Carter. He's reaching out to me. This postcard says nothing but says so much all at the same time. It isn't flashy, it isn't loud . . . it isn't anything that can be traced, but its enough. It's a whisper that only I can hear. I think Carter is alive. They all are but they can't come back here, unless that case goes away."

Exasperated Breeze flopped down on one of the bar stools that lined the kitchen island. "D.E.A is all over us. The workers are snitching, they have photos, and evidence . . ."

"The case is strong," Leena finished. "If their return depends on that we'll never see them again."

"The case has to go away," Miamor said.

"And then what?" Leena asked. "I'm so tired of this life. This isn't how I envisioned my life. Even if this case goes away and they get to come back . . . it is only a matter of time before something else tears this family apart. I don't know about the two of you, but I've had enough of the drug business. We have money. We have respect. It's time to move on from this."

Breeze was quiet as she pondered Leena's words. The Cartel had been her life for as long as she could remember. She had been born into it. Continuing the legacy allowed her father to live on, even in death, but was it worth it? By honoring their father, their family was diminishing before Breeze's very eyes. The streets would eventually make the Diamond clan extinct. *She's right, it's time for a change,* Breeze thought.

"The guys aren't here to guide our footsteps ladies. It's time that we made the decisions that we think are best for this family. It is time to take The Cartel legit. I don't want to lose any more loved ones. I want to live without worry and as long as we're in the drug business that will never happen."

The three women sat in silence, each haunted by their own thoughts. The ache in their hearts from their missing partners resonated within them.

Miamor looked around at their fractured group. They needed their men back.

"I'll make this case disappear, one way or another. After we bring the men home we'll talk about getting out of the game . . . for good."

Chapter 3

"Day or night, I'm available to you."
—Yasmine

Nothing had ever been so foreign to Zyir. He was Flint bred and Miami crowned. He preferred to stay where the native tongue was one that he understood. Call it closed minded, but Zyir just called it smart. He was a young man who liked to be aware of everything moving around him. As soon as he stepped off of the private jet an uneasiness settled into his bones. It was instinctive for him to reach out to Breeze. He missed her. The fact that they had been at odds ate away at him the entire flight. He knew that she was suffering because he could feel her strife. He was across the globe and was still emotionally connected to his shorty. She was his rib, he just wished that he could tell her that everything was going to be okay. Stone faced, he emerged from the plane and the first thing he saw was men carrying assault rifles lined up in front of two luxury SUV's. They were dressed in traditional, long flowing cloaks made of the most beautiful fabrics. Their heads were wrapped as well, only revealing their menacing facial expressions.

"They don't look too friendly fam," Zyir whispered to Monroe as they made their way down the stairs.

"You strapped?" Monroe asked.

"You know it," Zyir replied.

They were ready to go out guns blazing. It wasn't like them to tread lightly, but they followed Carter's lead. He was the captain of this ship and as long as he appeared comfortable they would remain that way too. Should he even show the slightest wrinkle of concern on his face, they would get it started. They were clearly outnumbered but Monroe's marksman aim evened the playing field a bit.

The door to one of the SUV's was opened and a distinguished man with a full beard exited. He wore gold garb and held out his arms in receipt of his guests. "Welcome to Saudi Arabia," he said in perfect English. He stepped forward and met the men halfway, showing good faith. He walked right up to Carter. "You must be Carter," he said as he held out his hand. "You're the spitting image of your father. He and I had some good times in America as young men. Before the wives and the children." The man paused and inhaled long and deep as he reveled in the fond memories. "To be young and rich again," he said. Carter gave him a firm handshake.

"You must be Mr. Baraka," Carter replied. Polo had made the connection so Carter knew that they were in safe hands. "This is my brother Monroe and my good friend Zyir. Thank you for extending the invitation."

"A son of Carter Diamond is a son of mine. I owed your father my life. He was a good man. I was very saddened to learn of his death," Baraka stated.

"As were we," Carter replied, keeping it short. "Thank you."

"Shall we?" Baraka said, extending his arm toward their awaiting vehicles. "Monroe and Zyir can ride in the first truck while I discuss specifics with you on the way to the resort."

"Resort?" Monroe questioned.

"Yes. I own Saudi Arabia's largest resort and casino. Five star. I have a penthouse set up for each of you," Baraka revealed. "It will be most comfortable."

Monroe nodded and headed for the truck as Carter climbed inside with Baraka.

The scenery outside of his window was mes-
merizing. He was in a desert Oasis. It was so hot
outside that he could see the heat waves creating
a hazy view on the other side of the glass. The
tan sand dunes around him made him feel out
of place. This was unfamiliar territory but it
was also a safe haven. He was out of reach of all
of his enemies, legit and otherwise. He felt the
tension dissipate from his chest. Fear of cap-
ture had been real until this very moment, but
now that he had touched Saudi soil he realized
exactly why Polo had suggested this place. He
was worlds away. The air didn't even smell the
same on this side of the planet and despite the
fact that he missed Miamor and his son, he wel-
comed the change.

"I couldn't get any details from Polo as far as
the troubles you are in," Baraka said. "Please tell
me."

Baraka was mild mannered but Carter could
see nothing but boss status and old money when
he looked at him. He didn't know many old men
who walked around with armed guards on a
regular. Baraka was important and the rubies
sitting on his ringed fingers told Carter that he
came from extreme wealth. Carter had every
intention on laying low but he was like a sponge.
He soaked up knowledge and stored it for future

use. He was all about expanding and building a usable and influential network. Something told him that Baraka was someone that he wanted on his team.

"The D.E.A. is trying to prosecute us on drug charges. They have evidence, mostly circumstantial and witnesses. There was no time to hinder their case against us. They want us behind bars to try to contain our influence over Miami. If we were free than their witnesses would never testify. We had no choice but to flee. We need time to regroup, maybe establish some networks over here," Carter said smoothly opening the door for potential business.

"Well you are welcome to stay here as long as you need to," Baraka said.

"Thank you," Carter replied. "I don't come empty handed however. We aren't in the business of taking handouts. Any business I conduct is mutually beneficial. There's a saying that in a good deal both parties walk away feeling like they sacrificed a little bit." Carter handed Baraka the briefcase that he had carried off of the plane. "A million dollars to show our appreciation for your hospitality."

Baraka gave Carter a chuckle as he took the case. "You are your father's boy," he commented.

"So I've heard."

***

The word penthouse did the accommodations no justice. They were being put up in mini-mansions in the sky. Each one came with a group of personal hand maidens, butlers, and a personal chef, not to mention the private plunge pool. This was the luxe life and Carter could appreciate the fact that the hideout felt more like an escape. He hadn't been expecting much but this set up exceeded his wildest dreams. He had seen opulence in his day but nothing quite like this. The Cartel reigned in the fields of drugs, war, and even real estate, but it was apparent that they hadn't amassed wealth on this level . . . yet. If Carter had anything to do with it they would make the transition soon, after his legal troubles subsided. After finishing the tour of Carter's penthouse Baraka turned to his guests. He stood tall, strong, with his hands clasped in front of him. "I hope you find your accommodations most suiting," he said. "Each penthouse is identical."

Monroe nodded and Zyir spoke, "No detail was left undone. Appreciate it."

Baraka smirked. He could spot a protégé in the making. Zyir was a chip off of Carter's block. Their swag was almost identical. They may not be brothers by blood but they were definitely family. Always had been . . . always would be.

The sound of a key card opening the door to the suite caused everyone in the room to look over their shoulders. When they saw her, they became breathless. The foreign beauty was the most beautiful creature that God had ever created. Her Miss Universe smile illuminated the room as she walked confidently pass the group until she was tucked safely under Baraka's arm.

Damn, Carter thought. He ran his hand down his goatee and exhaled as he shifted his stance. Her long, butt length hair was dark and mysterious, matching the charcoal colored eyes that pierced upon first glance. She was slim with a model's physique. Her only curve was the perky c-cups that sat up out of the custom tailored Dolce pant suit she wore. Her skin looked like honey and Carter couldn't help but wonder if it tasted just as sweet. He shook the thoughts from his head as Baraka spoke. "This is my daughter Yasmine," Baraka introduced. "She knows my hotel better than I do. She is the hospitality manager. If you need anything she can take care of it for you. No matter how sensitive the matter, she can handle it and keep it in strict confidence. Do not hesitate to ask."

"Good to know," Carter replied as he extended his hand to her. "Nice to meet you."

There was seduction in her eyes as she took his hand. He could practically feel the heat of her touch melting into his skin as she rubbed his hand slightly. "I look forward to pleasing you," she said with a hint of mischief dancing in her eye. "Day or night, I'm available to you."

Carter smirked as he cleared his throat, bringing a balled fist to his mouth.

"I know your journey has been long. We will let you gentlemen rest," Baraka said. He led Yasmine out of the suite. The handmaidens remained stationed in the corners of the room, ready to serve.

Monroe and Zyir stepped up next to Carter. "This shit is wild bro," Monroe said. "Servants, butlers, and shit . . ."

"Don't take advantage," Carter instructed.

"From the looks these Arabian women been throwing our way, I'd say we are the ones at risk of being taken advantage of," Monroe replied with a handsome grin.

Zyir smirked but remained silent. He had caught the vibes as well and knew that this would definitely be an interesting trip. *An interesting trip indeed,* he thought.

Chapter 4

*"We are the law Aries. You're a Murder Mama.
This suburban neighborhood with manicured
lawns got you confused ma."*
—Miamor

The serene country street was void of all threats as Miamor sat in the rental car outside of a modest two-story home. The small city in middle of nowhere, Idaho, was quiet, peaceful, and completely off the map. Miamor completely understood why it had been chosen. It was where you would go to run from your past. It only existed to its own residents. Outsiders had no knowledge of the place whatsoever. She secretly wished that she could find a place that she could run away to with her family. How nice it would be to leave it all behind. Solace. She watched as children rode their bikes up and down the paved streets. The houses all matched. The lawns were perfectly manicured as automatic sprinklers swished sounds of home ownership into the air.

Miamor saw no sign of trouble, no sign of drugs, guns, murder. There was absolutely no mayhem on these Idaho streets . . . just good people, living normal, safe lives. *Must be nice,* she thought. She exited the car and hesitated as a car passed her on the street. The driver smiled and waved. *People are friendly here,* she thought as she waved back. She crossed the street and approached the house that sat on the end of the block. It was beautiful and well taken care of with flowers planted around the perimeter of the large country porch. The creaking of a swing whistled in the wind as a little boy sat with shoulder length dreadlocks, rocking slowly as he played with toy trains. He kicked his feet joyously as the swing creaked with every movement.

Miamor gasped at the sight of him and then her heart filled with warmth.

"Hi," she greeted. "Is your mom home?"

The boy stopped swinging and on cue the front door opened with a gun immediately pointed at her face. The mother inside was so on point that she knew that an intruder had interrupted her son's habitual swaying back and forth. Miamor stared down the barrel of a .357.

"Miamor?" a voice of disbelief rang out, but the recognition didn't cause the gun to lower. It was aimed at her, steady, unflinching, and ready.

"Hello Aries," Miamor greeted. Aries held the gun firmly in her grasp as she stared into the eyes of a cold-blooded killer. Miamor was the devil in a dress and she hesitated before she decided to take a chance and lower the gun. Confusion filled her eyes.

"Miamor . . ." Her brow furrowed.

The little boy stood up and ran to his mother, clinging to her leg. Aries peeled her son off of her. "Go to your room sweetheart. Lock the door and watch cartoons," she instructed, her voice stern.

The little boy nodded and disappeared inside of the house.

"You think I'm going to hurt you? I would never bring harm to you Aries. You're my friend." Miamor's voice didn't reveal the stab of anguish she felt in her heart. If her own friend feared her, she must have been a monster. *How did it come to this?* she thought.

"Yeah well I thought you were dead and I don't let my guards down these days . . . for anyone. Even friends," Aries replied.

Miamor looked down at her body. "I'm wearing Prada and five inch heels Aries. You really think I came to put in work looking like a super model?"

Aries icy demeanor chipped away a little bit and she smirked. "Bitch nobody said you look like a super model. I see we're still arrogant huh?" Aries cracked. Her face melted into a smile. "You look great for a dead woman," she cracked. Aries put the gun on safety and embraced Miamor. "You have a lot of explaining to do," she said.

"I know," Miamor replied. "Are you going to invite me in?"

Aries stepped back into the house and Miamor followed.

"I'm proud of you," Miamor admitted as she looked around the home. Everything was in its place. Modest, but extremely beautiful, Aries house felt like a real family lived in it. Plush carpet absorbed her feet, beautiful venetian blinds shaded the windows, while leather furniture sat on top of an opulent French rug. A stab of jealousy vibrated through her, but it only lasted for a moment. This was the life and she was glad that one of the Murder Mamas was blessed to live it. It wasn't about the money or respect, it was about peace of mind. After the sins that they had committed Aries was lucky to find it. "You made it out. You have a home and a child. I assume there is a man?"

Miamor sat down at the kitchen table as Aries went to the cupboard to start a pot of tea.

"There used to be someone," Aries said. "He was killed. The past knocked on my door and he got mixed up in some bullshit. I bounced around from place to place. Went back home to the Islands, then to Montana to settle a score, to Arizona, and finally decided to settle here. I ditched the accent to blend in and I started over. This place felt the safest."

Aries filled the kettle with water and placed it over the blue and orange flame on the stove. Miamor admired her. *She's so normal now*, Miamor thought. She then took a seat across from Miamor. "What happened to you Mia?" A dark cloud seemed to shift over their heads as the mood changed. The reunion had turned dark as the thought of their dead friend loomed over them.

"I was in hiding," Miamor admitted. "Running from Mecca. I only came back after Carter killed him."

"But we got your hands sent to us in a box," Aries whispered.

Miamor shook her head. "It's a long story but they weren't my hands."

"You left us," Aries whispered. "We were in the middle of a fucking war and you just dipped. You left us stuck. Where were you when they took Robyn's life?" The reunion between the two of them was bittersweet. Miamor had been their leader. Aries couldn't help but think if she had stayed things may have turned out differently.

"I cried for a week straight when Robyn was executed. I'm sorry Aries. I should have been there," Miamor whispered. "You all were my sisters."

Tears accumulated in Aries eyes. "They put her down like a dog," she whispered. She quickly swiped the emotion away. "You have a child?" she asked.

Miamor frowned. "How do you know that?"

Aries chuckled. "You put on some weight. The bad bitch I know don't play that. You wouldn't gain a pound. A baby is the only explanation. Can I assume that you're back with Carter?"

Miamor smiled. She missed this intimate interaction with Aries. No one had known her better than the Murder Mamas. They were family. Despite her love for Carter and her growing bond with Breeze and Leena, she was never as intimate with anyone as she was with her crew. "I am. Which is why I'm here. I need your help Aries. There's a case against Carter, Zyir, and Monroe . . ."

"Monroe?" Aries questioned in shock. "What the fuck? Everybody is just rising out of their graves in Miami?" The revelation hit her the same way it had everyone else when they first found out Money was alive, like a ton of bricks. "I saw that man in his casket."

"He's alive," Miamor confirmed. "He lay in a coma for five years but he breathes just like you and me. The case that the Feds have brought down on The Cartel is solid enough to send everyone away for life. They're on the run . . ." Miamor wouldn't have shared that information with anyone else, but she had trusted Aries with much more. Miamor hid no truths from this old friend. They had done and seen it all . . . together. "I'm being watched or I would put the work in myself. This fucking prosecuting attorney would love to catch me up in the RICO case. You're not on the radar though Aries. You could get in and out. Help me make this go away."

"You want me to murk a P.A.? Have you lost your mind Miamor?" Aries asked. They had gotten away with their share of murders in their day, but this situation reminded her too much of the one that sent Robyn to the death chamber. "You know this is how Robyn got caught up. We aren't bigger than the law."

Miamor's gaze toughened. "We are the law Aries. You're a Murder Mama. This suburban neighborhood with manicured lawns got you confused ma? Anybody can get it. Niggas, bitches, children . . . white, black, fucking purple. I will do anything to bring my man home."

"Yeah but you're not Mia. You're asking me to and I just can't. I'm out of the life," Aries protested firmly.

"Maybe but this certainly isn't living Aries," Miamor's tone softened as she sympathized with her friend. "You have to be lonely here. You have no family, no friends . . . just you and your son. Come back to Miami with me. I want to be a part of your son's life. I want you to be an aunt to mine. We are the last two standing," Miamor said genuinely.

"Miami is Cartel territory Miamor. You can forgive and forget because you love the nigga that's in charge of it, but I still remember. I remember the war. The beef . . ."

"They are good people," Miamor interrupted. "And I need you there. Carter's half way across the world and he won't ever come home unless I make it happen. I need you to help me get this case off his back."

Aries shook her head. "Nah, Miamor. That's your problem, not mine. I'm not ever coming back to Miami."

Miamor wanted to press the issue but out of respect she didn't. They had done a lot of dirt together and it wasn't Miamor's right to push Aries into re-entering the life. "Okay," she said. She stood to her feet thinking that there was nothing left to say. Miamor needed Aries, but she did not blame her for declining the proposition. Aries was loyal, she always had been; Miamor knew that it would not be easy to get her to change how she felt about The Cartel. Love had caused Miamor to become soft, but Aries was still Aries and she would forever throw the middle finger to the organization who killed Anisa. It was just the way that she was built.

Miamor began to walk toward the door but was halted by the sound of her name. "Mia . . . you want to at least meet your nephew before you leave?" Before Miamor could answer the whistle of the teapot erupted in the air. Aries went to the stove poured two cups as steam drifted from the spout. She handed one to Miamor. "Come on," she said. Miamor followed Aries up to the little boy's room and when they opened the door they found him fast asleep on his bed.

"You don't have to wake him," Miamor said. She walked over to the bed and knelt over the small child. "Auntie loves you." She planted a kiss on his forehead.

"His name is Tre," Aries said.

Miamor stood and went into her clutch. She removed a piece of paper and pen. "Take care of yourself Aries. I am so proud of you. If you ever need anything just call me." She wrote down her number and address before handing it to Aries.

"Thanks for coming by Mia," Aries responded. She took the paper but they both knew that she would never use it. She was shutting the door on her past life and silently Miamor wished that she could do the same.

"I love you Murder Mama," Aries whispered sadly.

Miamor closed her eyes for a moment and thought back to when they all were together; there had been five of them at a point in time. She was flooded with instant grief at the fact that three of them were no longer breathing. *Did I lead us here? Are their deaths my fault?* She thought. It was a burden that she would always carry on her shoulders. The loss of her sisters weighed heavily on her conscience. "I love you too Aries. Always." Miamor opened the door.

"Mia . . ."

Miamor turned around to Aries.

"Don't try to kill the P.A. or the judge or none of that. It's too dangerous. There's more than one way to skin a cat. A dead public official will only make the government go for more blood. You need leverage," Aries said. She shrugged.

"But hey what do I know? I'm just a suburban housewife. Good-bye friend." Miamor nodded and walked out of the house filled with hurt. It was a pain that she had never felt before because she knew this was the final good-bye. She was headed back to Miami to fix her problems on her own, but not in the way that she had intended. Aries had given her some words of wisdom, ones that would prove valuable in time.

Chapter 5

"He on that real suit and tie type shit."
—Fly Boogie

Two Weeks Later

Murderous thoughts filled Miamor's mind as she thought of ways to tamper with the federal case. The role of motherhood had settled her a bit. It forced her to think first and react accordingly, but it did nothing to scratch the itch she had to make bullets rain from the sky. It was like a junkie craving a fix; when Miamor had a problem she solved it, period. Erring on the side of caution was like pulling teeth to her. As much as she wanted to reinstate her murder game, she could not. Miamor had to think about her son and if she went off the handle she wasn't sure she would ever be able to recover. Murder was like heroin for her. The familiar feeling of revenge was hard to shake. Once she got a taste of her old lifestyle it would be hard to revert back to a normal life. Motherhood and the game didn't mix and Miamor desperately wanted to get that part right. She wanted to be the wife and mother that her family needed, not the goon that streets required. She had to fix things. It was up to her to put her family back together but there were certain risks that she wasn't willing to take at the moment. Although she didn't see them, she knew that there were so many eyes on her that if she so much as jay walked they would bury her under the jail. In the past this problem would have disappeared already. It would have been nothing to tie up a wife or kidnap a kid to make a judge throw the case out, but in those days she had lived recklessly. Now, she had a child who depended on her and she would not sacrifice him in order to save Carter. She had to play it smart this time and use caution before she proceeded. She hadn't heard anything further from Carter and she knew that she wouldn't. It was too risky. Any communication between the two of them could cause exposure. Her mind spun with worry as she thought of him. He consumed her every waking moment. *I have to make this go away.* The doorbell rang and Miamor arose from her seat. Her housekeeper Magdalena had quit after being interrogated for hours by the D.E.A. so she was left to take care of the massive estate on her own. She hastened her steps to stop the guest from ringing the bell again. She couldn't have the sound intruding on her infant son's sleep. She pulled open the door and stepped aside as Fly Boogie walked inside. Neither she, nor, any of the girls could move freely so she had put Fly Boogie on the prosecuting attorney. She had eyes on him at all times as she slowly gained information about him.

"What do you know?" Miamor asked, cutting directly to the point of his visit.

"Not much. This mu'fucka is squeaky clean. He on that real suit and tie type shit," Fly Boogie said as he dug his hands in his pockets.

"Nobody is completely clean," Miamor responded. "Everybody has dirty laundry, we just have to find the closet he's hiding it in."

Fly Boogie shook his head doubtfully and handed her his phone. "Take a look for yourself. I've been stalking this nigga for days. This is all I've got, a bunch of pictures . . . but nothing stands out."

Miamor swiped her finger across the screen as she flicked through photos. She peered at the images with a critical eye. She sent each one to her email before moving to the next shot.

"I'm telling you there's nothing there. You should just let me get at the niggas who turning state. No witnesses, no case," Fly Boogie said.

"I don't know what you're talking about," Miamor said quickly. She hadn't told Fly Boogie her exact agenda. She didn't know him well enough to trust him with the details. He was Zyir's man and off of that strength she decided to use him to her advantage.

"Yeah a'ight. Look I know a nigga young and fly and all that, but one thing ya' boy Fly ain't is dumb," he answered. "You trying to find something out about the prosecution to shake shit up. When all you got to do is cut off a few pair of loose lips, nah mean? A nigga with no lips can't do no talking."

Miamor smirked at the young hustler's remarks. He was confident as if he had a cloak of invincibility. That type of bravado came with youth. She had lived many days with that same cockiness, but she was older and smarter. She knew better. She couldn't kill everybody. This case was sewn up tightly. Too many low level hustlers and mid-grade buyers were exchanging testimony for deals. Most were hidden away in witness protection. One witness in one safe house was feasible, but multiple murders without the aid of her old crew was impossible.

"Again, I don't know what you're talking about," she reiterated.

Fly Boogie nodded and then proceeded to the door. "I can put in work and I'm not like these other li'l homies out here. Zyir is my man. Whatever I got to do to prove my worth, I'm with it. You can trust me."

"Good-bye Fly Boogie," she said with a half-smile. The kid was growing on her and his charismatic personality paired with his knack for the streets was appealing. He was a young goon, and a hustler by any means necessary. He was Carter Jones before the Italian cut suits, drug kingpin status, business acquisitions, and overseas connects. Fly Boogie was gutter but had so much potential. He was ride or die. If they ever came out of this she would definitely tell Carter how helpful Fly had been. *And if Carter never comes home, I'll put Fly Boogie on my team,* she thought, preparing herself for the worst.

The sound of the grandfather clock ticked slowly as the pendulum swung back and forth. Leena tapped her nude, manicured, nails against the wooden arm of the office chair as she waited patiently. The nude jumpsuit she wore along with six-inch heels, stood out amongst the poorly dressed businesswomen around her.

Their cheap threads paled in comparison to the immaculately styled attire she wore. While well composed in appearance, she was unraveling on the inside. She had become acquainted with the night hours since Monroe had gone away. Worry and stress etched permanent lines on her once youthful face. She was no longer a young girl in love with a bad boy. She was a grown woman, dealing with the consequences of loving a man whom conflicted with the law. Her choices had led her to this point. The choice to stay involved with The Cartel had been hers and now she was suffering, heart empty, future unpredictable. She was a dope man's wife and to a young girl it was a dream . . . to a grown woman it was a nightmare. The position was glitzy on the surface but dulled the person she was within. Leena wanted out and as she sat waiting for the Diamond family accountant to summon her, she was determined to find her exit.

"Leena Deveraux, Mr. Odom is ready for you now," the receptionist announced.

Leena stood and followed the thin, brunette to the back office. She nodded gratefully as the woman stood to the side and extended her arm so that Leena could bypass her. Mr. Odom stood, clad in a Brooks Brothers suit. He was distinguished with smooth, black, skin and a clean baldhead. The dark features of his goatee and thick eyebrows stood out on his face, perfectly groomed. His persona yelled wealth and he had a presence that made everyone around him attentive. He was the complete opposite of what Leena had expected. A rich, successful, black man paving a way in a legit atmosphere was so foreign to her. All she had been around for years was men involved in the game. This black man in front of her was refreshing. He smiled and extended his hand. The scent of his clean cologne awakened her senses.

"Thomas Odom," he introduced. "You must be Ms. Deveraux,"

"Call me Leena," she replied.

She sat down and placed her handbag in her lap as he walked around his desk to take his own seat. He folded his hands on top of his desk, the lines of the suit hugging his broad shoulders.

"What can I help you with?" he asked.

Leena cleared her throat before she spoke, trying to swallow the lump that had formed. She wasn't a dumb girl. In fact, she had a bachelor's in business, although it did very little besides collect dust in a box. She had allowed herself to be sucked into the lifestyle of the rich and infamous. Leena had completely abandoned the concept of a normal life, but there was only so much she could take. After the catastrophe of her wedding day and Monroe disappearing into the sky, she could no longer take this life.

"My fiancé was Monroe Diamond," she started. "I'm here to speak to you about Diamond enterprises. I know that he along with Carter and Breeze have a lot of money put into that corporation. I'd like to talk about investment opportunities. The family is interested in going in a different direction."

Odom studied her as she spoke, admiring her beauty. "First let me express my condolences to you and your family. I'm sure this is a very hard time for you, but I can not speak to you about Mr. Diamond's financial affairs. He wasn't a client of mine. He was a loyal client of Jamison Wildes. Perhaps you should be speaking to him about the Diamond affairs."

Leena went into her Birkin and removed a manila envelope. "I thought you may say that Mr. Odom . . ."

He waved his hand. "Thomas," he said, dismissing the formalities.

"Thomas, well Jamison Wildes only handled the domestic accounts for Monroe. You are far better versed in foreign money, which is why Monroe hired you to handle any international transactions, including Swiss and Cayman accounts. Here is Monroe's living will," she said as she passed it to him. "As you can see he left his third of Diamond enterprises to me. Along with that is the living will of Carter Jones. I already have his beneficiary along with Breeze on board. We want to change the way that our money is earned. I know that Monroe trusted you with his money because of that I trust you."

Odom pulled his tie and sat back in his seat, crossing his leg over the other. "I have done business with the Diamond family for many years. I tried over a decade ago to steer Carter Sr. away from his way of business. It saddens me that it took so much loss to come to this," Odom said. "Unfortunately the government has seized all accounts associated with your family. There is no money."

Leena smirked. "That's funny. What you have to understand Thomas is that our men prepared us for this day. You don't fall in love with a man like Monroe Diamond without preparing for the inevitable fall from grace. I want the money that's tucked away in the Swiss and Cayman accounts. I want it in cash and I know exactly how much it is so please don't try to short change me."

Odom smiled as he got comfortable in his chair. Intrigue danced in his eyes. Leena's hard exterior covered up a bleeding interior as her heart beat rapidly. She hadn't had a sleep filled night since the Feds had come around. Leena needed the money to take The Cartel corporate. She didn't know how yet, but she knew that the move was completely overdue and absolutely necessary.

"Stand please," Odom said.

"Excuse me?" she asked, suddenly thrown off.

He motioned with his fingers smoothly for her to stand. She put her hand bag down on the floor and stood, as did he. He rounded the desk, his tall figure walking toward her. Fragile and heart broken Leena's thought drifted to Monroe. Until now, she had never had to take the lead. She was so comfortable following. Thrust into power, it was her place to now manage the money that Monroe had left behind. She needed to square her shoulders, put fire in her eyes, and boss up her entire life but instead all she felt was emptiness.

As Odom stood in front of her he seemed to see through her. "You're beautiful Ms. Devereaux. It truly pains me to see a woman like you so broken. You are worthy of much more."

Leena sucked in a sharp breath. *Am I that transparent? S*he thought. Odom was handsome and she had his full attention. Leena silently wondered what life would have been like had she met a man like him. He was what Monroe would have been had the war with the Haitians not happened. Instead she had been caught in a web of drugs, lust, and money. She had fallen for not one but two Diamond brothers. She hadn't stood a chance.

Sensing her discomfort he switched the subject. She was clearly mourning. She smiled demurely. "I'm fine. A bit uncomfortable standing in six inch heels when I could be sitting comfortably," she replied.

He cleared his throat. "I'm sorry. I just need to be sure. Please hold out your arms."

Leena frowned but did as she was told. His hands began to roam. "You think I'm wired?"

Odom didn't answer, but he continued to search her. When he was sure that she was clean he nodded.

"I apologize. The IRS and other bureaus have been combing through my records trying to make me an accomplice in this case. I can't be too careful. Now let's talk about the money . . . perhaps over dinner?" Odom asked.

Leena was stuck for a moment. *Did he just ask me out?* She thought. He sensed her hesitation. "I realize that you are basically Monroe's widow.

I was in attendance at the wedding turned massacre remember. It's just dinner and good company while attending to business."

"Okay," Leena said. She wanted to say no, but until she got the money in her hands she decided to keep things comfortable between them. He wouldn't be the first accountant to clean out a client, so she decided to play it safe to hinder any foul play. "I'll send a car for you tonight at 7:00 p.m."

Odom's eyes widened in surprise.

She chuckled slightly as she grabbed her bag. "I'm the Cartel Mr. Odom. I have to control my surroundings. Guess I picked up a few tricks to the trade being around Monroe."

"Apparently," he quipped. The way he eyed Leena, she knew that she would have to be careful with him. He had never met a woman like her and she knew that he never would. She was one of a kind and held a power that even she did not yet realize. Her mind was so sharp that she could outthink the majority and now it was her time to come into her own. A new regime was emerging. The streets had forced Miamor, Leena, and Breeze into a sisterhood. Together, they would takeover.

Chapter 6

*"I forgave you because my brother loves
you but I don't fuck with your clique."*
—Breeze

Breeze stepped out of the chauffeured Maybach with oversized Bulgari shades hiding her
true emotions from the cameras. She was the
surviving child of the infamous king of Miami,
Carter Diamond. She was a living legend and
everyone wanted a piece of her. Controversy circled the family like vultures waiting for death.
The news reporters stayed on her particularly.
Everyone wanted a comment, an interview; even
Time Magazine had offered her money for a sit
down. Street fame was turning into actual fame
for Breeze; she wanted none of it however. The
only thing Breeze craved at the moment was
Zyir. Loneliness consumed her days while the
only companionship she had at night was grief.
Leena and Miamor were lucky. They had the

seeds of the men they loved to cultivate. Even in Carter and Monroe's absence, the children they left behind provided comfort. Breeze was alone. Breeze was not a mother. She had no piece of Zyir, besides her memories and even those weren't enough. She wanted her man. She was skeptical about his well-being. A part of her didn't believe that he was alive, but Miamor seemed so sure that it kept a tiny spark of hope blazing in Breeze's chest. Breeze was the weakest link but she hid it well. Sunglasses were a permanent veil to cover her red, puffy, eyes. Her expensive clothes distracted the masses from her hunched shoulders. She disguised her burden well because she made sure she was always put together right. It was how her mother, Taryn had raised her. "You have to always be a bad bitch." It was words she had lived by her entire life, but in the absence of all the people who had sworn to be her protectors, they never rang more true. The hired goon stood suited in Italian threads while concealing American metal in his holster. His six foot five inch frame pushed the reporters out of the way as she trailed him into the building to meet the federal prosecutor.

"Ms. Diamond, how does it feel to be the last member of The Cartel standing?"

"Is it true that your family is responsible for seventy percent of the murders in Dade County?"

"Ms. Diamond can you comment on the mysterious plane crash that killed your brothers and live-in boyfriend?"

Breeze kept her head low as she held onto the back of her bodyguard's shirt. The thirsty media was so focused on breaking open the story of the largest crime family in the South and they were relentless in their tactics. Relief came as she stepped inside of the rotating doors.

"Wait here for me," she instructed.

The average person would have been shaken by a request to meet with the law, but Breeze was fully prepared. She had a pit on a chain in the form of her attorney, Rosenberg and like a loyal dog ready to bark he stood waiting for her in the lobby. He had represented the family for years, dating back to Big Carter and Polo. He knew of their dealings intimately and had protected them from persecution for a few decades. He had attended family barbecues, holidays, and birthday parties. Breeze felt completely safe in his care.

"Breeze, how are you?" he asked as he greeted her with a firm handshake.

"I'd be better if I didn't have to be here. What is this about?" she asked as they made their way to the elevators.

"This is a fishing expedition," Rosenberg replied. "You can let me do all the talking. That's what you pay me the big bucks for." He gave her a wink and she smiled, feeling relaxed as she followed one of her father's oldest friends into the lion's den.

Rosenberg led her directly into the office of Daniel Broome, the P.A. assigned to take down her family. Her internal alarm immediately went up.

"Rosenberg, I didn't realize you would be joining us," Broome said.

The two guests took a seat without being asked and Breeze folded her legs, making herself comfortable.

"You should know better by now Daniel," Rosenberg replied, showing disrespect by using his first name.

Daniel Broome was an American bread golden boy. Son of a senator and an ivy-league grad, he came out of law school with a readymade position. He had assisted on many cases, including the original case that the Feds had brought against Carter Diamond. When they didn't convict, Broome had a hard-on for The Cartel and now that the children of the man whom had eluded the law were in his clutches he was determined to bring justice. He was a young, ambitious, lad . . . too ambitious for Breeze's taste.

"Why am I here?" Breeze asked.

"Breeze as you know I've been following your family for quite some time. This case is strong, completely rock solid. Before the death of your brothers and your boyfriend my focus was on convicting them. Their deaths don't mean that this case goes away. Someone still has to pay for the damage that has been done to the streets of Miami."

The P.A. pulled out a manila folder and began to pull out still photographs. "Your family, your father, your brothers have destroyed this community," he said. He placed a picture of a young boy laid out in his own blood before her. Breeze didn't flinch. He then placed a picture of a young toddler who had been hit by a stray bullet. Again, Breeze was unmoved. There were casualties in war. "Innocent people have lost their lives behind the melee of The Cartel."

Breeze felt badly for the people in the pictures, but she was raised up in a game where death was an everyday factor. She had lost everything and no one was sitting back mourning for her . . . feeling sorry for her. Breeze had experienced it all and she was still here, standing tall. She gave no fucks about anybody who was outside of the scope of The Cartel family. If her brothers had executed anyone, they had deserved it. As many losses as The Cartel had taken, she felt no qualms about the losses of others.

"These are sympathy tactics you use on a jury Daniel. Cut to the chase. What do you want?" Rosenberg asked.

"I would like to put a deal on the table," Broome said. "When I get the jury to convict, you will go away for the rest of your life. You are a young woman Breeze. You don't want to grow old in prison. If you give me the cocaine supplier we can shift the focus of this case to a larger entity."

Breeze remained stoic as she sat back judging the suit and tie, white-bred, lawyer. *He has no idea what he is up against,* she thought. *I'm never going to cooperate. This is a waste of my fucking time.* Snitching wasn't an option. Emilio Estes supplied The Cartel so she would only be freeing family to enslave family. It was a catch 22.

"Can I have a moment with my client?" Rosenberg asked.

Breeze raised her hand. "We don't need a moment. There's nothing to talk about. We'll pass," she said.

Breeze stood to her feet, signaling that the meeting was over. Rosenberg followed her lead. "See you in court."

Breeze walked out of the office and bumped directly into a girl.

"Excuse me," the girl said. She quickly turned her head and kept walking but her presence made Breeze freeze in her steps as she watched the girl make a hasty retreat.

Goosebumps formed on her arms as her heart beat rapidly as her fight or flight instincts kicked in. It was as if she had seen a ghost. The girl had only spoken two words to Breeze but that was all that was needed for Breeze to recognize the voice. There was a murder mama in town and as Breeze high tailed it out of the office fear chilled her to the bone.

"Breeze! Is everything okay?!"

Rosenberg didn't even get a response. All he saw was Breeze's shaken facial expression as she disappeared behind the closing elevator doors.

"Miamor!!!"

Leena and Miamor stood to their feet in alarm as they heard Breeze's distressed voice break through the mansion.

"What's wrong?" Leena asked as Breeze entered the kitchen, where they had congregated for lunch with the children.

"Ask her," Breeze said as she pointed toward Miamor.

Miamor frowned as she withdrew the bottle from baby Carter's mouth. "Lower your voice please before you scare the kids," Miamor said with authority. "Have a seat, pour yourself some wine, and calm down before you talk to me."

"Fuck the wine. I saw your friend today at Daniel Broome's office. She walked different and she talked different but it was her. The bitch who helped kidnap me was in his office! I bumped right into her."

"My bitch," Miamor said with a smile.

"What? You knew she was here?" Leena asked distressed.

"Let's pour some wine. Let me explain," Miamor said. "But first are you absolutely sure it was her?"

Breeze shot Miamor a look that could kill. "It was her but why is she here?"

"I went to visit Aries to see if she could help me get to the P.A. She turned me down, but I guess she's had a change of heart," Miamor replied.

"Listen Miamor, I forgave you because my brother loves you but I don't fuck with your clique. I don't know them. They brought harm to the people I love. She is not welcome in Miami. If I have to I'll put money on the problem to make it go away," Breeze said threateningly. Had Breeze been any other person making any other threat Miamor would have bodied her, but Breeze was her sister. She had to remedy things between Aries and Breeze in order for everything to work.

"I need you to trust me Breeze. You are my family and I love you as such. She is not here to bring any more harm to you. I promise you on my son's life that she is here to help," Miamor reasoned.

"I don't care what she is here for. I don't rock with Aries," Breeze said. "And I don't deal with people who deal with my enemies."

Breeze stormed out of Miamor's home livid as hot tears burned at her eyes.

"Breeze?!" Leena called.

Miamor sighed. "Go after her. Make sure she's okay. Li'l Money can stay here with us. You have to meet the accountant tonight anyway. You can pick him up in the morning."

Leena kissed Miamor on the cheek. "I hope you're right about your friend being in town to help. We don't need anymore betrayal amongst us."

Miamor watched as Leena departed. She immediately picked up her phone and dialed Aries' number. Her presence could only help bring Carter back home . . . that's if Breeze didn't put her newfound power into play first.

***

Candles flickered and the scent of sea salt filled the humid air as Leena walked into the five-star restaurant. White clothed tables and couples in love filled the space as Leena made her way to the table where Odom was seated. She was conservatively dressed in a flawless vintage Chanel pant suit. She didn't want to give the wrong impression, but her beauty made it hard to hide her appeal. Her curves were sharp and as she walked she turned the heads of everyone around her. She came up behind Odom and said, "I have to say, I don't appreciate the change of venue. I was expecting a more appropriate environment."

She shifted uncomfortably, visibly displeased. Odom stood and placed his hand on her back as he guided her to her chair. He pulled it out for her before reclaiming his own spot. "I'm a fan of the steak," Odom dismissed.

"Hmm," Leena smirked. "We're here to talk about business. Lets be clear."

"Relax Ms. Devereaux . . . Leena, I understand your position. That doesn't make me any less intrigued by you. I must be honest. You seem more like a woman who prefers legitimate money."

"Money is money," she responded.

"I guarantee you Leena it isn't. No cop, no district attorney, no enemy can come and take my money away," Odom said. "My wife will be secure forever."

His words evoked something within her because she completely understood what he was saying. Just because it was truth didn't take the sting out of the words.

"An accountant's money can't afford me," she replied, slightly offended.

Odom smirked as the waiter walked up with a tray full of food. "I took the liberty of ordering."

"You don't even know what I like," Leena said.

"That's why I got a little bit of everything. It's good to try something new every once in awhile Ms. Deveraux. You never know, you just might like it," Odom answered suavely. She cut her eyes at him but the scent of the five star-cuisine invaded her senses as the waiter set the meal out in front of them. If this had been a date, she would have surely been intrigued by Odom. He was an eligible bachelor . . . charming, handsome, and well-off but he was too slow for Leena. The white-collar job was too safe to ever make her panties wet. While his efforts were flattering, they were in vain. In the end, all she wanted was the money. Odom thought that Monroe was deceased, otherwise he would never have the moxie to push up on his lady. While Leena was determined to draw a professional line clearly in the sand, Odom seemed insistent on crossing it.

"Tell me Leena, how does a woman like you end up in such a delicate predicament?" he asked.

"What's delicate about it? I have access to more money than people see in two lifetimes. Monroe left no stone unturned. My son and I will be well taken care of," she reminded. "Once you hand over the funds that is."

"It is very hard to produce that much money in cash without implicating myself. It would be much easier if I could arrange a trust for the three of you and your children," Odom said seriously.

"We want cash. Cash is untraceable," Leena said.

"Liquid cash is also dangerous. A trust makes you legitimate. That's what you want for The Cartel am I right? Legitimacy," Odom countered. Leena's mental wheels turned as he spoke. She was savvy when it came to business and she knew that he was right. If he set up the trust correctly, he could make it appear as though it was earned from legal sources. Cash would be risky. Every purchase would be scrutinized and they would be able to secure no lines of credit.

The cash would make them hood rich but Leena and the girls were trying to establish an empire that could rival the likes of the Trumps and the Rockefellers.

The sounds of Nina Simone cut through the air as a live band began their set.

"Dance with me," Odom said, his white smile decorating his face nicely.

Leena cleared her throat and reached for her wine glass. She took a sip, extending her long neck upwards as she took her time responding. Her red lipstick left a kiss of seduction on the glass.

"That would be inappropriate," she answered.

"Maybe, but it would also be fun." Odom stood to his feet and extended his hand to her.

Leena smiled. She would have to watch this man. He was too smooth for his own good. "You gone leave me hanging. Don't make me tuck my tail in embarrassment. One dance," he said.

Leena rolled her eyes and gave him her hand while simultaneously throwing her napkin on the table.

"One dance," she shot.

She stood and he escorted her onto the floor with the other patrons who were gently swaying to the music.

Odom pulled her close, but still left space between them so that she was comfortable. "When is the last time you had fun?"

Leena's mind went down memory lane but she knew that it had been so long ago that she couldn't recall exactly.

"Every day of your life should be fun Leena, carefree, comfortable," he said. He lifted his hand and spun her, then pulled her back close.

"Maybe in another lifetime," she said. "I'm sure you are a very good man. In fact you seem like the perfect man, for a different type of woman. I am flawed. My life isn't black and white. I've been living in the gray for so long that I could never go back. A square life doesn't suit me."

Leena let go of his hand as the music faded. "Now if you don't mind, let's talk more about this trust . . ."

The water parted like the red sea as Monroe's hands moved rhythmically as he swam with aggression. 50 laps had become light work for him. The early morning sun was just rising. He could feel it warming his muscular back. He came up on the edge of the pool, panting as he finished his a.m. workout. He admired the orange rays of morning light as they slowly seduced the slumbering earth into awakening. He eased his body out of the water and stood in tight swim shorts, the V-cuts of his lower abdomen toned and defined. Monroe was built like a Greek God. He was completely conscious of what he put into his temple. After surviving a near death experience he wanted to take care of himself and live as many years as he could. He was still playing catch up for the five years he had lay in a coma. Feeling his pulse racing as he pushed his body to the limit made him feel alive. He did any activity that made his heart pump blood to his organs. Yoga, swimming, basketball, golf, weights, it didn't matter . . . movement made him feel most alive. He grabbed the towel from the Saudi Arabian woman who awaited poolside. Draped in beautiful fabric she was his personal assistant. The Saudi's had been very accommodating to them and he felt completely comfortable in the far away land. Carter had instructed them to put home in the back of their minds but being the control freak that he was he always kept an eye on Miami, even from Saudi Arabia.

Monroe walked over to the poolside spread that lay out for him. Breakfast and a USA today were neatly placed out for him. It was a routine that he had done since leaving the states. It was his way of staying abreast in a world that was now so foreign.

"Shall I set a place out for Mr. Jones?" his lovely assistant asked, causing Monroe to raise his head. He saw Carter emerging from the immaculate resort and headed toward him. He wore a casual confidence on his face and a controlled arrogance led the cadence of his footsteps as he approached. For the first time in years Carter wasn't strapped. He was completely carefree in Saudi. No one posed a threat. They were amongst allies and it felt good. The only thing that was missing was his Miamor. In her absence one thing was very certain, the ladies still swooned over him. Even within a society where religion was so thick and women were held to a higher standard, he still turned their panties to puddles whenever he entered a room.

"Yes, you can set up a place for him. Thank you," Monroe replied. "Its kind of early for you huh bro?" he greeted. "I know you ain't trying to join me with the morning routine. From the looks of things Saudi is treating you good. Nigga getting a gut and all."

Carter chuckled. "I don't do that sweating shit bro. I leave that for you. I'm feasting like a king, this that money gut play boy," he cracked jokingly.

Carter sat across from Monroe and graciously accepted the coffee that Monroe's servant poured for him. "Is there anything else you need Mr. Jones? I would love to oblige any request," the girl cooed as she batted her eyes.

Monroe smiled as Carter shooed the girl away, requesting privacy.

"Get your own desert girl. That's all me," Monroe said.

"Ladies recognize real muscle. That gym shit ain't working bro," Carter teased. The men shared a friendly laugh but Monroe could see there was something Carter had come to get off his chest.

"I know you ain't up at the crack of dawn to banter. What's up fam? Speak your piece," Monroe invited.

"I know I've told you and Zyir to dead all communication back home, but I've kept my eyes and ears open to the circumstances of The Cartel . . ."

"As have I," Monroe admitted.

Carter pulled a burner phone out of his pocket and pulled up a picture before passing it to Monroe.

The average person wouldn't have been able to see the anger that suddenly struck Monroe but Carter noticed the tension that had filled his jawline. As Monroe stared at Leena dancing closely with their accountant Odom, he was livid.

"Apparently, Odom hasn't given up the money in the Swiss accounts yet. I'm told that Leena is being compliant to his dinner requests, his impromptu business meetings, just to keep things running smoothly until he turns over the cash. He thinks your dead. Leena is a beautiful woman."

Monroe slid the phone back over to Carter. "Don't worry about it," he said arrogantly. "That square ass nigga don't got a chance with my girl. If a nigga can pull my bitch he can have her."

Carter nodded. "Just wanted to let you know what Leena and the girls are up against."

"Who do you have as your eyes in Miami?" Monroe pondered.

"F. Boogie, who else?" Carter answered, matter of factly. "Miamor doesn't even know that I'm in communication with him yet."

Monroe nodded. "He's a smart kid. Definitely need to promote him for his loyalty when we return," Monroe said. "I'll get with you later fam."

Monroe headed up to his penthouse suite. Although he didn't wear his heart on his sleeves he was highly bothered by Odom's blatant lack of morals. He hadn't been "dead" long enough for anyone to push up on his lady, especially not a close family friend. There were two things that Monroe didn't play games about. His money and his woman.

Chapter 7

"The young diamond princess always
has been easily shaken."

—Aries

Miamor knew Aries well enough to know that when the time was right she would make her presence known. After Breeze's spotting Miamor decided not to call her old friend, but instead to give her room to work. *What the hell do you have up your sleeve Aries?* Miamor wondered. She looked at the text message she had received from an undisclosed sender. Anonymity did little to hide the identity of the sender, it was Aries. As Miamor went to the place she used to call home so many memories flooded her system. Miamor was headed to her old condo in Miami. It was the one that she had sat in with all of her girls, including her sister, plotting in. It was the place where she had first realized that her love for Carter was real. It was familiar to Miamor and when she pulled in front of the building she smiled. It was nothing like the castle she lived in now, but at one time in her life it had been home. She left her car on the street and fed the meter before heading up. She was cautious because she feared being under the federal scope. She drove around in circles for at least an hour before heading to her true destination. She took the steps, an old habit from her hit-woman days. She never liked closed off spaces. Elevators left her vulnerable. She would rather go up and down a million stairs than to be a sitting duck in a confined space. Her calfs burned until she conquered the fifteen flights that led to her old doorstep. A light sweat had formed under her clothes and she gave herself a moment to still her racing heart.

"It's a lot of steps right?"

Aries voice echoed in the stairwell causing Miamor to spin around. Aries was one flight above her. She was the only other person in the world who would have opted for the hard route. They were one in the same.

"Bitch I should have known," Miamor said. "Now you mind filling me in on how you weaseled your way inside the P.A.'s office? You nearly sent Breeze on a tirade after she bumped into your ass. Thanks for the heads up!"

"The young diamond princess always has been easily shaken," Aries recalled. "Let's go inside, I'll explain everything. I think I have something that can help you."

Miamor watched as Aries unlocked the door and walked inside. The apartment was white walls and white carpet; bare with the exception of a blow-up mattress that filled the space.

"What made you decide to help me?" Miamor asked.

Aries placed her hands on her wide hips and shrugged. "I knew your crazy ass would have tried to do it yourself if I didn't help. Through it all Miamor you are my sister. We are the only ones left."

"Where's your son?" Miamor asked.

"Somewhere safe," Aries said shortly. "I'm not here to stay. I will never move him to the place where I have done so much dirt. Once the job is finished I'm going back into the shadows."

"Understood," Miamor replied. "How did you get a job at the prosecuting attorney's office?"

Aries reached into her skintight jean pockets. They hugged her thighs so snugly that her hand barely fit into the pockets. She pulled an ID badge out and handed it to Miamor. "Shit I don't work for the prosecuting attorney. I snagged an ID badge, clipped it to my shirt, and walked in the building like it was home. There are so many interns running around there; fetching coffee and making copies that no one even batted an eye. They just think I'm another face to do their odd jobs and make lunch runs."

"You are a bold bitch Aries, I'll give you that. If one finger print is traced . . ."

"It won't be. I'm careful," she asserted.

Aries pulled out her phone and opened her email. "I've been around the office for a few weeks now and at first I couldn't find anything. The fact that Broome was so squeaky clean is what made me determined to keep digging. Nobody has no dirt. There is always something. A cheating spouse, a kid or parent on dope . . . your homeboy Broome was pulling up too clean."

"So how does this help me?" Miamor asked, impatient.

"I started clocking his movement, his emails, his calendar and on Thursdays at 4:00 p.m. there is a firm meeting he leaves the office to attend. I logged into the system with his ID but I couldn't get an idea of who he was meeting, so I followed him," she said. Aries went into the hall closet and retrieved a leather MCM back pack. She removed a DSLR camera, unscrewed the expensive lens, and then passed the body to Miamor. "Flip through the pictures," she instructed. "You know who that is?"

Miamor went through the still images. "I can't tell. You don't have any of his face. Is he gay? He's meeting with his lover? I don't understand . . ." She kept moving the images until finally, Timmy "Two Time" Bono appeared on the screen.

"He's meeting with the mob," Miamor whispered as her brow furrowed and her fingers clicked the buttons anxiously, while she gripped the camera tightly. She was speeding through the pictures so fast that they began to play in front of her like a movie. Broome was passing Timmy Bono a stuffed, yellow, envelope but before she could inquire about the contents the next flick showed Timmy Bono pulling money out and thumbing through it.

"Are they paying him off for a case?" Miamor asked.

"He's placing bets," Aries said. "He's into horse racing bad."

"How can you be sure?" Miamor asked with a gasp and a glint of mischief in her eyes.

"Gamblers have a language of their own. My husband used to gamble. If you sit back and listen they don't talk about favorite sports teams, they focus on the numbers. The over, unders, the spreads. They talk about the breed of a horse, its bloodline. I know an addict when I see one. Timmy Bono is the biggest Italian gangster in Florida. He retired here from Chicago. He's not into the drug scene, but he's head of the largest underground gambling ring on the East coast. Everybody places bets with him. Athletes, actresses, rappers, and apparently prosecuting attorneys."

"The question is what is he betting on?" Miamor asked.

"The races," Aries replied, matter-of-factly. "The Kentucky Derby is coming up and he's preparing to put it all on the line. I told you. He's got a bad itch for horses."

"Than let's put him in a position where he has everything to lose," Miamor whispered as she painted a beautiful picture of deception in her head.

The smell of money laced with cigar smoke and manure filled the air. Elaborate hats with feathers and jewels sat atop the heads of the women in attendance and everyone had brought out their finest wears. Aries and Miamor blended with the eclectic crowd. They didn't want to gain attention so they kept their presence demure.

"The entire front row around the entire track is big fish," Aries schooled. "Mostly Asian. They always have the most money in the pot."

"This shit is unreal," Miamor said as she looked around the massive track. She had thought the Miami championship crowds were thick. The entire city came out whenever the popular team played, but the entire world seemed to show up for the derby. She bumped into so many people that her shoulder was beginning to feel sore.

Miamor had to check her temper and keep a level head. *Everything is riding on today,* she thought.

Inside of her Birkin she had an envelope filled with 75k. More money than any stable hand would ever see at one time. Miamor was sure that this would get her next to Mona Lisa, the prize winning, legendary horse that Broome had placed $100,000 on. When Miamor found out that Broome was a gambling man, she knew she had him. The question was, how had he come up with such a hefty sum of cash to place the bet in the first place. After much digging, Aries discovered that Broome had borrowed the cash from the evidence locker in a federal case. His horse was what the gambling world would call a favorite. All of the odds fell in its favor. Once Broome collected his winnings he would be able to replace the cash while keeping fifty thousand that he had flipped in the race. The plan would have been foolproof had it not been detected. Now Miamor was about to ruin his life.

They were oblivious to the festivities. Miamor and Aries kept their eyes on the horses. They watched the jockeys. They watched the people behind the gates as a horse retired after its race. Their eyes caught everything, until finally Miamor chose her mark.

"Her," she said with certainty.

"How do you know?" Aries asked.

"I just know," Miamor said.

Aries had seen the determined look on Miamor's face many times before and she trusted her friend's intuition. She shrugged with indifference. "All right. Let's do it."

The duo waited for hours until they finally noticed the woman they had seen earlier at the track, emerging and headed toward the parking lot. Her long hair fell in one length past her middle back and was pulled into a sloppy ponytail. Her dirty clothes revealed the fact that she had worked closely with the horses all day. The woman slightly hunched over, her posture poor as she walked tiredly to her car.

"Follow her," Miamor instructed Aries and like clockwork they pulled out of the parking lot right behind their mark. Miamor and Aries worked like two hands, one washed the other. It was as if they had fallen right back into their old ways. They were parts of a well-oiled machine. Their work was efficient and flawless. "Hurry, don't lose her," Miamor urged, anxiously.

They tailed her for half an hour before pulling across the street from a small blue house with worn shutters and peeling paint. The front screen door was hanging half way off the hinges, but the woman beamed gratefully as she got out of her car, as if she was going home to a palace.

Miamor waited until the woman placed her key in the lock before she exited her car. Aries looked left, Miamor right. The streets were bare. Cloaked in the night's shadows, their identities were concealed. It was the perfect stage for treachery, but Miamor hoped that things played out smoothly. Miamor hurriedly walked up the walkway and just as the woman was pushing her door open, Miamor was forcing her inside.

"Agh!" the woman yelled startled.

"Shhh," Miamor said as she cupped her mouth. "Is there anyone else inside this house?" she asked.

The woman's eyes were filled with terror when Aries brandished her .45 while she looked around cautiously. She shook her head.

The home was barely the size of a small apartment and Aries checked it quickly. "No one is here," she informed.

"Good, that'll give us privacy to talk," Miamor said. "I'm going to take my hand from over your mouth. You can't scream. If you scream then my friend here is going to have to silence you . . . permanently. Nod your head if you understand me."

The woman nodded frantically and Miamor let her go.

"What do you want? I'm a poor, old, woman, I don't have anything of value," she said.

"You have something that is of great value to me," Miamor said softly. "I'm not going to hurt you. I'm here to offer my help in return for yours."

The woman stood clutching herself as her eyes danced back and forth between Miamor and Aries.

"I . . . I don't understand," she stammered.

"Please sit," Miamor said. The woman did as she was told while fear corrupted her heart.

"You have access to the horses in tomorrow's 6:00 p.m. race," Miamor started.

The woman nodded nervously.

"I need the Mona Lisa sabotaged and I'm willing to pay $75,000 for your assistance," Miamor said bluntly.

Flabbergasted the woman immediately shook her head. "I . . . I can't . . . I could never . . . I love those horses."

Miamor looked down at the stack of bills on the entry table. "It looks like you could use the money. No offense but this is hardly living," she said, referring to the house. She was trying to get what she wanted by using sugar before the situation turned to shit.

The woman stood. "Please, you have to leave. I don't want your money. I'll get by. Please I'm not interested" the woman pleaded fearfully. She was obviously frightened as she tried to usher her unwanted guests to the door. Miamor hated to put this burden on the woman's heart. She seemed nice and Miamor knew that she had grown soft. In the past she wouldn't have cared about her mark, but today she felt compassion for the disheveled woman before her. Not many people would turn away from such a large sum of money. The woman had principles and Miamor respected it. It wouldn't help the woman out of the situation, but still Miamor gave the woman a few points for trying to stand her ground.

"Okay remember I tried it the nice way first," Miamor said, her voice suddenly cold. She walked around the living room as if she owned the place until her gaze fell upon a mantel of framed pictures. "What do we have here? Children? I'd bet you would hate to see anything bad happen to them."

"Please . . ." the woman's eyes were wide and filled with tears as her bottom lip trembled.

"Look bitch let me make this perfectly clear," Aries interrupted as she placed her gun to the woman's head. "You're going to inject Mona Lisa with a shot tomorrow directly before the race.

Simple, quick, and easy. If you refuse by the time you leave the tracks little miss blondie up there . . ." Aries pointed to the picture of the woman's daughter. "and those two ugly little grandkids of yours will be dead before you get home. Don't think we can't find them. We've done this for quite some time. I assure you, we're quite good at it," Aries threatened.

Miamor stepped up. "All you have to do is inject one shot. It'll be the easiest $75,000 you ever make," Miamor finished. "Do we have a deal?"

The woman nodded in trepidation as her tears finally broke free and fell down her face.

"Relax. You do this and you'll never hear from us again. You don't and we'll be back, next time for blood. You tell anyone about this little visit and you'll be burying your entire family by the week's end," Aries threatened. Miamor handed the woman a shot of a drug called Lasix. Some breeders used the drug to stop their horses lungs from bleeding while racing. It was three times the normal amount that breeders usually give their horses before a race. It would dehydrate Mona Lisa so badly that the horse would most likely die before ever meeting the finish line. Once Broome was broke and desperate, Miamor would have him right where she wanted him. It was only a matter of time . . .

***

Odom pulled his Aston Martin out into traffic as he loosened his necktie. The day had been long and stressful. Gathering the money that the Cartel had stacked for a rainy day had required all of his focus. He had needed to ensure that he didn't leave a paper trail that would lead him to the big house. He had set up two trust accounts, one for Miamor and the other for Leena. Because they weren't directly related to the Cartel he could create whatever financial history he wanted them to have. Since Miamor had practically lived under the grid since her teenage years, her credit was non-existent. Leena had worked in cash so her credit was neither good or bad. It was easy for him to manufacture perfect credit scores for them both. Breeze on the other hand was another story. Her family was deeply rooted in the drug game and any trust that he set up for her would have been immediately seized. Her money was placed in Leena's account for safekeeping, but he wasn't ready to hand over the key to their new fortune just yet. Odom was smitten with Leena and wanted nothing more than a shot to court her. She had accepted the dinner invitation but he knew that once she had access to her own money she wouldn't need him anymore. He needed a little bit of time to show her that a legit life wasn't so bad. His attraction was strong and he was trying to get to know her. The late night text messages that he would send her were always politely returned. His early "Morning beautiful" lines answered immediately, but always safely. He understood her hesitance. She was a new widow. Her last relationship had left her lonely, overwhelmed, and hurt, but Odom was determined to crack her. He wanted to introduce her to something new. Her consistent no's only made him more persistent. A man of the upper class, he was used to getting his way. Most women let him have his way with them with just the flash of his black card. He was attractive, successful, important, but he lacked the raw edge that Leena was drawn too. In the end when she was around him she didn't feel that familiar pulse in her pussy. Mecca had made her feel it at first sight and Monroe had made her wish she didn't. Odom knew that he had his work cut out for him, he was up for the challenge. He was hoping that the unexpected bouquet of roses he had sent over to her home would at least be rewarded with a call. He had been anticipating her response all day. He picked up his phone and saw that he had no missed calls.

"Fuck it," he whispered to himself as he took matters into his own hands. *There's nothing wrong with going after what I want,* he coached himself.

The phone rang twice before the husky melody of her voice filled his ear.

"Hello?" she answered.

"Just the sound of that voice brings so much joy to what has otherwise been a shitty day," he said.

"Oh really?" Leena replied. He smiled because he could hear the laughter in her voice. "It couldn't have been that bad. You had the time in your schedule to send flowers to my door."

Odom chuckled and replied, "You're quite a distraction Ms. Devereaux. You don't quite seem like the roses type of girl, but they are beautiful all the same. I thought I'd play it safe."

"They aren't my favorite flower," she admitted. "But the arrangement was beautiful. Thank you. When can we expect to have our affairs in order?"

"We can arrange an affair anytime you are ready," he joked.

"Odom . . . you are a really nice man, but I'm . . ."

"Easy Leena. Don't stick me with the fork yet. I'm not done. It was only a joke. I understand your situation. I just want it to be known that I plan to wait. As long as it takes for you to get over your loss. I'm very interested in making you mine."

Her sigh was heavy on the other end of the line.

"Maybe I can take you to lunch. We can discuss the trust. All of the money is in two accounts. I can explain everything to you tomorrow. Maybe just maybe you will tell me your favorite flower. That way next time I know what to send. You pick the place this time and I promise I'll stick to your plans."

"I'll think about having lunch with you," she said after a long pause. "After we close out our business. I'll meet you at your office at noon."

"I'm looking forward to it," Odom said, flirtatiously.

"Good night Odom," Leena finished.

Odom could hear the sweetness in her tone and he ended the call with a half smile, feeling hopeful. Hope quickly faded into alarm when he saw the hooded figure rise out of his backseat.

"I don't know what the fuck you smiling for playboy. That little lunch date ain't happening," Fly Boogie retorted as he pressed cold steel against the back of Odom's neck. "You was putting all your game down too. My bosses feel that is a bit disrespectful. Slime-ball mu'fucka."

"Look you can have whatever you want. I have money . . ."

"I don't want your money. I have a message from Monroe Diamond," Fly Boogie said "His bitch ain't on the market."

Odom's eyes doubled in size as he realized this goon had been sent by a ghost himself. "I meant no disre . . ."

Fly Boogie hit Odom hard against his skull causing him to wince as his head jerked forward and the car momentarily went off course.

"Pull this mu'fucka over!" Fly barked.

"Please . . ."

"Dig this," Fly Boogie said calmly as the car rolled to a stop on the side of the road. "Tomorrow you're gonna hand over the money to Leena and cut off all communication with her going forward. If not I'm going to visit your mama out in Aventura off of Biscayne Blvd. Am I clear?"

"Crystal," Odom replied. He didn't have to ask how Fly knew his mother's address. He knew exactly who he was fucking with. The caliber of the Cartel's reign hadn't been seen since the days of the New York and Chicago Italian mobs. The Diamond family was heavy in Miami. He didn't know what he was thinking approaching a widow of The Cartel. He had let his little head get him into a beef when in actuality he wasn't built for that life.

"Good, now get out of the car," he ordered.

Odom stepped out of the car and out into the shower of rainfall that fell from the sky. Fly Boogie got out, gun trained on Odom.

"Please don't kill me," Odom said calmly, realizing that he was fucking with an entirely new type of drug dealer . . . one that neither the Feds nor death could catch.

"Get on the ground," Fly Boogie hollered as he kicked in the back of Odom's knee causing it to buckle. He fell to the wet ground, gritting his teeth and kicking himself for being so unaware of his surroundings.

"Better cut Leena loose tomorrow mu'fucka or its lights out for you," Fly Boogie said. "Sincerely, Monroe Diamond."

Fly Boogie climbed into the driver's seat and rolled down the window. "Ol' pussy ass nigga," he spat an insult before pulling off recklessly. Water back splashed onto his expensive suit as he watched Fly Boogie speed away from the scene.

"Fuck!" Odom shouted as he climbed to his feet throwing his fists at the air in frustration. He had clearly fucked with the wrong man's wife.

Chapter 8

*"I've got a thing for a woman
with aggression."*

—Carter

Carter erupted out of his sleep, immediately reaching for the handgun that lay at his bedside. It was instinct for him, especially during times of high stress. He would rather pop first and ask questions later than to be caught slipping. Only this time it was only Yasmine's face he saw. Her expression was fearless and held a bit of impatience as she raised an eyebrow at him. "You're going to shoot me?" she asked.

Carter lowered his weapon and swiped his tired eyes with his hands as he shook his head to wake himself up. *What the hell was she doing in his suite?*

"My fault ma. Its habit," he said as he climbed out of the comfort of the plush bedding, exposing his shirtless body. "You don't knock huh?"

"People knock when they are guests. I own this entire property. No need for me to tip toe around my own establishment," she replied with a smile. "I didn't mean to alarm you."

He could see the amusement in her eyes. "I'm funny?"

She shook her head. "Not at all Mr. Jones," she replied. "I find you quite intriguing. Men here, don't carry the same air of confidence that you do. You're . . . dangerous." She said.

"You shouldn't sneak up on dangerous men than," he replied.

"I happen to like danger," she answered flirtatiously. "How did you sleep?"

"Well."

"My father explained to me the circumstances that brought you here. I can only imagine the stress that you've built up. I've arranged something for you and the others. I think you'll find it very pleasing Mr. Jones," she said.

"Call me Carter," he corrected.

She nodded. "Carter," she said. She walked up on him, standing closely as she placed a finger on his chest. "Shower, get dressed, and then follow these instructions. It's my job to fulfill your needs."

He felt his manhood jump at the insinuation of her words. He would have to tread lightly around this siren. Images of her petite body bent over in front of him flashed through his mind, causing him to harden. It had been awhile since he had been inside of a woman. Miamor had been recovering from the delivery of their child. He had been on the run for his life. He hadn't realized how backed up he was until he felt his desire building in this moment. She stepped closer, pressing her body against his, feeling his wanting. "Hmm," she moaned softly. "You are definitely not like the men in Saudi Arabia."

Not one to let his little head do the thinking for him, Carter stepped back, putting room between them.

"I'll see you in half an hour. Monroe and Zyir have already received their invitations," she said. She turned and strutted out of the room and Carter couldn't help but wonder about what was underneath the clothes that she wore. He shook his head, hoping that he hadn't just run from one problem only to bump right into another. It was obvious that Yasmine was trouble just waiting to happen. He wasn't a young man. The potential for lust didn't distract him from the task at hand. He needed to lay low and he was interested in finding out more about Baraka's business practices. He wouldn't allow a woman to get in the way of a potentially fruitful partnership. He would keep her at arm's length because he had a feeling if she ever got her hands on him, he wouldn't want her to take them off. She was a temptress but he was a man of principle. He didn't shit where he slept which meant that the beautiful Arabian women around him were off limits, especially Yasmine Baraka.

The smell of vanilla filled the air as the smoke from the lit incense floated mystically into the air. The lights were dimmed as Zyir walked into the suite, surveying his surroundings. Women were everywhere. Hedonistic, sexy, uninhibited, as they partook in various sexual activities. A magnificent spread of food was presented on a long dining table. Fruits, wines, cheeses, meats . . . it was a king's feast.

"I hope this is to your liking."

He turned to see Yasmine enter the room with a friendly smile as Monroe followed her. "I arranged a bit of convenience for you gentleman. These harems are here to service you in any way. Your every desire, your every wish is their command," she said.

Zyir was led away by a naked woman just as Carter walked into the room. It was a full out orgy of woman on woman action. The scent of sex lingered in the air, hidden by the musk of the vanilla fragrance. Monroe looked back at him with a raised brow. "You see this shit?" he asked. "They treat us like kings over here."

"You are a king Money. Make sure you act like one. Take care of those who take care of you. Tip well for good service. These women work hard for their money fam," Carter said. Paying for pussy wasn't his thing and although this was being gifted to him, he still wasn't too interested. He liked to pursue a woman, wine and dine a woman, sweet talk the panties off a woman as she tried her hardest to resist. He enjoyed the art of the chase. This wasn't his vibe. "Enjoy brother, we all could use a release. Strap up," he warned.

He turned to leave.

"You don't like?" Yasmine asked.

"Its not my thing," he responded.

"What is your thing?" she asked curiously. The moans that filled the air caused him to look over his shoulder. Two of the most beautiful designed women he had ever seen were feasting on one another. One of them capturing the other's swollen clitoris in her mouth, sucking gently. Carter definitely needed a stress reliever but this wasn't his idea of a conquest. These women were following orders for the sake of a dollar. They weren't his type. Physically they were flawless but mentally they were weak.

"I've got a thing for a woman with aggression," he replied.

"Well I'll have to see if I can accommodate that?" she said. "Since this isn't your type of party, maybe you'll join me for the evening. I can show you around."

Carter reluctantly agreed. The last thing he wanted was to offend Baraka's daughter. They were his hosts and if it hadn't been for them he would be in police custody by now. He nodded and followed her out of the room. She led him to the front of the resort and out to the valet where an armed body guard waited for her.

"I don't think I'll be needing you tonight Aki," she said to the six foot nine inch, threatening presence. "I think Carter can protect me just fine. Although you will have to drive."

"Why is that?" he asked.

"Women aren't allowed to drive in Saudi Arabia. I have an SUV and a driver to escort me at all times, but I thought you would like to test out my Lamborghini?"

"Your father instructed me to escort you whenever you leave the property Ms. Baraka," her bodyguard spoke. He was a mammoth of a man and Carter didn't doubt that he provided excellent protection. His menacing looks alone would probably deter anyone from pushing up on Yasmine.

"I've got it homie," Carter said coolly as he placed his hand on the small of her back and guided her into the car. He walked around and jumped into the driver's seat before speeding away from the resort.

"Why do you have a lamb if you can't even drive it?" he asked.

"Because I can ride it," she responded seductively. "Big toys, fast toys, they're *my* thing. I get off on the finer things in life." She maneuvered in her seat as if her thighs were on fire and in actuality they were. She yearned to be touched by a man like Carter. The darkness of his skin, the confidence in his stride, the smoothness in his words . . . it all made her panties wet. She wondered what it was like to be the girl on his arm, to feel his hands on her ass as she rode him slowly. Saudi men were too damned docile. She wanted a man that would pull her hair as he slid into her from the back. One who would bust his gun if another lusted after her too openly. She desired a man with swag and Carter Jones was dripping with it.

"You're bad ma," he said with a chuckle.

"I'm so good at it too," she replied.

He shook his head and increased his speed, feeling the horsepower of the engine. "These ain't the kind of problems you want ma, trust me," he said, his thoughts flashing to Miamor.

She was a live wire and he loved it. It was her touch, her companionship, her wit that he was craving. Even if he used Yasmine in the bedroom, she could never make up for the other roles that Miamor served in his life. Without her he felt a void . . . sexually and otherwise. He was missing his lady and it showed.

Yasmine noticed the look of concern on his face and couldn't help but to pry. "Did you leave a girlfriend behind? Perhaps a few?"

"There's only one," he responded. "And she's not up for discussion," he replied vaguely. He didn't want to bring Miamor into his thoughts too much. She was his weakness and he didn't want to expose that fact.

The look of pure adulation in his eyes couldn't be hidden. A man who truly loved his woman couldn't deny it if he tried. Yasmine didn't know Miamor, but she couldn't help but envy her slightly.

She's not here. What a fool of a woman to let him venture so far away from home. Especially when there is a woman like me, waiting for her to slip up, Yasmine thought.

Yasmine guided him to the local market where rows and rows of the cities finest craftsmen set up shop each day to sell their goods. Carter stood out amongst the sea of cloaked men and women.

The heat beat down unbearably on him, causing him to remove the jacket to his Gucci suit and unbutton his Oxford shirt slightly.

"I should have warned you about the temperatures," Yasmine chuckled. "This isn't America. Its like a melting pot in this desert climate." She removed a linen scarf from her purse and reached up to wipe the sweat from his brow. Their eyes connected and she gave him a coy smile before withdrawing her hand and leading him through the rows of vendors.

The people of Saudi Arabia flocked to him as he walked the streets. Barefoot kids ran behind him offering to sell him goods that he didn't need, or even wanting to perform tricks for tips. Carter's heart went out to all of them. He purchased from every one who stopped him because he knew that the small change he was spending meant nothing to him, but so much to them.

"America! America!" they called to him, trying to lure him over to their shops and small stands. They spotted him from a mile away. His ritzy Rolex and shiny shoes gave away his wealth. He didn't mind spreading it however. He was having the time of his life. He held babies, and shook the hands of the local men as if he were the president himself.

"They like you," Yasmine said. She was highly impressed by the humility of this man. Not only was he a boss, but he had compassion and it only made her infatuation for him thicken.

He shot her a smile as a little boy behind him fell down suddenly. "Oww!!" his yelp was ear piercing as Carter turned his attention toward him. The kid couldn't have been older than six or seven. He had been trampled by the older ones trying to keep up. He was holding his bare, dirt covered, feet in agony. Carter bent down, resting his elbows on his knees so that he was eye level with the kid. The rest of the kids circled around the two of them as Carter helped him up. "You okay li'l man? Looks like you could use some shoes," he said. The boy looked at him in confusion and Yasmine quickly stepped up to interpret for Carter.

When the boy responded, Yasmine relayed the message. "He said his mother doesn't have money for shoes."

Carter picked up the young kid and placed him on his back, not caring that his thousand-dollar suit was now soiled in sweat and dirt. "Tell them all to follow me," he said.

Carter took over the streets of Riyadh Providence as he led a bunch of street kids from booth to booth picking them out whatever they wanted.

He made sure that each child left with a pair of shoes.

He was so distracted by the crowd that had accumulated around him that he never saw the men that had been lurking in the distance. Saudi Arabia was known for its oil. Many households lived in extreme wealth because of the industry but in this part of the city they were surrounded by nothing but poverty. It was where the poor resided and with him coming around flaunting his money, he became a quick target. Kidnapping was the name of the game. Wives of rich men were often held for extreme ransoms and with Yasmine as his escort she was in jeopardy. As the crowd thickened he lost sight of her. It wasn't until he heard her screams of distress did he realize that something had gone drastically wrong.

"Carter!"

Her voice broke over the crowd as Carter instantly turned to look for her. He spun left then right as he pushed through the crowd. It wasn't until he broke the edge did he see her being stuffed inside a raggedy van. She was fearless as she resisted the entire time, kicking and screaming as the man tried to force her into the car.

"Shit," he uttered as he ran, full speed back to the lambo. If he lost sight of the van there would be no getting Yasmine back. This wasn't his country, he didn't know the land or the language. All it took was for them to get away from the scene of the crime for her to be lost forever. He couldn't afford to have her abduction on his conscience. He would be solely to blame and the hospitality Baraka provided would quickly turn to hate, putting not only himself but his brothers at risk. He hopped into the car and sped off recklessly, burning rubber as he pushed the gas to the floor. Carter was sweating like a pig and he was slightly irritated. It had been a long time since someone had come at him on some rah rah shit but even though he was out of practice it was like riding a bike . . . he always remembered how to pop off. His temper flared as he caught up with the van with ease. There was no way the raggedy contraption could outrun the half-a-million dollar car. He passed the van and cut it off, stopping sideways in the middle of the deserted street. The van came to a screeching halt and before the driver could reverse in the opposite direction Carter hopped out of the car and let his canon bark.

BANG! BANG! BANG!

He couldn't really see through the nasty windshield of the van but he knew exactly where the driver was supposed to be sitting and when he heard the horn blare out of nowhere he knew he had hit his mark. Suddenly a second man hopped out of the van, holding Yasmine at gunpoint.

She was already gagged and bound as the man held a pistol, point blank range at her head.

His face was wrapped in Arabic garb, concealing everything but his menacing eyes. He screamed at Carter, making demands that Carter couldn't understand. There wasn't time to think, no time to do anything but react and as Carter pulled his trigger his heart stopped momentarily.

The bullet lifted the man off his feet and laid him flat. He rushed to Yasmine's side, snatching off the blindfold to find her hysterical underneath. It wasn't until he looked down did he see that he had hit the man between the eyes. Yasmine clung to him as he picked her up and carried her back to the car. "Let's get out of here," he whispered as she hugged his neck tightly. She pulled back and looked him in the eyes before placing her lips on top of his. His adrenaline pumped as sparks flew between them. A few seconds passed before Carter turned away.

"I can't," he whispered as he placed her in the passenger seat. He cupped her cheek. "You okay?"

She nodded and turned her feet inside as he closed the door. Carter ran his hands over her neatly waved Caesar cut and blew out a sharp breath. *What the hell am I getting myself into?* He thought. He hopped inside and pulled away from the bodies that he had left leaking in the middle of the street. He was supposed to be lying low, not adding to his body count. As he glanced over at Yasmine he realized that he was putting himself at risk in more than one way. *Its time to press chill,* he thought. *Today could have ended badly. It could have easily been me circled in chalk.*

"Please don't tell my father," she whispered as they pulled back up to the resort. "I just want to forget that today even happened and if he finds out he'll increase my security. They suffocate me as it is."

"How old are you ma?" he asked, curiously.

"Twenty-five," she responded. "Too old to have a babysitter."

Carter looked at her seriously and replied, "Men protect priceless possessions. You're irreplaceable. It's important to keep you safe."

She blushed and replied, "Thank you for saving my life today. If you hadn't been there . . . "

"You wouldn't even have been there if it weren't for me. I appreciate you taking me down there and showing me your city, but don't jump out of character for me. I get the feeling that you've never shook the hands of a poor person in your life. You were put in danger because you were out of your element," he replied.

"Yeah well everything about you is out of the ordinary for me Carter," she said. "and I don't plan on staying away."

Carter sighed and began to respond but was interrupted when the valet opened his door. He exited as did she and he guided her back into the comforts of luxury. As soon as they entered the sound of slot machines rang out in the air.

"Have a good night," she said. She wanted to kiss him and he knew that she wanted to, but they both also knew that he would stop her.

"You too," he said before retreating to his suite.

Chapter 9

"I'm attracted to the bad boys."

—Leena

BANG!

The sound of the loud bell sent the beautiful horses bolting as the race began. The beautiful stallions were like well oiled machines as their strong bodies darted around the track. Dirt kicked up from beneath their hooves as each jockey swatted their individual beast, pushing them to their limit. The crowd was loud, rowdy, and watching in pure marvel Miamor and Aries sat back, watching anxiously as the jockeys rode the horses with expertise around the track. Timmy "Two Times" Bono stood to his feet as he and his cohorts cheered along the sidelines, in the first row of the stadium seating. Miamor had no doubt that they stood to make a pretty penny on the race, or at least they would have if she hadn't tampered with the odds. Despite the 85-degree weather, various members of the Italian mob were dressed to the nines in expensive suits. Miamor's heart raced in rhythm to the sound of the the hooves hitting the dirt. She could hear the stampede in her ears and feel adrenaline pumping in her chest as she fisted the guardrail in front of her. Mona Lisa was in the lead and Miamor had to admit it was an exquisite animal. It was strong and determined as its nostrils flared while its legs moved swiftly. Miamor was enthralled. She anxiously stood to her feet. "Why isn't it working?" she wondered as she watched as Mona Lisa neared the finish line. "Aries . . . its not . . ."

Before she could finish her sentence Mona Lisa suddenly bucked and raised on its hind legs. The entire crowd stood and gasped as the horse seemed to freeze in mid-air, kicking its front legs in distress. The jockey struggled to hold on but was thrown off as Mona Lisa fell with a loud thud to the ground. The stampede of other horses raced right by the champion bred animal. No one seemed to focus on the winner as an underdog stole the race and an emergency team rushed out onto the track.

Miamor glanced at the Italian mobsters and saw not a trace of jovial excitement in their expressions. They each had lost a fortune, as had most of the people in attendance. She had to force herself to keep the sly grin off her face. "Let's go Mia," Aries whispered.

Miamor tore herself from the scene as she thought of the next part of her plan. Now she had to set-up the proposition to get Broome to drop the case against The Cartel.

Leena sprayed her Dolce Blue perfume as she stared at herself in the mirror. The emptiness that occupied her eyes was undeniable. As much as she wanted to tell Odom he was wrong, she knew that he was right. He could see through the fancy clothes, chauffeured cars, and queen on the throne, persona. Leena craved normality. If she were a normal girl in a normal world, her man would still be with her. He wouldn't be faking his death or running from federal cases. Sadness was paralyzing and she had been forcing herself to live in a fog ever since Monroe had first disappeared from her life. Mecca and Monroe had consumed her with lust, with love, with money, and power . . . she had been sucked in by it all. Like a moth to a flame it all was so enticing. Now she had been burned and Odom was there, saying all the things that she wanted to come from Monroe's lips. No, she didn't want Odom, but she would love to experience life on the right side of the law. She stepped into her Donna Karan dress and maneuvered her arms awkwardly to zip it to the top. She placed a blazer over it and slid into six-inch heels. She exited her bedroom and descended the steps to find her son playing boisterously with Breeze.

"Thank you for keeping him," Leena said.

"He's my nephew Leena. This isn't considered a favor. We are family," she replied. She turned her focus to Monroe's son. He looked so much like him, but his demeanor was mischievous like Mecca's. Li'l Money might have been Monroe's seed, but he had a piece of Mecca inside of him as well. Breeze recognized it even at such a young age. "What did auntie teach you? Huh? Diamonds are . . ."

"Forever!" the three year old quipped loudly with nothing but youthful innocence. He had no idea how deeply rooted that statement was or how true it rang. He was born, Monroe Diamond II, he would grow into a powerful man. "We'll be fine. Just get the money, finish this business and tell Odom to quit stalling you."

Leena nodded and then kissed Breeze on the cheek before leaving. The attention that Odom showered Leena with was flattering, but instead of making her feel good, it made her feel uncomfortable. She wanted Monroe to do those things, she wanted him to say the things that Odom said so eloquently. She wanted a square life. She could not endure any more of the streets. Although they came with many perks, if Monroe wasn't there to enjoy them with her, it wasn't worth it. Leena smiled at her driver as he held open her door and she slid into the back seat.

Her thoughts were so plentiful that they distracted her and made the thirty-minute drive fly by. Before she knew it she was pulling up to Odom's office. Passersby stopped as they attempted to see who was pulling up as the driver hit his hazards and hopped out to open her door. All they saw was legs for days as she stuck her Manolo out first to steady her balance. Leena exited smoothly, ran her hands over the fabric of her dress to smooth the wrinkles and then double stepped it into the building. Oddly, butterflies filled her stomach. So much weighed on her shoulders. She had to be coy enough to not disrespect Monroe's legacy but open enough to Odom's flirtation to keep him from turning snake. *I'll be glad when he come up off this money,* she thought to herself. She was tired of the charade because honestly it left her confused at the end of the night. Odom seemed to spot the empty spaces of her life and put them under a magnifying glass. He made her question Monroe's love for her. *If he truly loved me would I even be in this position?* She thought. "Stop it, of course he loves you," she whispered, scolding herself. "This man is about to stop playing with my money. I'm not leaving here today until it's in my possession."

Leena's step was more confident as she marched into Odom's office with determination. "Good morning Ms. Devereaux," the receptionist greeted at first sight. The many calls she had been instructed to place and flowers she had ordered for Leena on Odom's behalf . . . the woman was very familiar with Leena. "Please go right in. He's expecting you."

Leena gave the woman a gracious smile and headed into Odom's office.

She went to close the door, but Odom interrupted her. "Leave it open," he said with a direct tone. Leena paused and looked at him. "Sit."

He passed her two manila folders, sliding them across the table. "This concludes our business. The account numbers and trust information is inside the folders. Thanks for coming by."

Leena was taken aback by his tone and change of attitude. *Just last night he was sending flowers . . .* she thought. She was confused. He was abrupt with her, almost rude. He didn't even look at her in the eyes as he spoke to her.

He looked up from his desk. "You're still here because . . ." he let the words linger and Leena jerked her head back, insulted. She flipped through the pages of the manila folder and saw that all of what she needed was inside. The jig would have been up anyway. Now that she had all of The Cartel's assets in her possession she no longer needed to play nice. Leena stood to her feet abruptly. There was a weirdness in the room as if there was an invisible elephant between them. *Fuck it, I've got what I came for,* she thought. She turned on her heels but the nagging feeling that something was awry wouldn't let her leave without finding out what the hell was going on. She stopped as she reached the threshold of the door. Turning to Odom she opened her mouth to speak, but Odom held up his hand to stop her.

"Just leave Leena. I don't want that kind of trouble. You're off limits," Odom said, visibly shaken as he lacked his usual confidence. He was abrupt, almost rude, and obviously intimidated. This wasn't the flirtatious Odom that she had come to expect. In fact, it was almost as if someone had set him straight and she only knew one man that would do such a thing on her behalf.

Leena smirked as her entire chest warmed. She knew that Monroe had sent a message to

Odom. He had reached all the way across the world to put a man in his place for coming at his lady. It was then that she realized that no matter the burdens, she loved the swag of being with a dope boy . . . especially one that had risen into infinite power. Monroe had status and because of that so did she. Odom never stood a chance.

"You see Odom. That's why you would have never been able to get even a whiff of this. I'm attracted to the bad boys and the fact that you were so easily scared off shows exactly how much bitch you have in you," she said with a laugh. "And to think . . . I almost bought what you were selling." She shook her head back and forth before adding, "Good-bye Odom."

Leena strolled out of the office with complete confidence that her man was alive and well. She just hoped that Miamor and Aries did what they had to do so that he could finally come home.

Chapter 10

"Stop bluffing."

—Yasmine

Carter shook his head in disdain as the blackjack dealer swept up the losing hand. Saudi Arabia had given him a new ritual. He spent his mornings at the card tables trying to beat the odds but today he was nothing but bad luck. He felt a presence behind him as the scent of Yves Saint Laurent invaded his space and Yasmine came into his peripheral view.

"Looks like you need a break, the tables are murdering you," she said in her husky tone. Carter looked up at her and she flashed him an amused smile.

"You find my losses funny," he cracked with a half-smile.

She pinched two fingers together and scrunched her face. "Just a little bit. I've been in the camera room watching you lose all morning," she said.

She chuckled and reached down to pull him from his seat. "Let's go. Join me for brunch," she said.

Carter stood to his feet and pulled a wad of money from the pockets of his Brooks Brother slacks and placed three hundred dollar bills on the table. The dealer broke change but when he went to hand Carter the chips, Carter waved his hand. "Keep it," Carter said. He always tipped the dealers well and they loved him for it. "See you tomorrow morning Mr. Jones," the dealer said, never losing count as he dealt a new hand to the remaining players.

Carter nodded and then placed his hands in his pocket as he followed Yasmine out of the casino. The blare of slot machines filled the massive space and the smell of tobacco smoke clung to his clothing.

"I need to get out of these clothes, take a quick shower. I don't want to ruin your meal by smelling like an ashtray. I can meet you in a half hour," he said.

"Nonsense, we can stop by your penthouse on the way," she said.

Carter nodded. He didn't know her well but from what he could tell, she wasn't accustomed to the word no. The pampered Arabian princess always got her way.

"Fine," Carter said. "You remind me of my sister, Breeze."

"Well Breeze must be fabulous," Yasmine responded. "Now let's get you changed before I starve to death."

They laughed as they conversed on their way to the top floor. When they arrived Carter's two hospitality servants stood ready to wait on him, hand and foot.

Each woman was equally beautiful, but Carter made sure not to take advantage. "Mr. Jones is fine for the time being ladies. You are dismissed for the day. I promise to take good care of him," Yasmine said.

Their disappointment was apparent but they didn't dare object as they left the room. "I think your staff is quite fond of you Carter," Yasmine said in amusement.

"They are just doing their job," Carter responded as he unbuttoned his shirt, revealing his chest and stomach.

"Oh don't tell me you don't notice the affect you have on women? You're quite intriguing," she said. Her eyes revealed her own interests and Carter shook his head with a smile.

"You're trouble," he said.

"Men like trouble," she said with a wink.

Carter disappeared into the bathroom. "I'll make this quick," he said. He showered, the warmth of the water easing the tension from losing as steam filled the bathroom. As he placed both hands against the shower walls he lowered his head beneath the stream. Making it quick he lathered his body and rinsed. He reached for his towel and exited, wrapping it securely around his waist. Carter dripped water across the floor as he made his way to the large walk-in closet that adjoined the master bath. Surprisingly Yasmine was already inside.

"I thought I'd choose something debonair for you to wear," she said. "You have great style."

Carter smirked and walked around her. "Thanks but I can piece my own shit together ma. Women like to incorporate too many colors, too many fabrics. I'm simple. Black Ferragamo pants, black button up, nice Mocha shoe, preferably, Prada," he said as he pulled each item down.

"Nice choice," she commented.

"Glad to have your approval ma," he said with a wink as he held his towel in place. "Now do you mind?" he nodded toward the door.

Yasmine gave him a flirtatious purse of the lips as she turned on her heels. "Don't make me wait too long. I lose interest easily," she said and somehow he knew that she wasn't talking about brunch.

Carter knew that he would have to tread lightly with Yasmine. She had been very hospitable during his time in Saudi Arabia. He spent more time with her than he did anyone else and he enjoyed her company. She flirted, he enjoyed it, but he would not cross that line. He was grateful to her father for his assistance in their hiding out and thought that in the future he could make a great ally. Pussy wasn't worth the destruction of a great business relationship. No matter how pretty the face it was attached to may be.

"Good morning daddy," Yasmine greeted as she looked up from her mimosa to see her father approaching over Carter's shoulder.

"Somehow I knew I would find you here," he said as he leaned down to kiss his daughter on the cheek. "I'm sorry to interrupt, but I thought I'd invite Carter here to a game of poker."

"I'm not much of a card playing man," Carter admitted.

"Then you must learn," Baraka insisted. "It's the kind of table that you want to have a seat at. Not everyone is accepted to play."

"Count me in," Carter agreed.

"Very good," Baraka said. "Seeing as how the two of you spend so much time together, Yasmine may as well teach you. She's quite the accomplished poker player. Maybe it will keep her out of the city and safe behind the walls of comfort I've built for her, eh?"

Yasmine's mouth dropped as she realized that her father knew about the attempted kidnapping. "Father, I . . ."

Baraka raised his hand to silence her and turned his attention to Carter. "I appreciate you taking care of her and bringing her back unharmed. For that, I owe you a debt. We can discuss more this evening. It seems you are a good man to have around. Just like your father," he said. He shook Carter's hand and gave him a pat on the back before walking away.

"How did he know?" Carter asked.

"He runs this town. He knows everything," she shot back. "And everyone worth knowing. The card game is important. Dignitaries, king-pins, investors . . . very powerful men come to my father's monthly game."

Carter licked his lips and replied, "Then you better show me what you got ma."

I'll show you all right, she thought. While Carter was trying to learn the game, Yasmine was trying to learn him. She loved being in his presence and the more time she monopolized of his, the more she wanted him for herself. *Forget his girlfriend. He is here and she is all the way there. Its not like she is his wife,* Yasmine thought. *By the time I'm done with him, he won't remember her name.*

Yasmine had a poker table set up in her suite and dismissed the dealer so that she could teach Carter one on one. After hours of drinking and lessons she finally said, "I don't think there is anything more for you to learn. You're kind of horrible at this." She laughed and he shook his head in amusement.

"You know you are the only person who I've let laugh at me in years. You know that right?" he replied with an embarrassed smile.

"Oh, well perhaps you have soft spot for me in there after all," she concluded.

"Perhaps," he whispered back as he lifted the glass of cognac to his lips.

She came from behind the table and said, "Don't worry. Poker is all about the bluff anyway and you are very good at that."

"I don't bluff ma," he shot back.

"You most certainly do," she replied. "You've been telling yourself that there is nothing between us since the day you met me. That's the biggest bluff of all."

He eyed her as he stood, challenging her words as he moved closer to her, invading her space. "You're very good at bluffing but you can stop now." She leaned in and kissed his full lips and it felt so good that her legs buckled slightly. She creamed in her panties instantly as his strong hands lifted her off of the floor. She wrapped her legs around his body and pressed her pelvis into his manhood. It was big and bulging against the zipper to his designer slacks. The friction alone threatened to make her explode. He laid her across the poker table as he ripped open her blouse, popping every button until her voluptuous honey colored breasts were revealed.

"I can't," he said, tormented as he pulled away, but she wasn't letting him get away this time.

"You can," she whispered lustfully. "My pussy is so wet Carter. Stop bluffing." She pulled her panties to the side and rubbed her blooming clit. It was swollen and he could swear that he could see it pulsating in desire. It was begging him to conquer her. "Nobody has to know Carter. I can be your little secret."

Carter loved Miamor, but he was a man and the sight before him was too much to resist. He undid his belt and stepped out of his pants quickly. She wanted it. She had been begging him for the dick since he had arrived. She was a beautiful girl. He had to. Carter couldn't stop himself as he slid into her wetness.

"Oh shit. Damn ma," he groaned as her walls formed around him like saran wrap. She threw the pussy up at him as if she were an all star pitcher and he knocked it out of the park every time. She smelled so sweet and felt so good that the remorse he felt was overshadowed by the pleasure. He hated to say it but this was the best he had ever had and she was willing to take it any way. The veins popped out of his manhood and she felt his girth as she moved her hips, bucking against him as he grinded. This was the type of sex she had craved. He was hitting her spot and commanding her body. She had known that he would make her go crazy and now that he was finally inside of her she was in complete bliss. She was sure that now that he had gotten a taste of her, he wouldn't be able to stay away and eventually their lust would transform into a love that no average chick from Miami could compete with. What Yasmine didn't realize was that Miamor wasn't an average chick. While Yasmine was relying on sex to keep Carter's interest, Miamor was putting in work to prove that she was the only woman in the world who could ever truly hold him down.

***

Carter didn't fare well at poker. He lost
$75,000 in the course of an evening but it was
the price to pay to get into a room full of prestigious men. The table of ten ranged from a Saudi
prince to an oil tycoon to a Wall Street banker
from New York City. He was the only dope boy
in the room and it worked to his advantage.
By the time the games were over he had made
connections with those whom he felt would be
useful and had exchanged contact information
with those whom felt he could be useful to them.
Baraka was impressed and as they exited the
private playing room he said, "Once your legal
affairs are in order, we should do business. I
don't make many trips to the states anymore. My
wives aren't fond of the long trip, but I want to
expand my casino into the Nevada market."

"Las Vegas," Carter said.

"Yes, I'll need a partner. In fact, I just want
to invest and see a return. I've seen the way
that you handle the dealers, your wait staff,"
he paused and looked Carter square in the eye
before he added, "my daughter. She listens to no
one but she minds you. If you two weren't worlds
apart and your line of work wasn't so dangerous
I would find you quite suitable for my Yasmine."

"She's a lovely girl Baraka, but it's not rocking
like that between us," he replied. "I don't like to

create potential conflict in business and your backing is something that I highly value. Nevada could be a great look for The Cartel."

"I can't get in that market alone. Las Vegas is old mafia money, built up. I don't have the muscle to fight my way in, but you do," Baraka said. "Let's table this discussion until you figure out your affairs with this government case. Just keep me in mind. When the time is right to make the transition, you have my support."

With the shake of a hand the deal was solidified. All he had to do now was figure out how to get his neck out of the federal noose so that he could get to the money. Drug money was like peanuts in the scale of things. Owning a casino would legitimize him in a way that the streets never could. *Not bad for a young nigga from Flint, MI.* he thought. He adjusted his cufflinks and headed toward the elevator bank with a smirk on his face. *Not bad at all.*

Chapter 11

"Take the bass out of your fucking voice before I let you hear a tiny whisper that'll leave you speechless."

—Miamor

Daniel Broome rolled out of bed when the smell of fresh bacon frying hit him in the early morning hour. His bare chest was muscle-less and hairy, accompanied by a slim frame, and small waist. He wasn't much of a man. But what he lacked in stature, he made up for in reputation. His tenacity and ambition had gained him an excellent conviction rate at work. He was the most fast tracked prosecuting attorney the region had seen in quite a while. He ran a hand through his messy hair and made his way out to the kitchen where his wife and young daughter were already seated around the table.

"Morning honey," he said as he gave her a soft swat on the behind and a kiss on the cheek. She never turned from the stove as she prepared breakfast.

"Mornin'," she responded. "Breakfast will be done in a sec. There's coffee in the pot."

"I just need to grab the morning paper first," he replied. He stepped out onto his porch and retrieved the Miami Herald. Wandering back into the house, he grabbed the hot cup of brew that his lovely wife now had waiting at his seat.

"Morning daddy," his daughter piped, finally looking up from her coloring project.

"Morning sunshine," he answered. Making himself comfortable, he unrolled his paper and took a sip of the brew.

Before he could even dive into the reporting he frowned as a photo fell from within the pages. He gasped when he saw an image of himself handing money to Timmy "Two Time" Bono.

"Is everything okay?" his wife asked as she turned briefly from her cooking.

"Uh . . . yeah," he stammered as he quickly stood and grabbed the picture. "Yeah, yeah. Everything is fine. Look I'm going to head in early for the office. I've got a heavy case load today," he lied, eager to get out of the house. He rushed back to the bedroom with the newspaper and photo in hand. "Fuck!" he cursed. He tossed the paper on his bed and noticed a bet slip from the horse race. He picked it up. On it in big bold letters he read the words . . .

GOTCHA!

Thoughts ran through his mind a mile a minute as he fumbled with his clothing. He didn't even bother washing off yesterday's stink before dressing and rushing out of the door. Before he could even reach his car a black sedan pulled up at his curb. He paused, his car key grasped between his thumb and pointer finger, as he diverted his attention to the vehicle.

Honk!

The beep of the horn made him eerily aware that the surprise visitor was for him. He looked around and then unsurely made his way down his driveway and toward the tinted car. The back window rolled down and Miamor sat wrapped in an expensive silk scarf. The large Chanel sunglasses she wore hid the intention that shone in her eyes.

"Get in," she said, the tone of her voice leaving no room for him to decline. She popped open the door and moved over to the other side of the car. Broome fisted his hair and sighed heavily before hunching down to enter.

"It seems you're in quite the predicament Mr. Prosecuting Attorney," Miamor began. "You lost money, evidence money, on a horse race. It was supposed to be a sure bet, but it wasn't. Now you have to come up with the money to replace the borrowed evidence before anyone realizes its gone missing."

Daniel Broome, the young cocky P.A., with his American boy wit was speechless. He turned beet red as he realized Miamor had his balls in a vice grip. "I don't know what the hell you're talking about!" he roared. His heart felt like it would implode as an ache of devastation vibrated through his chest. He could see his entire future being flushed down the drain. His college boy gambling fun had turned into a nasty habit, one that had led him straight into the arms of the devil.

"Simmer down Mr. Broome," Miamor said as she looked out of the window without a care in the world. "You feel that? Your tie feels like it's cutting off your oxygen and your hands suddenly became moist. Your stomach is a bottomless pit and your throat as dry as the Sahara," she described. "That's how I felt when you brought a case against the man I love. It felt like the walls were falling in around me. You had all the power, but now . . . I have the power and I'm a ruthless dictator . . . I don't rule fairly. The only thing that stopped me from running in your house and tying up your kids and slitting your wife's throat while you watched . . . was the fact that you had so many fucking Feds watching me. So consider this route the easy one. You can keep your career and no one has to know about the missing evidence if you play this by my rules from this point forward."

Broome's entire body was tense and he was pressed so closely to the door that Miamor thought he would fall out of the car. She recognized his fear. He was afraid of her. Many had been before, but she had never felt satisfaction like this until now. Before her murder game had been a job. This time it felt personal. Part of her wanted to say the code word so that Aries could fill Broome with bullets from the place where she rested in the trunk, but she held her composure. She needed him alive, at least for the moment. She needed him to drop the case.

"You are threatening an officer of the court! I will . . ."

"You will take the bass out of your fucking voice before I let you hear a tiny whisper that'll leave you speechless," Miamor said as she placed a chrome pistol with a chrome silencer in her lap.

Broome's eyes watered as he was instantly brought back to reality. "I'm here to make you an offer. I'll give you the money you need to replace the evidence."

"Your accounts are frozen," he whispered.

"You're a fool if you think we don't have access to greater assets," Miamor laughed. "If you drop the case against us, our men and the entire Cartel syndicate, I will give you the money in cash. You can replace the evidence and no one will ever have to know that you took it. If not, I'm going to ruin your career."

"I can't just drop the case, there are witness statements, evidence . . ."

Miamor interrupted him. "Give me the locations of the witnesses. I can make them disappear. The statements will be recanted or silenced. Carter, Zyir, and Monroe aren't dead. Once you drop the charges they will come home. You can reduce the charges if dropping them seems too fishy. Reduce them all the way down. I'm talking slaps on the wrist, a few months in jail at the max. No real jail time."

Broome was in a state of shock as his chin hit his chest. It was at that moment that he realized that he was in over his head. How three men had evaded federal arrest was beyond him. Not only that, they had been smart enough to make the government stop pursuing them. He wanted to stay on the right side of the law but there was no way he could get out of an evidence scandal without ruining everything he had worked for.

"Do we have a deal?" she asked. The car stopped moving and Broome peered out of the window to see that they had pulled right back to his house.

"How do I know you won't cross me after the case is dropped," Broome said.

Miamor reached into the front seat grabbed the bag off of the passenger seat. She passed it to Broome. "There's your evidence money. The rest, you'll just have to trust me on. The fact that I have something over your head will keep your cross hairs off of The Cartel. If we ever go down, you'll fall with us," she assured.

Daniel Broome nodded his head in understanding and then exited the car. As he watched the sedan pull away his wife came up behind him, taking him by surprise.

"Holy Hell! Donna!" he screamed on her, jumpy as ever.

"Who was that?" she asked.

"Nobody," he mumbled. "I've got to go to work."

He hurried into his own car and pulled off, leaving his wife standing in their front yard

watching him leave in concern. He drove all the
way to the end of the block before the stop sign
halted him. Gripping the steering wheel with
two hands he lowered his head and sobbed like
a baby. He had just gotten in bed with Satan and
he knew that no matter how the situation played
out, he would eventually be burned.

Chapter 12

"That Murder Mama shit is sexy."

—Carter

"Hmm," Carter moaned as the feeling of warmth tightened around his strength. He could feel the veins popping out of his shaft as his manhood grew inside of her mouth. Being awakened out of his sleep to the best head of his life was like heaven. Yasmine was good for not knocking before she entered. He had meant to pull her to the side and discuss what had happened, to prevent it from going further. In a conscious state he would have been able to decline this favor, but she had caught him off guard. She had slipped into his bed while he was asleep and wrapped her pretty lips around his dick. As he brought his hands to her head he fisted her hair as he straightened his legs while curling his toes in ecstasy.

"Shiit," he whispered. He had so much tension built up in him that he could feel himself pulsating in her mouth. Her tongue circled his head causing every nerve ending in his body to awaken. Her hands reached up and rubbed over his chest while her head traveled south as her tongue massaged his loins. Carter sucked in a sharp breath when he felt her tongue dip too far and he tightened his grasp on her hair to pull her up. He finally opened his eyes and lifted his head to the most beautiful sight he had ever seen.

"Hey you," she said with a smile.

"Miamor?" he whispered. He wanted to think that he was dreaming . . . that she was a figment of his erotic imagination but the pleasurable feeling she was giving him felt too real . . . too familiar to be fake. "What are you . . ."

"Shhh," Miamor whispered as she placed a finger over his lips and pushed him back onto the luxurious sheets. Miamor pulled her dress over her head and spun her body so that she mounted Carter backwards. She snaked her hips and his eyes followed as her waist and behind winded to a silent beat. By the time her depth drowned him he could barely hold off the orgasm. A rush washed over them both as her mouth fell open in an O and she drew in a sharp breath as he stretched her walls. He was thick and strong.

The feelings of his hands on her hips set the tone as she began to rock and roll, slowly. Carter had a front row seat and he had to bite into his bottom lip to keep himself from losing his cool and moaning too loudly. Miamor rode him like she was the star cowboy at a rodeo show. Each time she bucked back he saw the pink of her pussy bloom as her voluptuous ass cheeks spread. It was a beautiful sight to behold. He reached out and palmed her backside, massaging it as she made his length disappear and reappear, again and again in her slippery abyss. She was warm and the honey scent that invaded his senses was the sweetness that only a woman could possess.

"Let's play a game," Miamor whispered as she turned her neck and looked back at him. The coy look in her eyes was seductive yet flirtatious and as she subtly looked down at her own ass she twisted her hips simultaneously. Carter smirked because she knew that he loved every moment of her sex play.

"I ain't been inside this pussy in months baby, later for games," he whispered. Miamor tightened her walls until her muscles shook, begging for release, but she kept them locked around him. "Have you given my dick away?" she asked.

"You know this your shit ma," Carter replied as he sucked his teeth, toes curling. Miamor eased up the pressure, manipulating her grip on him while winding. She tightened again as she rose upwards. "Did a bitch have her mouth on this dick?" she asked.

"Never that, all I want is this right now. What's with all the talking?" Carter asked.

Miamor lowered her hips, rocking slowly, sensually. "That's too bad," she said as she tightened once more. She sped up her pace, turning their love making into passionate fucking as sweat glistened on her body. This was carnal. It had been too long for them both. "If you had said yes, I would have told you to let me watch," she whispered. The image of himself intertwined in the depths of one of the foreign beauties as Miamor sat and watched was too much for him to handle.

He roared and his entire body tensed as he released himself inside of the woman he loved. Miamor kept her pace despite the fact that she was spent. She was too close to her own orgasm to stop now. Carter sat up and reached around her body to thumb her clit. The friction of his hand was all it took. He stroked her swollen knob until it pulsated. Her back arched and her head flew back as he grabbed her neck, then her breast. "Give it to me ma," he whispered.

Miamor rained all over him and her body went limp as she leaned against him. His manhood went limp and easily retreated out of her as he pulled her backwards until she lay beside him against the sweaty silk sheets.

"How did you know where to find me?" he asked.

"I'm resourceful when I need to be," she said as she stared at the wall as they spooned, while he ran his fingers through her hair. "I used to hunt niggas for a living. Hunt and kill. Finding you wasn't hard, especially after you sent the post card clue."

"Were you followed?" Carter asked seriously. "Does Leena and Breeze know where you are?"

"Breeze is home with the kids. Leena is in Monroe's room I'm sure doing something very similar to what we just did," Miamor said with a laugh.

"This was stupid ma," Carter said sternly in her ear, but he couldn't help but to nuzzle in the crease of her neck. "Damn, I missed you."

Miamor savored the feeling of his touch and she closed her eyes, planting the moment in her memory. Now it was hers forever. She turned to him.

"I came to bring you home," she whispered.

He sat up on one elbow. "You know that can't happen."

"I took care of it," she whispered as she stared at him intently. "The charges have been reduced. You, Zyir, Money, you all can come back to Miami. You can come home Carter."

His eyes turned cold. "What did you do Mia?" he asked. "My son needs a mother."

"And your son's mother needs you. I need you Carter. I look at our son and I cry because he doesn't know you yet. He's a baby yes, but I want him to have you. There was no way I was sitting around while you ran for the rest of your life. Like it or not you're in love with a murder mama Carter. When shit pops off I react. Now I couldn't make it go completely away. I tried, but to avoid suspicion you guys will have to do some time. 5 years. That's lightweight though compared to the life sentences they were trying to throw your way. You come home, you knock out the fed time for tax evasion, and I'll be waiting for you when you get out. I just want you back," she professed. As she spoke tears fell down her cheeks and Carter could see that his absence had taken a major toll on her. They had spent years apart and had vowed never to separate again. Carter didn't want to see the inside of any prison but for his family, he would do those five years. If that's what it took to get back to Miamor and Carter junior, he would.

He wiped the tears from her eyes. "Don't ever put yourself at risk for me ma. I'm not worth your freedom. I'm not worth tearing a mother away from her son. You hear me? I can take care of myself. Our li'l man can't. That's your job while I'm away. He is me and I am him. He is my weakness Miamor. So make him strong. Make him your first priority from now on. I come after that, you understand?"

She nodded. "Yes and that selflessness is one of the many reasons why I'm in love with you," she whispered.

Carter smiled and gave her a small laugh.

"What?" she asked as she frowned in confusion.

"That Murder Mama shit is sexy," he whispered. "You rode out for yo' man."

"Always," she replied with a laugh. He watched her as she gave him a mischievous grin and disappeared under the sheets. They had been apart for too long. She had to remind him of all the things about her that he loved so much. It was time for round two.

Monroe stared out of the window of the penthouse suite as he leaned his head against his forearm. The sun was rising indicating a new day, yet Monroe still hadn't let go of the old one.

His mind was restless. Sleep didn't come easy for him these days and the beautiful servant massaging his shoulders did little to calm his worries. A constant burden rested on him. It was the cause of all of his tensions. No amount of rubbing would make those go away.

"Can I do anything for you?" the Arabian goddess asked sweetly.

Out of nowhere a voice responded. "You can remove your hands before you find yourself without any."

The servant immediately let go of an astonished Monroe as he turned to see Leena's not so sweet face. Her scowl was harsh as she stood with her arms folded across her chest.

"Really?" she asked as she cocked her head to the side.

Monroe didn't justify her displeasure with a response. He rushed her, picking her up, his arms wrapped under her behind as he lifted her. His excitement couldn't be contained as he pushed her against the wall, knocking expensive French paintings to the floor. Their kiss sent them to another world as the servant stood awkwardly, watching them. She cleared her throat.

"Hmm, hmm."

Monroe waved his hand, dismissing her without ever losing focus of Leena and the servant fled the room. As his hands explored her body, he realized he hadn't been homesick. Monroe had missed his woman. He lifted her skirt and ripped her panties as she fumbled with his pajama slacks.

He filled her up to capacity as he pulled back, moving her hair out of her face gently. Her mouth was slightly open and he slid his tongue inside as he made love to her against the wall.

"I missed you," she whispered. "Oh God, I missed this."

Monroe had so much anger, so much emotion, so much love, so much everything . . . built inside of him that he was more passionate than he had ever been with her. Monroe had left Miami on bad terms with Leena. They had fought, they had been beefed out when he had been forced to go on the run. Leaving her while they were in distress ate him up inside. He didn't like to leave loose ends untied and it had been weighing on him. The last time they had seen each other, hateful words had been spoken. He needed her to feel his love for her and he was trying to give it all to her in that moment. Her legs were wrapped around his waist and he pinned both wrists above her head, with one hand. He placed the other hand around her to pull her love into him. Her wetness soaked him as his hips went in and out. Leena was a prisoner to his stroke. At his mercy, she could do nothing but close her eyes and let him take her on the orgasmic high. Monroe moved from her lips to her neck, to her breasts, as he kneeled before her. He kissed her belly button, her stomach. She gasped. She held his head and braced herself because she knew where he was headed. He found her throbbing clit and took it between his moist lips. "I'm sorry," he whispered. "I'm so sorry."

Before he even said the words, all had been forgiven, but she didn't tell him that. She let him pour all of his woes into her as he licked and sucked her gently. "Agh," she moaned. "Money, wait."

"No baby, just cum," he said.

Leena brought her knees up and pushed it into his chest, sending him onto his back. Straddling him in a Sixty-nine, she placed her flower back over his face as she eased his manhood into her mouth. She could taste her sweetness on his tongue as she pulled on him with her tongue. Deep, then shallow, then deep, and wet . . . oh so wet, until finally he reached his peak. He sucked her clit mercilessly as he pulled her hair, causing her to lift her head as his seed spilled. He knew she had gotten hers as well when he felt the tremble of her thighs.

She climbed off of him headed toward the bathroom. "Come shower with me?" she asked.

Monroe arose and followed her into the bathroom. The steam from the shower quickly filled the air as they stepped in together. "How are you here right now?" he asked.

"I could never stay away from you Money. I love you," she said. She took the soap and squeezed some on a towel and began to wipe his broad chest.

"I'm sorry ma, about everything. I don't want to fight with you. This shit has eaten away at me since we left Miami. I couldn't reach out to you, couldn't hear your voice. The last time I saw you, we were yelling and saying shit that we should never say to each other. I love the shit out of you Leena. I want you to know that, every minute of every day. I just got ghost on you and I didn't know if you knew. I needed you to know . . ."

Monroe gripped the back of her neck as he spoke. Their faces, inches apart, their soapy bodies close. They just wanted to be one.

"I knew," she replied in a husky whisper.

"No ma, you don't know," he said as he looked in her eyes. "I can see it in your soul. You couldn't feel me. You didn't know because I didn't show you good enough. Marry me."

"What?" she said as she pulled back.

"You heard me ma, I'm not speaking French," he laughed.

"When?" she asked.

"Now," Monroe replied. He eased her under the stream of water as the remnants of their lovemaking circled the drain. Cleansed and feeling pure Monroe didn't know if he was caught up in the emotion of their reunion or if this had been his plan all along. All he knew is that he wanted her to be his. He wanted her to know that what they shared was nothing less than authentic.

"Let's go," he pulled her out of the shower. "I want to be married tonight by the time to sun sets you will be a Diamond," he said.

"What? Money!" she exclaimed. "This is crazy! We can't do this. Not here."

Monroe paused. "Is this what you want?"

Leena was suddenly breathless but her smile was infectious. "More than anything in the world."

"Then that's all that matters," he said.

Miamor looked over at Carter and smiled. He gave her a wink causing her to blush as they sauntered through the desert atop of the humps of brown camels, wearing all white. Monroe rode in front of them and Zyir behind them. The day was slowly slipping away as the sky transformed from blue to beautiful mixtures of orange and red. The tan sand dunes around them served as the only backdrop. Dusk was upon them and happiness was in the air.

Leena rode last. She was carried on a canopy-covered platform, escorted on the shoulders of four men. Her identity concealed as they made their way into the desert where her wedding ceremony awaited. She couldn't believe that this was happening and so suddenly at that. She peered out of the canopy to see the imam, who stood patiently, waiting for them to arrive. Although she wasn't a practitioner of Islam, the Muslim religious leader, was the only option. There wasn't enough time to fly her own priest out so she would be wed under the blessings of the Muslim tradition. Her heart beat out of her chest. She was nervous but nothing about her was unsure. The connection that she shared with Monroe was incomparable to anything that she had ever felt for another human being. Their friendship was deep like a bottomless ocean. Not even they had explored all of its depths and secret places. She looked forward to embarking on the journey of intimacy together in the years to come. *Damn, I'm about to become someone's wife,* she thought. A few tears built up in her eyes. She had never been a princess. She didn't know what it felt like to be entitled, to be royalty. Her entire life she had always dreamt of the day that her prince would come. The reality was so far from the dream that it made her emotional. She always envisioned marrying into a traditional family. She imagined baking cookies with her mother-in-law or giving corny sweaters to her father-in-law for holidays and birthdays. Monroe's family was incomplete however. His mother, his father, and Mecca were pieces to the family puzzle that would forever be missing. In a perfect world, they would have been front row at the wedding but today their absence was blatant. She could only imagine how hurtful that was to her man. She wiped her eyes. She didn't want to ruin her flawless make-up or put a damper on the day but she couldn't help but wish that they came from a more traditional world. A world where street wars and chaos didn't exist. She let the fabric close and took a deep breath as she felt the four men who acted as her carriage, stop moving. *This is it,* she whispered. "You're about to be Leena Diamond," she whispered. Leena knew how big of a responsibility came with the name. Carter Diamond's children had been raised to believe that diamonds were forever.

The name rang bells in the streets of Miami. She was about to take on the legacy of another man . . . of her husband, and while it was one of the most joyous things she had ever felt, she also felt overwhelmed. She realized that she was about to make this thing official and that there was no turning back. Once she was in, she was in and the only out was death. Leena wondered if she was making the right choice. Their love wasn't perfect, but life was not a fairytale. It was time for them to solidify as one. She couldn't ask for a better mate. The curtain opened and she stared into the eyes of Zyir.

"Hey Lee," Zyir greeted with a smile.

"Hey Zy," she replied with an equally dazzling grin. She was a woman in love and it showed. She was truly glowing on this day.

"You ready?" Zyir asked.

She nodded. "Doesn't feel quite right doing this here without Breeze and the babies. My parents," she admitted.

"Right now all that matters is that you and Money are here. Everyone else is just extra," Zyir schooled as he extended his hand.

Leena placed her hand in Zyir's. For years he had acted as brother to Leena and uncle to her son. He was truly loyal and Leena was glad that he was there to escort her to her awaiting groom.

"Here goes nothing," she said as she beamed while Zyir reached up and lifted her into the air before placing her on her feet. Her Carolina Herrera dress was long, made of soft silk. It was simple. No poof, no train; just a long flowing fabric that hugged her body just right. The thin straps held it up against her lean yet curvacious frame. She stood next to her Zyir as she hooked her arm within his. All eyes were on her. Carter and Miamor stood lovingly to the side while Monroe stood beside the imam. If she had any qualms before they were all erased the moment she saw his face. He calmed her soul with just one glance and she knew that it didn't matter who wasn't in attendance. All they needed was each other. That's what true love was all about. Zyir escorted Leena all the way to Monroe. A sense of peace washed over her. The closer she got to him the more her smile brightened. Zyir stopped and extended his hand to Monroe.

"Congratulations . . . family" he told Monroe with a nod.

"Thank you bro," Monroe replied. The gestures were a far cry from the bullets that had been flying at each other the last time Leena had attempted to wed Monroe.

Monroe turned toward Leena and grabbed her hand as they stepped in front of the imam.

Her fingers merged with his as if they were two pieces of one puzzle coming together. They turned to one another as electric compatibility sparked through them. The imam cleared his throat and began speaking in Arabic. The English translator who stood behind him brought clarity to his words.

"We stand here under the laws of Saudi Arabia and the blessings of Allah to join this man with his first wife. The couple has requested to recite their own vows as they enter into this union," the translator expressed.

Monroe stepped toward Leena closing the small space between them as he gently caressed the side of her cheek. His eyes drank her in, admiring her. "You've never looked so beautiful," he said. He was overcome with emotion as he peered at his bride and she could see tears accumulating in his eyes. She wiped them away for him as he began his vows. He pressed his head against her forehead as he cupped her face and closed his eyes. He was visibly overwhelmed. "No woman has ever given me what you give me Lee. I promise to protect you and keep you well because when you are safe, I feel whole. When you hurt, I hurt, and I promise to never do anything to hurt myself. You give me a reason to breathe Leena. You're the air in my lungs. You fill my spirit. You steer me straight and bring morality to the world of wrong that I live in. You have intrigued me from the first day I met you. I promise to never let that intrigue die. To always reinvigorate our love and keep it fresh as the years go by. I promise to appreciate you, to nurture you, to support you, to honor the woman that you are. I will cherish you and walk with you faithfully. I vow to never burden your spirit with disloyalty. You have my fidelity until the day that my body fails me and I am no longer of this world. Even still my spirit will always walk with you. I will forever love you ma, from day one until the death of me."

Leena was filled to capacity with joy. His words were so heartfelt and unrehearsed. They weren't perfect, but they were Monroe. They symbolized everything that embodied the man he was and she loved them. No vow had ever sounded so sweet. His words sent the sentiment of love into the air.

Leena's mouth fell open. At a loss for words, her tears finally freed themselves. It was his turn to wipe hers away. "I don't know how to follow that," she said overcome with a small chuckle, causing Monroe and everyone witnessing the ceremony to laugh and erupt in applause.

"I'm simple Lee. You know what I need to hear," he whispered while gazing lovingly at her.

"I will love you," she whispered. "I vow to love only you until I die."

"That's my girl," Monroe said with a coy grin. "That's enough. That's all I'll ever need from you. I've got the rest." He turned to the imam and nodded his head.

Again in Arabic he spoke as the translator assisted. "By the powers given to me by Allah, you may kiss your lovely bride."

Monroe's lips graced hers so delicately that she melted into him. They were now husband and wife. A new family, a subsidiary of The Cartel, had just been forged . . . not by blood, not by money . . . but by love.

Chapter 13

"Kiss good-bye to our freedom for
awhile gentlemen."

—Carter

Monroe and Leena were surprised by the
elaborate reception that had been paid for and
gifted to them by Baraka. Although they didn't
know most of the guests there, they partied all
the same. There were belly dancers, and flame
spitters, and more presents than they could
possibly open. The day couldn't have been more
perfect, but as it wound down, they all knew that
sunrise would bring about a new era. Carter sat
alone at the bar as he watched Miamor dance
happily with Zyir. She looked so carefree and
genuinely at peace, even if it was only temporary.
Carter knew that she deserved this feeling of
contentment to be permanent, and he vowed to
give it to his lovely Miamor.

"So that is your girl friend?" Yasmine said as she slid into the barstool next to his.

Carter smiled. "That's her."

"Looks average to me," Yasmine commented as she sipped from her champagne glass. She was obviously irritated and slightly intoxicated, equaling a loose tongue.

Carter smirked as he removed her champagne flute from her hands. "I think you've had enough," he said. "You're talking reckless. Besides, green doesn't look good on you ma. You're bigger than that."

Yasmine cut her eyes at him playfully. "Everything looks good on me Carter, even nothing, but you know that already, don't you?" she asked seductively as she rolled her eyes and walked away, clearly pissed.

Zyir and Monroe approached him next as they all watched Yasmine make her exit. "You better be careful with that one bro," Monroe said.

"And you better reign her in before Miamor catches wind," Zyir added.

"There's nothing to catch wind of," Carter assured. He looked at the glass of champagne that he had taken from Yasmine and downed it.

"Just watch out for that one. She's been at your side since we got here and she don't seem too happy to find out about Miamor," Monroe said.

"I've got it under control. Luckily this is our last night in Saudi. Tomorrow morning we will be on a plane back to Miami. We've got to be prepared for the arrest. Get your heads together. We'll be going inside for a few years. Doesn't sound like much compared to the life sentences they were trying to throw at us, but I promise you it won't be a cake walk. We'll need protection. In prison its all about numbers and reputation. I'll make sure we have that," Carter said. "I need you two to be on the same team . . . we don't have time for division from within."

"That's water under the bridge. We're good," Zyir said as he extended his hand to Monroe. Monroe pulled Zyir in for a hug and Carter nodded his head.

"Good," he said. "Kiss good-bye to our freedom for awhile gentlemen. Tonight will be the last night you'll enjoy for a long time."

"Zyir," Breeze whispered as she saw the caravan of black, chauffeured, SUV's pull into the gates of Leena's home. "Thank you God." She held her nephew, little Carter in her arms. Monroe Jr. clung to the ends of her skirt. "Come on boys, your daddies are home," she said happily. She was so eager to see them all that she could barely contain herself. When the cars stopped before her in the circular driveway she descended the steps. Miamor and Carter emerged from the first car.

"Welcome home brother," Breeze greeted with a wide smile.

"Thank you B," Carter replied. He reached down and scooped his son from her arms. "He looks like me," he whispered. The infant had grown in the months that Carter had been away and now his features were clearly visible. Carter felt pure pride as he admired a mini-version of himself. It was every man's greatest desire to have a son and Miamor had given him that. He would be forever grateful to her for such an amazing gift. This little person he held in his arms was his heir . . . the carrier of his last name, of his legacy. Miamor stepped to Breeze's side and kissed her cheek. She then bent down to pick up Monroe Jr. knowing that Breeze was eager to get to Zyir. "Go get your man," Miamor said with a wink.

Zyir emerged from the second vehicle and Breeze ran to him full speed. He picked her up and kissed her lips sensually. "I should kill you," she whispered as tears flooded her eyes. "I really thought you were dead. Do you know what you did to me?"

"I know," Zyir replied as he held her tightly. Nothing but love pulsed through him as he realized how incomplete he had felt without her. "I'll never make you a widow Breeze," he promised. He moved her hair out of her face and placed her on her feet. "I love you."

As soon as the words left his mouth they were followed by the sounds of sirens. Breeze peered over his shoulder in alarm as she saw the many police cars pulling onto the property.

"Why are they here so soon?" Monroe asked as he emerged from the car. He rushed over to his son and pulled the toddler into a warm embrace.

"Daddy!" his son shouted in excitement.

"I love you Money," Monroe said. Tears built in his eyes because the short lived reunion was hardly enough. He had hoped to spend a few days with his son before turning himself in. "Take care of mama for me okay? You're the man of the house. Daddy has to go away for a little while longer, but I'm always thinking about you man. I'll always come back for you. You're my strong man?" he asked. His son nodded his head. Monroe knew that the young boy couldn't comprehend exactly what was happening, but he felt obligated to say all these things before he was taken away. Monroe was becoming emotional at the fact that he was about to miss the next five years of his son's life. It was a long time to miss of a young child's upbringing. This was a long good-bye and he only hoped that one day his son would understand. Leena knelt down next to them.

"Tell daddy you love him Money," she said. She grabbed Monroe's hand as they embraced their son.

"Love you daddy," the toddler spoke.

"We both love you Monroe and we'll wait . . . for however long it takes," she promised.

Monroe kissed both of their foreheads and then stood to his feet. Carter and Zyir came to his side as the wives and children stepped back.

Carter handed his son off to Miamor and etched her face into his memory. He kissed her lips. "Everything will be okay. I'll be there, visiting you, writing you, whatever you need," she assured. Carter nodded and in that moment held so much respect for her. A lot of women made the promise to ride it out but very few actually came through. He knew that this was one thing he didn't need to worry about. If Miamor said it, she meant it and suddenly he was plagued with guilt for betraying her with Yasmine. A part of him wanted to confess his sins to her but he knew her too well. She would hate him forever because while she had been back in Miami fighting for him, he had been fucking the next chick. That resentment would only grow while he was locked up and it would tear them apart. He needed her. He loved her, even when his actions spoke otherwise. Miamor would be his motivation to keep his nose clean inside. Prison was a whole new world. Once you went behind the wall there was never a guarantee that you would emerge. five years could easily turn into forever if they caught a new charge. Miamor nodded her head and blew Carter a kiss as he was taken into federal custody. It was now up to the three of them to keep The Cartel afloat and to move them into the next era.

Leena picked up her son and turned around. "I'm not staying to witness this. We're done with this street shit," Leena said firmly. "When they get out, I want them to come home to something legit. I never want my son to see his father off to prison again."

Leena stormed into the house as Breeze and Miamor shot each other a glance of sympathy. The two women huddled close to each other as Miamor cradled her son. It was a new day and as their men were carted away like common criminals Miamor knew that Leena was right. It was time to move forward in a different direction. It was time for maturation.

Chapter 14

"This feels like the end Mia."

—Carter

Miamor sat next to Carter as she clasped his shackled hand. Their attorney, Rosenberg spoke on his behalf. Money and Zyir had already signed their plea deals. Carter was last up and although in her heart Miamor knew that this was necessary, it still didn't feel right. *Maybe it would have been better to let him stay on the run,* she thought. *At least than he would be a free man.*

As Broome ran down the terms of the plea bargain Carter was stoic. His expressionless face was hard to read. He almost appeared numb to it all. Prison was a place that he had promised himself to never go. He would have much rather let his legend die in the streets, under a hail of bullets, than to let it become obsolete in a prison cell. He didn't want to be another hood

legend forgotten. The steel bars and brick walls
had a way of keeping you out of sight and out of
mind. He feared that the most. Everything that
he had built, everything that The Cartel had
accomplished would become a memory. For an
inmate, life froze in place. The only two days
that mattered was the day you went in and the
day you got out. On the outside, however, life
moved on and he knew that eventually even his
woman would disappear. He wanted to think of
her as the exception, but time waited for no man.
Miamor was beautiful and smart, not to mention
cunning. Another boss with another organization, perhaps in a different city would eventually
spot her and claim her as his own. She was a
kingpin's perfect prize.

"Carter," Miamor whispered, sensing something was wrong with her man. He looked up at
her. She frowned because in all the time that she
had known him, she had never seen him look
so unsure. Indecision, was not a quality that he
often exuded.

"Please clear the room," she said. "I'd like a
moment alone with Carter before he pleads out."

"That isn't protocol," Broome began.

Miamor shot him a look so deadly that it silenced him into submission.

"You have two minutes," Broome said as he
stood and escorted Rosenberg out of the room.

"This feels like the end Mia," Carter admitted. "The end of The Cartel, the end of us, the end of it all. Shit is fucked up. There is no way I can keep control from the inside."

"This is the beginning Carter. Five years is not long enough to scare me away. You don't worry about anything. I will keep it all together. You just have to trust me," Miamor said.

Carter nodded and kissed her lips. "Whatever you do you keep it out of my ear. I don't expect you to wait, but I expect you to be respectful. Don't tarnish my name ma," he stated seriously. He was a realist. He had seen this same situation play out too many times before not to know how it ended.

"I only want you," she reassured. What he didn't realize was that he was it for her. She truly only had eyes for one man. "I don't want you to doubt me Carter. I'll do whatever you need me to do, in order for you to trust me. Let's get married. Right here, today. You know me. I'll never break that vow."

"And you know me, I'd never trap you with that vow," Carter replied. "When I marry you, you'll be in a white dress. You'll have the violins and white doves and hundreds of guests . . . because you deserve that. I'll never trap you. I don't want you stuck with me because you have to be . . ."

"I want to be stuck with you forever Carter. Whether you're next to me every night or not. I'll wait and I don't need no fancy shit to do that. I just need your promise to love me and to be faithful to me," she said sincerely.

"I'm about to be property of the federal government for five years ma. You realize that?" he asked.

"I will ride with you through whatever," she promised. "If this is what I have to do to prove that than let me. Or am I just not the type you think of when you think of a wife?"

Carter leaned into her, but the handcuffs that bound him to his chair stopped him from fully reaching her. She met him halfway. When they kissed Miamor could have sworn she heard angels singing. That's how pure their love felt. "You know better than that," Carter replied. "No other type could ever be my wife. It's always been you."

Broome opened the door and entered with Rosenberg on his tail, interrupting their brief moment. Miamor realized it would be a long time before they ever truly had privacy again.

"We want to fill out an application for marriage. We'd like to make it happen before he goes in," Miamor said.

Broome loosened his tie. She had him by the balls and all of her requests were making him appear weak to his colleagues. She was pushing the limits of their arrangement, but what could he do? Since Carter had not yet pled guilty, the approval of the marriage request was up to Broome's discretion, not some warden. Before he could respond Miamor said, "Make it happen, we'll wait. After we are married, Carter will sign your deal and enter his guilty plea."

Carter was amazed at how Miamor was running the show. She had the P.A. jumping through hoops at the drop of a dime. As a judge was summoned, the couple stood in front of one another. "Are you sure this is how you want to do this Miamor?" Carter asked.

She nodded. "I've never been more sure of anything. I love you. I don't need the pomp and circumstance," she assured.

Her answer held nothing but truth and as they stood two people reciting vows in a downtown federal building, they became one. It didn't matter if it wasn't as she had imagined. They were perfect for each other and it didn't matter that they were being thrust into imperfect circumstances.

"I now pronounce you, man and wife," the judge said dryly. It wasn't perfect or romantic, but it was official and that's all that either of them wanted. Miamor smiled. "You may kiss your bride."

They didn't even give Carter the ability to wrap his hands around his new wife. They kept him handcuffed, but it didn't matter. His mouth found hers anyway and this one kiss elevated their bond to the next level. She could feel his energy pulsing through her body as if suddenly she knew what true love felt like. Broome gave them no time to celebrate before he got back to the task at hand.

"Hmm, hmm," he cleared his throat and slid the paperwork across the desk.

Carter felt Miamor's hand rubbing his back softly in support as he leaned over, fumbling with the pen because both of his hands were locked by the cuffs. He put his John Hancock sloppily on the paper in front of him and was instantly whisked off.

"I believe this ends our business," Broome stated as he looked at Miamor smugly. "Hope you have some frequent flier miles," he said. "I'm shipping those sons of bitches to a federal institution in Colorado." It was his way of making things difficult.

Miamor turned and walked out of the office. She wasn't angry, she had anticipated some type of kink in the plan. As she slid into her chauffeured SUV she dialed Aries.

"Miamor, is everything good?" Aries asked.

"As good as to be expected right now," Miamor replied. "I need you to put me in touch with Timmy Bono."

"Sure, but what do you have up your sleeve bitch?" Aries asked with laughter in her voice. She knew Miamor too well and could only imagine why she needed to be put in contact with the notorious Italian mobster.

"Nothing beats the cross," Miamor started.

"Like the double cross," Aries finished. "Consider it done."

Chapter 15

*"Look around. You're the only one of
your kind for a reason."*

—Man at the bar

The dimmed yellow light illuminated the smoky bar as incoherent chatter filled the air. The exclusive spot may as well have had a no-blacks allowed sign on the door because as soon as Miamor stepped foot inside, she was out of place. All conversations ceased as she walked toward the bar. Her expensive heels crunched peanuts under her feet as she made her way through the down home establishment. She slid into a stool next to a young Italian man. He gave her a once over and then poured the remainder of his drink down his throat in one swig.

"You lost sweet heart?" he asked.

"No, this is exactly where I need to be," she replied.

"Look around. You're the only one of your kind for a reason," the man said. "Although I must say I don't mind the view, you know what I mean?" He raised his hand and motioned for the bartender. The older Italian man had skin as rough as leather. His greasy, black, hair was slicked back off of his face, his top lip completely covered in a bushy mustache. Miamor could see the depth in his eyes and she would put her life on it that the hunch of his back was caused by the many secrets he had weighing down his soul. *These four walls have probably witnessed some crazy shit,* she thought.

"What can I get you?" the bartender asked as he glanced at Miamor.

"When's the last time you saw someone like this in the bar? Eh, Fred?" the man beside her asked.

The bartender tapped his finger on the bar and said, "A black girl in a bar is the least of my worries Sonny. Don't be a jackass," the bartender said sternly. He turned to Miamor. "What can I do for you sweet heart?"

Miamor lowered her voice. "I need to see Timmy Bono," she said

The bartender grabbed the bar rag and began to clean the countertops as he shook his head back and forth. "I don't know what you're talking about toots. I don't know anyone by that name. Sure you got the right spot?" he asked.

Miamor had expected to hit this roadblock so she had come prepared. She slid an envelope out of her handbag and placed it on the bar. She tapped it with her blood red fingernail. "After he sees this, he'll want to see me too," she said calmly.

The bartender discreetly grabbed the envelope and then disappeared without saying a word. Miamor kept her hand in her purse as she palmed the .45 that rested at the bottom of it. When she saw the wooden door that was hidden in the back shadows of the bar open up she knew that Timmy Bono was there. The bartender returned.

"Go through that back door there," he said.

Miamor arose from her seat and walked into the back. As soon as she stepped foot inside the door closed behind her. She spun to see two goons posted on the sides of the door. She looked at the man sitting behind the wooden desk in front of her . . . Timmy Bono.

"Please have a seat," he offered.

"I'd rather stand," Miamor said as she shifted uncomfortably.

"My men are going to search you," Timmy Bono said.

She held her hands out at her sides while gripping her bag in one of them as one of the goons stepped up. His hands searched her body gropingly, but he was so distracted by her curves that he neglected to go through her bag. "I'm clean, I'm not a cop," she spat harshly when she felt him palm her behind.

"So, what brings a pretty little thing like you into my bar?" he asked.

"I'm here to extend my friendship," Miamor said. She removed another envelope from her bag and placed pictures before him. "Daniel Broome has been building a racketeering case against you. All of the illegal bets that you have placed for him were caught on wire taps."

"Who are you? How do you know all of this? And what do you have to gain by telling me all of this. If I've learned one thing in my line of business it is that people who come in the form of friends are often truly enemies," Timmy Bono responded with dark eyes.

"I'm neither," Miamor answered. "I'm a woman with information," she said. "I choose my alliances very wisely and carefully. I'm sure you are familiar with The Cartel."

"The Diamond family," Timmy Bono said. "We call them the black mafia." Bono laughed heartily and his voice boomed loudly in amusement. "I am familiar with The Cartel."

"I am the head of The Cartel now and like I said, I would like to be friends," Miamor said.

"The head of The Cartel?" Timmy Bono asked. "What type of show are yous running over there?"

"That is not your concern. All you should know is that you have a problem with P.A. Daniel Broome. Don't say that I didn't try to warn you when the Feds come kicking in your door," Miamor said.

She turned and headed for the door.

"What's your name? Ms. new head of the cartel?" Timmy Bono asked.

"Miamor," she replied with a smile. "Don't let the good looks fool you Mr. Bono." She nodded toward the pictures on his desk. "Don't take my warning lightly."

Timmy Bono nodded as he watched Miamor walk from the room. She sighed in relief, but didn't release the hold on her bag until she was tucked safely in the car. As she collapsed in the passenger seat she looked over at Aries.

"Everything smooth?" Aries asked.

Miamor shook her head. "I don't know," she replied. She wasn't sure if Timmy Bono would act on her advice, but if he was anything like her he would eradicate Broome just to be safe. Revenge would be hers and she wouldn't even have to lift a pretty finger . . . all Miamor had to do was sit back and enjoy the show.

Chapter 16

"You're my world, Zyir."

—Breeze

Carter heard the sliding partition of his cell open and as he sat up out of the twin sized bed, he watched as a manila envelope was dropped inside. He stood and met the eyes of the C.O. who had acted as delivery boy. He gave him a nod, but said nothing as he walked over to retrieve the package. He bent over and scooped it from the floor but when he stood the C.O. was gone. It didn't matter however, Carter had already committed his face to memory. He was someone that Carter could use to communicate with the outside. Should the need ever arise, he now had a dirty officer that could do his bidding . . . for the right price of course. He opened the envelope and frowned when he pulled out a folded up newspaper. There was a lipstick print right next to the title.

THE MIAMI HERALD

He read the headline.

Prosecuting Attorney, Daniel Broome found dead.

"That murder mama shit is sexy than a mu'fucka," he muttered with a chuckle as he shook his head in disbelief. A sexy grin crossed his face as he rubbed the stubble of a beard that had begun to grow. "She wild."

He knew that Miamor was somehow behind the hit. She was more reliable than any hired hand and more gangster than the goons that made up the Cartel. She was his lady and although he knew that she could hold him down, it bothered him that she was still taking risks on his behalf. They had a son. She wasn't supposed to still be pulling triggers. He had failed her, but he promised himself that once he got out he would never disappoint her again.

Being locked up made him feel like he was weak and it made his family touchable. It wasn't the shackles that bothered him . . . it was the fact that he was so far away from everyone he loved. He couldn't protect his family if he weren't around. *I can't even send a kite to my niggas to let them know how to move because I'm in the*

middle of fucking nowhere, he thought. The
Feds had hidden him away in the mountains of
Colorado and to make matter worse they had
separated them. Zyir was in upstate New York
. . . Monroe was tucked away in California.
They had divided them in an attempt to conquer them. Without one another to rely on, the
five-year stretches would feel like forever. Each
day would be a hard one lived. Carter Jones
was considered the leader, head of the criminal
syndicate, The Cartel. Therefore he was shipped
to a maximum-security facility. He was locked
down for Twenty-three hours of the day. He
only showered twice a week and the measly hour
that he was allowed to leave his cell was spent
under extreme scrutiny. This type of time would
drive a man mad. He knew the intention of the
judge and he was determined not to fold under
pressure. His mother had always told him that
when life got too heavy for him to hand his problems over to the Lord. It was something she had
said repeatedly when he was a young boy and
he never truly understood what she meant until
now. This jail shit was for the birds and if he
didn't get his mind right he would never survive.
He worked out his guilt by getting familiar with
God. Praying for a resolution to the things that
ailed him . . . the biggest thing being that he was

missing out on baby Carter's life. He was a father to a black son and because of some bullshit case he was forced to be absent. He was missing everything and it pained him deeply to know that he had left the love of his life to raise his seed by herself. *What kind of man does that to his wife? To his son?* Behind steel and concrete Carter now realized that none of the millions he had touched had been worth his freedom. He had always thought he would die in the streets before he would ever let a pig take him to jail, but having a child had changed that for him. He couldn't blaze out with the Feds because he had a son to look after, but what good was he to anyone now. Caged like a rabid animal, Carter's head was all over the place. He wasn't young anymore. He was pushing thirty. He had done all of the things that he had set out to do in the game. He had reigned over the streets of Miami. His name rang bells and put fear in the hearts of many. It was over for all of that. He no longer needed the street life because when it was all said and done the streets didn't love him back. He made a vow to himself that when he emerged from behind the wall, he would go legit. He would take Baraka up on his offer and relocate to Las Vegas. In fact, he would put the plays in motion beforehand.

There was nothing left in Miami for his family but bad memories. It was time for Miamor to pack up their estate and make the trip west. Las Vegas was much closer to Colorado than Miami anyway. It would make the trek to visit him more convenient. It was time to reorganize his entire empire from the ground floor up.

Books. That's what got Zyir through his days. He buried his head in all of them. From the bible, to philosophy, to the street classics, it all fed his brain. He needed the words to take him on a mental vacation because his physical body was trapped behind the wall. If he stopped reading long enough his captivity haunted him. The only time he ever put the books down was when he was sleeping and even that he did with one eye open. Being shipped off solo to upstate New York, he was up for a challenge. He was locked up with a bunch of Tony Montana types. Every inmate in the joint walked around like they had something to prove. He wasn't even six months in and he had already been tested. These five years would pass by slowly because he didn't have the privilege of flying under the radar. His reputation had beat him there. Everyone knew he was affiliated with the infamous Cartel and they either wanted to be down or to challenge him.

The stretch ahead of him was daunting but he was no fool. He would eat the five because he knew that he was supposed to be serving life. He was no saint. The crimes that he had committed during his reign on the streets should have gotten him buried under the jail. His hood resume was official and he secretly missed the action of the everyday grind. He was like a caged bird and he knew that until he was free he wouldn't be able to rest easy. He would have to get used to the anxiety that now weighed him down. He only hoped that he survived his time. Prison life was unpredictable. No one knew what the next day held. Five years could easily turn to ten, even twenty if he made the wrong move. He would have to be careful how he handled niggas inside. A man serving life had nothing to lose and hated to see a young nigga like Zyir eventually go free.

"Rich stand up."

The unexpected visit from the C.O. caused him to stand.

"You've got a visitor," he said.

Zyir frowned. He wasn't expecting anyone, but he didn't mind taking a walk. The air in the visiting room was easier to breathe than the musty, muggy, stinking atmosphere where the cellblocks were located. He turned around and placed his hands behind his back, then back-pedaled so that he could stick his wrists through the slot on his door. Every time the metal cuffs bound his hands he cringed. This was slavery. He was in bondage and it hurt his pride as he grit his teeth.

"That's a little tight bro," Zyir stated with impatience as he shot a warning look over his shoulder. The C.O. didn't respond but he loosened the cuffs slightly. He opened the door and Zyir stepped out.

As they walked him through the cellblock the inmates peeked out of their holes, trying to get a glimpse of him. Some looked at him with hate in their eyes, others with respect, but either way they all looked. He made eye contact with no one.

When he saw her face his cold heart melted. Her smile always warmed him.

"I didn't think you would come," he said as he leaned into her, kissing her neck and inhaling deeply as the smell of her perfume intoxicated him. She was his Breeze. Only she had the power to blow the negative thoughts out of his mind and brighten his day without effort. All it took was her presence.

"Of course I came," she replied. "You're my world Zyir."

Breeze was effortlessly beautiful and the faded skinny jeans she wore and crop top fit her body

like a second skin. The other inmates in the visiting room couldn't keep their eyes from stray-
ing from their own guests. They were too busy
ogling over his wife. She was like a piece of meat
and Zyir's temper flared as he asked the inmate
next to him, "Fuck you looking at my nigga?"

Breeze noticed Zyir's aggression. He was
wound tightly and wore his stress all over his
face. She reached across the table, gripped his
chin and turned his face back to her. "Hey, look
at me Zy. Just focus on me. Forget what they're
looking at. It's me and you. An hour is hardly
long enough so lets make every single minute
count. Okay?"

Zyir nodded as he rested his face in her palm,
becoming emotional. Tears accumulated in his
eyes but his pride would let none fall. "I hate being away from you B. I love you so fucking much.
I'm sorry for leaving you."

"It's okay," she whispered. "It's okay. It's hard
but I'm fine. We will be fine and I'll be here every
visiting day. I'm thinking of getting a place in
New York until you're free."

There was nothing he would have enjoyed
more than to see her face twice a week, but he
wouldn't burden her with that expectation. "Nah
B, don't do that. You stay with the family. You,
Leena, Miamor. It's important that y'all stay
together. Wherever they go, you go. That's the

only way I know you'll be safe. I don't want you to come here again B. These niggas eye fucking you and shit. I'll catch beef over you ma and you deserve better than to have these bitch ass C.O.'s feeling you up every time you visit."

"I'm coming Zyir," she protested adamantly.

"Promise me you won't Breeze. You're my wife. You have to trust me. I want you to live. Don't fuck with no nigga because I swear to God when I get out I will put him in the dirt, but don't become a jailbird running up here to see me all the time. That's not who you are. Write me letters. Send me pictures, but my queen won't grace these walls again. Stay on your throne. You're too good for this," he said.

A tear rolled down her cheek and he brushed it away. "I love you."

"I love you more Zy," she responded.

Zyir spent the next hour enjoying the melody of her voice and drawing a mental picture in his mind because it would be years before he saw her again. He touched her, stroking her hand, her face, inhaling her scent. He didn't want to forget one detail. In five years she would be different. It was a long time to be away from someone, there was no way that either of them would be the same and he secretly feared what that change would mean for their relationship.

He loved her, like no one he had ever loved before and he hoped that this bid didn't destroy the bond that they shared.

Monroe was a part of the black La Cosa Nostra, it was a known fact. Even behind bars he was royal. There was no such thing as being low-key for Monroe. His face was known worldwide and because he was the surviving son of Carter Diamond and the blood born heir to Emilio Estes, his story was not easily concealed. He wasn't like Carter. He couldn't hide behind an illegitimate name. No one knew about Carter Jones except for those that needed to know. Everyone knew about the infamous twin sons of Taryn and Carter. Mecca was no longer here. Monroe was the last official son standing. He was a Diamond. He was Monroe Diamond. As soon as he was taken into custody, the media went mad. *The New York Times, USA Today, Miami Herald*, and all the bloggers covered his story. He was a modern day mobster and when Time Magazine plastered him on the cover he became famous. His name suddenly became a synonym for 'gangster'. The hottest rappers dropped his name in lyrics, his mug shot was printed on a popular t-shirt line. He became ingrained in pop culture but he never confirmed anything. He kept his mouth closed and ignored the speculation. He wasn't a fool. The Feds were just waiting for him to get cocky and confirm some of the illegal activities that had made him so popular. They would slap a case on him faster than he could bat an eye. Monroe Diamond would never be able to outrun his past because it had now been noted in the history books. It was a gift and a curse. The streets would forever mention his name but when he finally got out of prison he would never be anything but a drug dealer to everyone he met going forward. His future was already ruined. He was and would forever be a kingpin. On top of that he was a king pin that stood tall. He hadn't snitched, he hadn't turned state's evidence to get himself off of the hook. He lived by principle and he never did anything that he couldn't stand behind. He had sold dope on the streets of M.I.A. He had murdered on the streets of M.I.A. If that was his legacy, so be it. He had done it so there was no point in being ashamed now. His father had always taught him to stand behind his decisions. It didn't mean that he didn't have regrets because his head was filled with many, but he was man enough to live with the destruction that he had caused. Diamonds didn't fold. So these five years he would eat like chocolate cake.

As a result of his newfound fame, the inmates around him showed nothing but respect whenever he graced them with his presence. Prison life for Monroe was far different than what Carter and Zyir were experiencing. He did what he wanted, when he wanted. The locks and chains were merely a façade. Even the prison guards wanted to keep him happy in hopes that when he got out, he would remember the favors they bestowed. He was like a king inside. Being locked down only intensified his network. The Feds were better off letting him be, because when you put him with other wolves he ended up leading the pack. The relationships he was building behind the wall would only strengthen his muscle when he was finally released. At first his reach was slightly limited to Miami but he was locked up with criminals who had run their own enterprises, shaken down their own cities, murdered under their own circumstances. Once Monroe recruited and took them under his wing the Cartel would emerge better than ever. The Feds had tried to stop him but they had only helped to decorate his crown because he was picking up some valuable jewels while being locked away. It was only a matter of time before he put them to use.

Let the five-year bid begin.

Chapter 17

"Our reactions depend on your actions."
—Breeze

Year One

"We're moving to Las Vegas," Miamor said to the ladies as they moved around the kitchen, preparing Sunday dinner. It was a tradition that they had started as soon as the men went inside. It had only been a few months but Miamor knew that it was of utmost importance that they remain strong . . . united. When Miamor got the go ahead from Carter to transition out of Miami she knew that it would be a hard move. She was reluctant to leave all that they had built but she trusted Carter. If he said it, than it was law. Las Vegas it was. It was up to her to get all the pieces put in place. Upon release, Carter and the men would be convicted felons which would automatically black ball them from the Nevada market.

Anything they owned would be put in the names of their women.

"Las Vegas?" Leena asked. "No offense but I'm not moving across the country to jump into the pit of another fire. We know these streets. Why would we go somewhere else where The Cartel name has no clout?"

"In business you don't need clout, just money. When we move we'll be clean. Carter wants to open a casino," she informed.

"A casino?" Breeze questioned.

Miamor nodded. She was just as unsure as them, but it didn't show. She knew that if her skirt showed than they would worry. She had to appear as if she had it all under control. She didn't, but they didn't need to know that.

"What do we know about the casino business?" Breeze asked.

"Not much, but we have friends who know it well. Baraka from Saudi Arabia will invest. I have a meeting with him this evening. While I'm setting up shop, Breeze you need to liquidate our assets here in Miami. Sell it all. The realty company, this house, your houses."

"I'm not selling my house," Breeze said. "And I'm definitely not selling my parent's old home. This is where I grew up. This is where the next generation of our family should grow up."

"Where you grow up isn't usually where you grow old Breeze. There's too much history here. Miami won't give you a chance to grey. This city would rather see you dead. Keep the old Diamond estate if you like, but sell the others. This transition will be hard but I have a feeling that it will be worth it. Leena we'll need somewhere to stay when we get to Vegas. Think you can handle that?" she asked.

Leena nodded. "Yeah, I'll get on it right away."

Miamor approached her next subject tactfully. "There is someone else I need to bring in on this." She paused because she knew that conflict was to come. "I need Aries."

"No," Breeze replied without hesitation.

"Miamor!" Leena protested.

"Look without Aries, neither of you would have ever seen your husbands again. She helped bring them home. I can't run The Cartel without some bite behind my bark and I don't see the two of you putting in that kind of work. We need people like Aries to do our dirty work. She's loyal and I trust her," Miamor said, arguing passionately on her behalf. Breeze shook her head and rolled her eyes in disbelief.

"Breeze just give her a chance. Talk to her. One time. If you don't like it than I'll leave it alone, but remember that there are a lot of niggas in line for the thrones. With the three of us sitting on top this empire, we have to prove that we are not to be fucked with. If not, there is only a matter of time before niggas begin to test us. If everyone does their part we will be out of this city by the month's end and will have some loyal soldiers following us. Just let Aries do what she does best."

"Murder?" Breeze shot back sarcastically.

"She's protection Breeze and she's loyal. If she is on your side she is on your side. You don't have anything to worry about. The days of Ma'tee and that beef are long over," Miamor tried to convince.

"I'll meet with her, but I'm not making any promises," Breeze shot back.

"That's all I can ask," Miamor said. "Now which auntie is watching baby Carter while I take this meeting?"

"That's nothing," Leena said with a flip of the hand. "You know I got you."

"Pack a few days worth of clothes," Miamor instructed.

Leena frowned in confusion.

"The meeting is in Saudi Arabia."

***

After a long and tiresome flight, Miamor emerged from the private luxury jet a bit fatigued. The thick heat that seemed to blanket the air was the first thing she noticed as she made her way down the stairs. A driver waited at the bottom and he greeted her with a smile.

"Mrs. Jones, welcome to Saudi Arabia," he said.

Miamor nodded and placed her Versace shades over her eyes as she stepped into the vehicle. Miamor took a deep breath as she rested her head on her closed fist while propping her elbow on the windowsill. She would never admit it, but she was exhausted and completely overwhelmed. Since giving birth it seemed that her life had been moving at a rapid rate. She hadn't had a moment to breathe. Her emotions were all over the place and some nights she barely slept. If she didn't know any better she would have thought she was battling with a bout of post partum, but she was a 'Murder Mama' . . . nothing had ever gotten the best of her. She wouldn't start to accept defeat now. She wished that she lived in a world where everything was black and white; where she could be a mother to her son without worry of her past coming back to haunt her. A woman with a body count like hers was never supposed to bear a child. The child always paid for the sins of the mother and she feared that eventually her murder record would catch up to her. She could only hope and pray that it never did.

Lost in her thoughts, the hour long ride passed her by in no time and when she arrived at the resort she was escorted to the gardens, where a private luncheon was set up strictly for the occasion.

Baraka had a guard waiting at the entrance and she spread her arms out wide as she was searched thoroughly. He walked up to her wearing a tan cloak and matching head wrap. A friendly smile decorated his face.

"I have heard many tales about the infamous Miamor Holly, but your legend does not do you justice. It fails to mention how lovely you are," Baraka said.

She smiled. It never failed. It seemed that no matter their ethnicity, men always fancied her. Men found her irresistible.

"Thank you but apparently my legend hasn't been updated yet. My last name is Jones now," she replied, letting it be known that his flirting was in vain.

"Carter's wife?" Baraka said, obviously shocked.

She nodded confirmation but the sound of clicking heels caused her to turn her attention to see who was approaching from behind.

"Father, you didn't tell me we had a guest."

Baraka extended his hand to his daughter. "Miamor this is my daughter Yasmine. Yasmine this is . . ."

"Carter's girlfriend," Yasmine finished for him without a smile. She clearly wasn't happy to see her. "I know who she is."

"Appraently you don't," Miamor replied, sensing ill vibes from Yasmine. "I'm his wife," Miamor corrected, giving no smile of her own. Her intuition was in overdrive as she eyed Yasmine intently.

"Funny, he never mentioned that," Yasmine shot back.

Miamor scoffed. She wasn't going to discuss her man with a woman that was irrelevant. There would be no playing badminton with snide remarks. This wasn't a competition and if it was Yasmine would lose . . . Miamor killed the competition, literally. *You don't want to see any part of me little girl. Keep it moving,* Miamor thought. She focused her attention to Baraka, blatantly dismissing Yasmine.

"Shall we discuss business?" Miamor asked.

"Absolutely. I look forward to meeting with your representative," Baraka said. Arab men held women in low regard when it came to business. The men wore the pants. Period. Point blank. In Baraka's eyes Miamor's place was to be seen but rarely heard. "I assume since Carter is not available you have a family member, perhaps a brother, or consigliere to do things on your behalf?"

Miamor smiled, realizing the difference in cultures made her presence awkward. "I'm fully capable of handling this independently. Until Carter is free, I am the only person who has the authority to negotiate on his behalf. It's a bit different for you, I understand, but I think I can hang with the boys," she said charmingly.

A woman with such a strong presence was un-customary to Baraka and the way she used her femininity to enamor him left him with a stiff one. He was taken aback by her instantly. He had fallen under the murder mama spell. "I think that you can," he replied. "I like a woman who knows how to get what she wants," Baraka said. He held out his bent arm for her to latch onto. "Shall we?" She embraced him as he escorted her onto the grass until they reached their table.

Yasmine followed closely behind. There was no way she was sitting out of this meeting. If it concerned Carter, she wanted to be involved. She would do anything to be in his presence again.

The three of them sat and ate while having ca-sual conversation. Yasmine did most of the questioning . . . too much for Miamor's taste. *This bitch wants to know more about Carter than anything else. The fuck?* Miamor thought. Her patience was wearing thin so she fast-forwarded to more serious matters.

"I know that you originally had planned to open a casino with Carter. As you know Nevada gaming will never approve a license to him now that he has a criminal record. I on the other hand am squeaky clean," she said.

"I find that hard to believe," Baraka replied quickly and with intrigue.

"Where it counts Mr. Baraka," she added with a laugh. "On paper I'm as legit as they come. My credit is impeccable and I have no record besides juvenile stuff that was sealed long ago. Carter trusts me to be the front woman for this new venture."

"As do I," Baraka admitted. "You are sharp and fearless if everything that I hear is true."

"I'm sure that some of it is embellished," she said coyly.

"Tell me," Baraka leaned up, intrigued. "Is it true that you once severed a man's . . ."

"Don't believe everything you hear," she interrupted, not wanting to cop to anything. She didn't want her reputation to scare off his business. How the story had traveled all the way across the world she had no clue. She had to chuckle slightly to herself. She had been a wild girl before Carter had calmed her slightly. He really did bring stability into her life. *The good old days,* she thought.

"Besides that is something only a disgusting woman would do. Its quite barbaric, don't you think? Certainly not the type of woman that Carter would take as a wife," Yasmine shot.

"Sometimes barbaric is necessary when people don't stay in their place," Miamor replied with an underlying tone. "My husband can be quite brutal himself when the situation suits it."

"I will put up fifty million to finance half of the new resort and casino in Nevada. I take it The Cartel can come up with the other half," Baraka suggested.

"We can," Miamor said.

"Nevada isn't an easy town to takeover. I'm sure you are quite skilled in the art of war, but you will need an entire army. I don't have that type of support. This is where The Cartel would be beneficial," Baraka insisted.

"It's where we excel," Miamor replied.

"I'll write you a check and have my lawyers draw up the paperwork immediately. In the meanwhile . . ."

Miamor cut him short, "In the meanwhile you can get the money in cash." She pulled a folder from her Birkin bag and slid it across the table. "I had the liberty of having our attorney draw up the agreement. All you have to do is have your people look it over and sign."

Baraka laughed heartily at her wit and handed the paperwork off to Yasmine. He stood. "Please Mrs. Jones, enjoy a suite, rest up, do a bit of gambling if you prefer. We have excellent spa facilities. Whatever you would like. I will have the contract and the money returned to you by the time your wheels are up tomorrow. When you speak to Carter be sure to tell him that he is a very, very, lucky man," Baraka stated.

"He knows," she smiled graciously.

"Well than give him my best," Baraka replied.

When he walked away Miamor felt like jumping for joy, but instead she kept her cool. The financing was the hardest part. Now that she had gotten the ball rolling there wasn't much that would stand in her way to getting Carter's casino.

"Where d' fuck is dis' bitch?" Aries muttered as she sat inside of the restaurant waiting for Breeze to arrive. The waiter walked up and re-filled Aries drink.

"Slow day?" Aries asked.

The waiter gave a slight smile and a shrug before walking away.

Being back in Miami had brought the accent right back out of her. She was in her element and right back in the mind frame of a stone cold killer. She had forgotten completely about the suburban housewife and mother that she had forced herself to transform into. "De bitch is lucky I'm agreeing to meet her at all." Aries was losing patience. Breeze was twenty minutes late. Aries had already let the spoiled princess choose the time and place. She was feeling a type of way about being made to wait. *If it twasn't for Miamor, I would slit de' bitch's pretty little throat. Arghh! Waiting tis' for the fucking birds,* she thought. Aries had always had a temper problem when it came to anyone with the last name Diamond. She had a bitter taste in her mouth over Anisa's death. Their entire crew had fallen apart the day they set their sights on The Cartel. Distracted by her thoughts, Aries didn't notice the two large men heading toward her. She had been too busy looking for a carefree, sun-kissed, impeccably dressed socialite that was Breeze Diamond. What she didn't realize was that Breeze had grown up and life had hardened her. She didn't move without thinking nowadays. In fact, the place where they were meeting, Breeze owned. It was empty for a reason. Breeze had ordered it to be. She never left anything to chance anymore and as the two goons parted Breeze became visible. Aries motioned to stand but Breeze stopped her. "Sit down. If you make one move too quickly my pits right here," she paused as she nodded toward the two men who stood faithfully at her side. "They'll put a bullet in your head. Do we understand each other?"

"You grew balls," Aries stated with a smirk.

Breeze flew across the table and slapped Aries across the face with all her might.

Aries temper flared as they faced off.

"Jump bitch," Breeze instigated.

Aries' trigger finger itched uncontrollably as she bit her inner cheek. "Guess you not de' weak one anymore. If you brought me here t' kill me I would be dead already. I'm not your enemy girl."

"You aren't my friend either," Breeze replied. She rolled her eyes and continued, "The only reason why I haven't had my men kill you is because of Miamor. Sit down."

The two women eyed each other harshly as they both took a seat. Aries used the white linen napkin to wipe the blood from her lip. "This is the thanks I get for saving your ass from the Feds."

"Oh come on! You kidnapped me and tried to kill my entire family. I think we're even," Breeze stated. She crossed her arms over her chest stubbornly. "I don't trust you. You're Miamor's people but you're not like her. You can't be saved."

Aries laughed incredulously. "I'm just like Miamor. That's what you don't get. Mia and me. We're built exactly the same. She just happens to be on your team now."

"I had nightmares every night for a year. Ma'tee . . . he . . ."

Breeze paused and closed her eyes as the horrible memories came flooding back. She hadn't thought of it in years, but in the blink of an eye terror gripped her as if it had happened just yesterday.

"Ma'tee was a psychopath," Aries whispered. "Not everything dat I've done I'm proud of." Aries noticed how Breeze had seemed to fall into a daze as she thought of her torment and she immediately felt sympathy for the role she had played in her kidnapping. She had contributed to her fear. "Look Breeze. You might never like me. I get it but it wasn't personal. You may not relate to me but your father, your brothers, Miamor . . . dey all can. We are killers, Breeze. We live the street life. We live by de gun, we die by de gun. We don't think about de target. We just do de job. It was about de money, not about you."

"Why did you help set up the prosecuting attorney?" Breeze asked, slightly rattled as her hands shook. These old memories haunted her. She had forgotten the impact that they had over her until now.

"Because Miamor loves your brother and I love her. She is my sister. She needed my help. I was out of de life. I have a son. I had moved on and prayed for forgiveness for all de lives I helped destroy. But loyalty ties me to Miamor. I'm a Murder Mama and you don't walk away from that. She is aligned with you now. I don't like it. Your family took from me . . . from Mia too. We lost someone we loved from a bullet dat your brother fired. A war has two sides Breeze. Your family is far from innocent. You just happened to be the only good one caught in de middle," Aries schooled.

"I don't trust you," Breeze said clearly, not mincing words.

"Trust is earned. De feeling is mutual," Aries replied, frankly.

Breeze stood up from the table and leaned over Aries. "How do I know you won't cross my family as soon as we let you on the inside?"

"Miamor may be your family now, but she was my family first. I would never hurt her. Some loyalty you just don't break," Aries said.

Breeze grabbed her Louis Vuitton and turned on her heels. "Bring your son by the house. If you're family of Miamor's he may as well meet his cousins. Monroe has a young son he can play with." She began to walk away but stopped again. "I still don't like your ass though and I don't trust you as far as I can throw you. If I even feel like you're plotting on anyone I love, I'll have you put down the rabid beast you are."

"Touche'," Aries responded. "We all have dat one family member dat we can't stand, guess I'm the black sheep."

A truce had just been called. Aries was just the experienced gun that Miamor would need to help her conquer a new city. Las Vegas wasn't ready for the type of tyranny that The Cartel was about to bring.

The abandoned warehouse was eerily silent as Miamor stood, staring out over the fifty men she had assembled. It had taken a bit of time to weed through the massive following that their organization had. From runners, to shooters, to the cook-up crew, Miamor had observed them closely and cut the fat from the bone. Only the most thorough, the most gangster, the most loyal had been chosen. Now they stood before her

for one specific reason . . . to witness her gangster so that they would never test it. This was
a 'town hall' meeting in a sense. With a change
of leadership, new laws needed to be laid down
and she wanted to make sure there was no confusion. She could see the skepticism in their eyes
as they looked at the women who stood before
them. Breeze and Leena were at her side. They
were aesthetically gorgeous and the men were
distracted. They were too busy ogling over them.
Yes they were beautiful, but to cross them would
be deadly. Miamor needed that point to be made
here and now.

"The Cartel is transitioning out of Miami. Las
Vegas is the next move gentleman and there is a
place for each of you if you choose to accompany
us as we expand out West. Carter, Zyir, and Monroe are still very much the heads of this organization. Consider us their mouthpieces. If you had
loyalty to them, we have now inherited that. If
that is a problem, leave now because treachery
will not be tolerated. There is a punishment for
going against the grain," Miamor said. The doors
behind her audience clanged open as four, hood-
ed-figures, were escorted in at Aries' gunpoint.
The sniffling cries underneath revealed that
there were women underneath. Miamor pointed
up to the sky, where four men stood on rafters, a
noose hanging around each of their necks.

The women were lined up in front of Miamor and as she walked past each of them she snatched the hoods off of their heads.

"These women have done nothing wrong. Their only crime is marrying snitch ass niggas who folded under pressure instead of standing tall. The case that was brought against us, was held up on the backs of those men," Miamor stated as she pointed up to the sky where Fly Boogie was waiting for her signal. "Their testimonies helped the D.E.A. to gather evidence against us. I don't show mercy. Anyone that professes loyalty to the Cartel and then betrays us in any way will pay. I don't give a fuck about your wife, your kids . . . they will either suffer or be rewarded depending on your allegiance."

She looked up at the sniffling men. "Jump," she ordered.

Breeze turned her head and Leena just stared off into space as the men plunged from the rafters. The sound of them struggling to breathe as their bodies fought against the inevitable was sickening and it took everything in them not to flinch. This was the part of the game that they had not been exposed to. This is how the money was made. Order had to be established or anarchy would occur. The gruesome details had always been hidden from them, but Miamor knew the real. She knew that the necessary had to occur, but since becoming a mother something in her had changed. She had no sympathy for the men who had chosen their fates, but the women in front of her had done no wrong. Their only offense had been falling in love with the wrong type of man. They were probably mothers, just like she was. Her heart silently ached for them, but her face showed no emotion as she turned to Aries too and gave her the nod.

Aries went down the line. One bullet each, to the back of the heads of the women. The men shifted uncomfortably in their seats as they watched the cold-hearted sight. "Your family can either eat with us or die at our hands. It's all up to you."

Out of nowhere Breeze stepped up and began to speak. "We do not enjoy murder," she said, her voice a bit shaky. She paused to stifle her fear before she continued. "But it is a part of the game that we all know exists. My father, Carter Diamond, ruled with love and because of that he found himself in an early grave. My brother Mecca ruled with fear and he too met the same fate. So we will rule with both. Our reactions depend on your actions. Act accordingly and you can all avoid putting on those black suits. There is no need for flower bringing. Loyalty is all we ask." Breeze looked over at Aries. "Choose a few men and clean this mess up. We will cover the funeral expenses."

Miamor smirked as Breeze walked out of the room. She was like a proud mama because although Breeze didn't like it, she had finally come into her own. *Maybe she can help me run this thing after all,* Miamor thought. "We depart for Vegas at the end of the month. We'll be in touch."

She walked out and Leena followed suit as their stilettos clicked on the concrete floor as they made their exit.

Miamor's conscience had never played tricks on her but she couldn't get the faces of the women she had ordered killed out of her mind. As she sat in her son's nursery, watching over him as he slept, she wondered how many kids were now motherless because of her. Miamor was evolving. Ever since she had given birth and Carter went away she had been experiencing a vulnerability that was so foreign to her. She heard the ringing of her phone and she quickly answered it, to stop the sound from waking up her son.

"Fly Boogie?" she said in surprise as she checked the time. It was nearly three a.m. "Did something go wrong?" she asked.

"Nah, nothing like that. I'm at your door. I didn't want to ring the bell. Last time I did that you stuck a gun in my face," he said. "I kind of like my face." She could hear his smile and she shook her head as one melted across her face too. He had a way with her . . . he reminded her of what it was like to be young . . . reckless . . . brave. "I'll be down."

She eased out of her son's room and hustled to the front door. She checked the peephole to make sure that Fly Boogie was alone. She paused because a part of her knew that she should send him away. Whatever he wanted could wait until morning, but she didn't want to.

"Remind me again why you're at my door this late again?" she asked, placing a hand on her hip as she leaned her head against the doorframe.

"The bodies were taken care of," Fly stated.

She wagged a finger as she raised an eyebrow. "You talk reckless," she replied. "Take off your jacket and lift your shirt."

"You think I'm police ma?" he asked. I just put eight people in the ground for you for turning state's evidence and you think I'd turn around and set you up."

She didn't respond. She just looked at him as he sucked his teeth and lifted his shirt, revealing his toned abdomen. She eyed the V-cuts in his

pelvis and the .45 he had tucked in his waist as
she pursed her lips. Fly Boogie was young and
thugging it. She remembered the good old days
and she found his carefree attitude appealing.

"Satisfied?" he asked.

She nodded. "You have blood on you," she
said.

"That's cuz I put in work. Don't insult me ma,
I'd never switch up on you," Fly Boogie stated
seriously.

She pinched the bridge of her nose feeling
conflicted. "Sorry. I'm tripping. I don't know
what's wrong with me. I've never felt remorse
after murking anybody, but tonight it made me
sick to my stomach." She didn't know why she
was telling him this. Perhaps she needed to vent.
Carter was usually her listening ear, the one person that she could express her true feelings to.
With him gone, she had so much pent up emotion that it felt like she would burst.

"You're human. It can't be easy being a woman
and in your position," he said. "I know you're
official and everything, but you don't got to be
tough all the time."

"Come on," she said as she started down the
hall. "Let's clean you up." They walked into the
bathroom and she wet a towel with hot water
and wiped it across his strong chest, cleaning the
blood spatter and dirt off of him.

"You're beautiful," he whispered, causing her to tense up and stop. "Everything about you Miamor. You're dope as fuck."

"Fly you shouldn't . . ."

Before she could even finish her sentence he covered her lips with his. It had been so long since she had felt a man against her that she fell into the rhythm. She knew that she should have stopped him, but she didn't. She melted into this young tenderoni, allowing him to pick her up and place her on the sink as he cupped her face with both hands. It felt so good . . . too good. It was reminiscent of the way that Carter used to touch her. *Carter* . . . as soon as his name appeared in her thoughts she froze, pulling back. "We can't. I can't," she whispered. "This is a mistake. You can't look at me like that."

"Any man would look at you like that," he answered.

Miamor picked up the towel and wet it once more as she sighed. "Fly you're young. You need a young girl. I'm pushing thirty," she chuckled. "There's nothing fresh about me. You need to get you a good girl." She dismissed.

He went to speak and she placed a finger over his lips. "Don't Fly. You got one kiss. Let's just leave it at that. I like you. I don't want you to go down that road. It wouldn't end well for you.

Carter is away, but he'll be back and when he gets here I don't want your loyalty to be tainted. Just forget it ever happened okay?"

He nodded, but still stared intently. "Yeah, okay," he replied.

"Here let me clean you up," she said, starting again. She stopped when she felt the temptation of his hard body. She passed him the towel. "I'll wait in the living room."

When he came back out she stood against the wall with her arms folded "There was so much blood. You were covered in dirt. What did you do with the bodies? Dig a grave?"

"I dug four," Fly Boogie replied. She looked up at him in shock as he continued to explain. "I threw the bitch niggas who ratted in with the sharks. I buried the women in an old field. Nobody's going to find them don't worry and if they do they won't be tied to us. Tossing them in the ocean didn't feel right to me." Miamor looked up at him completely understanding where he was coming from. His compassion made him even more attractive. In her younger days she would have made him hers, but what she didn't know was that she had ruined love for him. Fly Boogie would never give too much of himself to any other woman all because of Miamor. She had him mesmerized without even trying and if he couldn't be her man, he would be her illest soldier. No questions asked.

"Have you ever killed anyone Fly?" she asked.

"I've hit a nigga off before for coming at me. Nothing like tonight though," he responded truthfully. "If that's what I've got to do, I'm with it. Whatever it takes to keep you on the throne ma. Anybody who got a problem with it can get it. You need a finger wrapped around the trigger, I'll pull it every time." She realized why he had come to her home. He was feeling the hangover of homicide and he wanted her to coach him through it. She took his hand in hers and placed them under the running stream of water as she cleansed him. She hated that she had tasked him with the burden of death. Fly Boogie wasn't a murderer. He would do it if he had to, but he didn't prefer it. He was just a hustler . . . a damned good one at that. She made a vow to herself not to turn his soul black. What she didn't realize was that Fly Boogie was committed to protecting all that Carter, Zyir, and Monroe had left behind, including their women . . . especially her. Although she was the one holding everything together he saw through her visage. Miamor hid her weaknesses well, but she wasn't superwoman and until Carter was home to hold her down, he would have her back.

Chapter 18

"I know a few Italians in high places."

—Miamor

Year Two

"It's so damn hot here! I thought Miami summers were bad, but this is almost unbearable," Leena huffed as her driver helped her out of the SUV.

Lisa Matthews, owner of Vegas' most prominent real estate agency, chuckled as she led the way into the condominium. "Living in the middle of the desert takes some getting used to. I've been here ten years and it still gets to me sometimes." She waved her hands around at the buildings around them. This is city center. It is the most luxurious property in the entire city. I think you will love it," she said as she led the way.

The beautiful Aria hotel was inspired by Chinese architecture and took her breath away as soon as she stepped foot inside. Everything was high quality, from the marble floors to the floating candles hanging from the fifty-foot ceilings. It was amazing and immediately excitement about this new venture filled Leena's chest. "If the condos are anything like this casino, I'm already sold," she said.

"I think that was the designer's intention," Lisa laughed. "Let the casino sell the real estate. This way please," she directed, walking swiftly.

They took the residency elevator all the way to the top floor where the elevator opened up to a plush, 5,000 square foot, two-story, condominium. It came already furnished, with the best view of the strip, and a private plunge pool to match. Leena smiled. This was living. *Maybe Vegas won't be so bad,* she thought.

"I love this," she admitted.

"I have two other ones just like it. One sits atop of the Mandarin Oriental and the other atop of the Vdara. Both the same size, different layouts, but equally nice. Designed by the same person. All you and your sisters would have to do is move in," Lisa said.

"It's a done deal," Leena said. "Let's talk price."

Leena was all about the numbers and by the time she was done negotiating she had walked the price down by a quarter million dollars for each condo. Lisa left out of the deal with only a fifth of her normal commission after Leena was done with her.

"We're also interested in commercial real estate . . . casino's in particular," Leena said.

Lisa stopped walking. She had been defeated in negotiations with Leena over the condos but the word casino renewed her. She had never been involved in the purchase of one, but she knew that it was the cash cow. She silently wondered if this lovely black girl in front of her even had enough money to enter the ball game. Vegas was a 'pay to play' type of city.

"I'd be happy to help you. I know of a few properties that are on the market but we aren't talking about million dollar properties here. You would have to have capital in excess of at least a $100,000,000," Lisa informed. "There are many moving parts when it comes to the casino business. I can handle the real estate side, but you'll need legal representation and you'll have to set up a board of trustees, amongst many other things. I can get in touch with a few colleagues of mine that can help me execute this type of deal, but the money would have to be readily available."

"That's not a problem," Leena replied cockily.

Lisa stammered, unable to form words. She had clearly underestimated Leena. She had assumed that she was the girlfriend or wife of some famous athlete.

"P-perfect," Lisa said, getting excited about the potential commission to be made. "I just need to see your purchase permits, liquor and gambling licenses as well to get the process started. It takes ninety days to even hear back from the gambling commission. Acquisition of a casino requires a letter of loan approval as well from the financial institution that's financing you. I'll write down this information and when you are ready, you can contact me. I'll be happy to assist you with the purchase of the casino, but I must warn you honey. You don't have the right color skin or the right jewels between your legs. That alone will stop you in a city like Vegas. Old Italian money runs that industry." Lisa handed Leena her card.

Leena placed it in her Louis Vuitton clutch and replied, "Yeah well new black money is moving to town. I would suggest they make room."

"Magdalena, please prepare a bottle for CJ," Miamor said as she walked around her new home. It was immaculate. All white with floor to ceiling glass windows and her view was amazing. The entire strip could be seen below her and the mountains were in the far distance. "Auntie Leena really outdid herself," she cooed to her baby boy as she bounced him in her arms. She looked at him. She was completely in love with her son. The past year and a half of her life had been pure hell without Carter. She missed him on a daily and discovering her way as a mom on her own had not been easy, but she had finally found her groove. With the help of Magdalena, she was doing just fine. She wasn't the typical Susie homemaker but she loved him all the same. There was something to be said about motherly instinct. Even the most wretched soul could be saved when it came to loving a child and Miamor completely adored hers. CJ was a perfect mix of his parents and he reminded her of Carter so much that she couldn't help but be completely putty in his hands. He was now one and a half and the bond they shared amazed her. She had been hardened by life's circumstances but when it came to her son she was a soft cookie. She couldn't wait for Carter to finish his bid and rejoin their family. Life would be so perfect. Until then she had to fill his shoes and command an army of goons as they took over a new town. The doorbell rang and Miamor carried CJ with her as she went to answer the door. Breeze and Leena were the only ones who knew where she lived. The rest of The Cartel members had been put up in Summerlin, a safe distance away from where the bosses actually rested their heads. The only members that were allowed to be close were Aries and Fly Boogie. They took up residence in rental apartments in the hotel portion of the resort.

"Hey," she greeted as she allowed them entry.

Breeze immediately scooped her nephew from Miamor's arms. They shared a bond like no other. Breeze loved on her nephews constantly, spoiling both Monroe and Carter's sons as if they were her own. "He's getting so big! I can't believe he will be two in a few weeks," Breeze said as she held him above her head while making love faces at him. "I'm throwing him a party," she said.

"Glad you have so much time on your hands," Miamor shot back with a smile. "While you're doing that, I'll be dealing with the gaming control board and gambling commission. They denied my application."

"We have to have that. You're being boxed out by the Italians," Leena said as she lifted Monroe Jr. up and sat him on the kitchen island. She removed his shoes, kissed his cheek, and then placed him back on the floor. Miamor shook her head as she realized that the three of them were truly multitasking. Raising children, running an empire, and holding down their men was no easy task but through sisterhood, they were making it. In that moment she was truly grateful for Leena and Breeze. It had been an unlikely sisterhood, but somehow it worked.

"We will get it. I'm going to make sure of it. I know a few Italians in high places," Miamor replied.

Miamor had known that she would need Timmy Bono sooner or later. A business alliance between the two of them could only prove to be fruitful. He owed her a favor and she was smart enough to only use it when it was absolutely necessary. *This greasy, olive oil smelling, mu'fucka is just what I need to get by in this town,* she said. Timmy "Two Time" Bono was old mafia and he had much respect in the game. Just because he had never been to Las Vegas didn't mean that the Italians who ran the city had never heard of him. They knew exactly who he was so when he requested a sit down, they obliged. They just didn't know that he was bringing a guest along with him.

"Let me do the talking toots," he said as he smashed out his cigarette on the brick exterior of the butcher's shop that they were about to enter. "Just stand next to me and look pretty."

She smirked but didn't respond. She would let him think that he was running the show . . . for now. As soon as she entered the shop the smell of blood overwhelmed her. Italians were all about their produce and fresh meats and cheese lay behind the glass freezer cases. It smelled like a slaughterhouse and her stomach turned as they bypassed the front, walking directly into the back.

A bulky, overweight, man stood off to the side and allowed Timmy to pass, but he stopped Miamor dead in her tracks, pushing her chest slightly.

"This is Gucci you fat fuck," she said in irritation as she slapped his hand away.

"She's with me," Timmy Bono said. His words were like magic. He might as well have said 'abracadabra' because suddenly the big man magically had a change of heart, letting her walk by. A card game was taking place inside a walk-in deep freezer and to her surprise a man hung in the corner, hog tied and hanging by his hands as he shivered uncontrollably. Miamor didn't flinch. She had done worse in her day so the bloodied man before her was all in a day's work.

This wasn't some rival drug crew in Opa-locka, or a hustler on the come-up in Carroll City. The Italians weren't running an amateur show. They were a crime syndicate that had reigned over Las Vegas for years. She was well aware of her adversary . . . but they were unaware of theirs.

"Who's the girl?" one of the men asked as he filled the air with putrid cigar smoke.

"A friend," Timmy Bono stated.

"Timmy "Two Time" you are always welcome in Las Vegas. Chicago is where the bosses reside. They've spoken highly of you. Your rank is recognized here. This mouliano we don't know. You shouldn't have brought her here."

"This mouliano's name is Miamor and I run The Cartel from Miami," she said, speaking up for herself.

The silence that fell over the room let her know that they had heard of The Cartel before.

"You're a long way from Miami," Mr. Cigar said as he held his cards close to his chest. He didn't give her the respect of looking at her as he spoke, but the other men at the table stared intently.

"I'm here to buy a casino. After being denied a license, I was told to come here. Apparently the gambling commission has a commission. I take it that this is it," she commented. "I come in

peace and offering five percent of my earnings to
you Mr. . . ."

"Salerno," the old man huffed.

"In addition to my five percent I come with a
gift," she said. She placed a suitcase in front of
him. "A million dollars. No pressure, just a gift.
I hope that my application can be reconsidered.
I've done square business with Mr. Bono. I know
that it is necessary for me to have an Italian
presence in my casino. I'm prepared to offer him
a position on the board, to represent the interests of the Italian community."

"Smart girl," Salerno stated. He didn't even
pop open the briefcase. He simply slid it to the
man sitting at his left and said, "Put that up. We
done here or you gonna interrupt my card game
all day?"

Miamor contained her smile because she
knew that by accepting the money he was accepting her terms. Had Carter walked into the joint
they would have never done business with him.
Italians hated black men, but they loved black
women and Salerno could get used to the pretty
young thing with attitude that had waltzed into
his butcher shop. He had a hard on for Miamor.
Her skin tone, the contours of her hips, her
breasts, even her pretty face . . . he lusted after it
all. There was no way he was turning her down,

at least not until after he had sampled what was between her legs.

"Have a good day," she said as she turned around.

"Bono, pull up a chair. Deal him in," Salerno stated. "Oh yeah and toots . . ." he said to Miamor just as she reached the door. She rolled her eyes. Apparently it was the nickname that all Italian men had reserved just for her. "Make that ten percent and if you ever cross me I'll cut your pretty fucking tongue out of your mouth and lick my balls with it, eh?"

Miamor smirked before turning on her heels and walking out, completely satisfied. She was one step closer to fulfilling Carter's dream. By the time he came home, his casino would be up and running.

"This is all you get in Las Vegas for $100,000,000," Leena asked skeptically as she turned up her nose at the old, musty, hotel and casino. The machines were old and outdated; the furniture rickety and rusty. Breeze, Leena, and Miamor looked around slightly taken aback.

"It was scheduled for demolition," Lisa Matthews said as she held out her hands. "You didn't pay for the building. It was the location that cost you. You are right on the South end of the strip.

Your location alone is worth at least three times more than what you paid. A little TLC will have this place up and running." The real estate agent tried to sound optimistic but even she wasn't buying the load of crap that was falling out of her mouth. "All the three of you have to do is sign right here on the dotted line and this property will be yours."

Miamor breathed deeply as a heavy feeling sank into her chest. This was the moment that they all had been waiting on, but she couldn't help but feel overwhelmed. She had never had to make moves on behalf of anyone but herself. She wished Carter was free. Letters and phone calls weren't enough to fill the void that he had left in her life. She had been making plans, executing plays, and moving on his behalf. There was no way to let him know about every thing that went down before she did it, so she was playing so much by ear in hopes that she was acting in accord to what he wanted. Was this the property that he would want? Would he be displeased that she had to cut a deal with the Italians in order to make it happen? Miamor was so unsure about so many things, but it was too late to back out now. She took the pen from Lisa's hand and reluctantly provided her signature. Leena signed next and then Breeze.

"Congratulations," Lisa said as she tucked the paperwork securely in her briefcase. "You are now the proud owner of . . ." The woman paused and said. "What are you going to name it?"

"The Davinci," Miamor replied.

"Has a nice ring to it," Breeze stated. "How did you come up with that?"

"Because I'm going to make this a work of art," Miamor answered surely. Leena pulled a bottle of Champagne out of her oversized bag and popped the top. The girls squealed in excitement as the bubbles overflowed.

"We don't have glasses," Breeze said.

"Than hit it like a thug B, stop being so prissy," Leena teased. Breeze laughed as she tilted her head back as Leena poured champagne in her mouth. The girls laughed as they each drank a bit in honor of their first official day as owners of The Davinci Resort and Casino.

Chapter 19

Three Years Later

Carter emerged from the prison and looked up at the sky. It was the first time that he had seen the sun without wires and barbs interrupting the picture. His appearance was different. He had grown a full beard and his body was chiseled to perfection from the time he had dedicated to his body. His face held a scar from a fight that had broken out on the yard, but still his swag was the same. His walk was still powerful, his stare still deadly, and his mind sharper than ever. The past five years had changed him and for the better. He looked back at the prison as he thought, *I'll never let a man put me back in a box. Ever.*

As he strolled over to the black Maybach that awaited curbside he frowned as he removed the prison issued shirt, revealing a white wife beater underneath. He was relieved to see Brock, his old driver. It wasn't the first face he wanted to see, but seeing as how he had been released 6 months early and wanted to surprise Miamor he would have to be patient.

"Good to see you Boss," Brock stated.

Carter slapped hands with the seven-foot killer and pulled him in for an embrace before stepping into the car. He smiled when he saw the Cubans waiting for him in the seat. He quickly clipped the ends and sparked a match as he puffed the cigar to life.

As the smoke danced in his mouth he savored the feeling of freedom as he melted into the leather seats. "I thought that would be your speed boss."

"My nigga you thought right," Carter said.

"Where to?"

Carter tossed the prison shirt out of the window as the car pulled away from the curb. "Take me to the nearest Neiman's my nigga. It's been four and a half years since I've seen my bitch. I want to walk back into her life and be the same as she remembered," Carter said.

Time seemed to stand still when he saw her. Five long years had passed and he sat back admiring her as she walked through the beautiful casino, smiling graciously at the players. The dealers seemed to fawn after her. He could see the admiration in their eyes as she blessed each of them with a bit of her presence, even if only for a second. The casino and resort was flawlessly designed. He saw Miamor's personality throughout the entire establishment. She had chosen every detail from top to bottom and its modern vibe was impressive. She had gutted the place completely and if the crowd was any indication than business was booming. He couldn't be more proud. Miamor moved around the casino like a fish swimming through water. This was where she belonged. She was in her element and he found her incredibly sexy. The way she commanded respect. The way her beauty stood out amongst the sea of people. She was radiant and in that moment he didn't think it was possible to love anyone more than he loved her. His eyes scanned the room and he immediately peeped Fly Boogie, sitting back hawking Miamor's every move. She was protected and he made a mental note to hit Fly Boogie off with some bread for being so on point. He didn't want to interrupt. Instead he turned around and walked back out of the door. Miamor was busy right now . . . busy holding him down . . . busy being the boss and he wouldn't interrupt that. He would re-enter her life when the time was right.

***

Miamor felt the hairs on the back of her neck stand and she turned around, scanning the room to see why she was suddenly paranoid. She felt eyes on her. It was the murder mama in her. She always knew when something in the universe was off. She felt like she was being preyed on. She tensed and as soon as her smile turned into a frown Fly Boogie was out of his chair and across the room at her side.

"You good?" he asked.

"Yeah, yeah," she said as she shook her head. "It just feels like someone is watching me."

"The entire room is watching you ma, you're the star of the show," he said.

"This feels different. I just need to go upstairs for awhile and regroup. I'd feel much more comfortable if I wasn't naked down here," Miamor said.

"You don't need your strap ma. You're protected within these walls. Anybody breathe on you too hard, I'm plugging em'," Fly Boogie stated. "Relax. Nobody's here to hurt you. The people come here to see you, because you make them feel like you know each one of them. You're like a drug ma. They can't get enough and as long as they see your face them wallets stay open. Do you. I got it."

Miamor nodded and continued to seduce the room, but she still couldn't shake the eerie feeling that had suddenly killed her vibe.

She saw Leena coming through the casino. Impeccably dressed and cuffing legal documents in her hands. "Hey, where are you headed?" Miamor greeted her. They kissed once on each cheek.

"I'm headed to financial to drop off these insurance papers and then I'm conducting interviews for a housekeeping manager," Leena said.

"Where is Breeze?" Miamor asked as Leena began to walk away, obviously in a hurry.

Leena shrugged. "If I see her, I'll tell her you're looking for her."

"And the kids?" Miamor asked, yelling after her.

"They're with Aries."

Miamor nodded and tried to go about her day but something was nagging her. She had no idea that Carter was free but she would soon find out.

As soon as Miamor stepped into her suite the overwhelming aroma of fresh flowers invaded her senses. Her mouth dropped in an O of surprise as she looked around. She was baffled. This was a romantic gesture and although she was aware that Fly Boogie was fond of her, he knew his place. *He would never cross that line. Would he?* she thought, confused. She picked up her phone to call him. If he was responsible for this she had to correct this problem. She didn't like how good the gesture felt. It was time to create some space. *I've got to put some distance between me and his charming little ass,* she thought with a smirk as she shook her head. Perhaps being her personal goon was becoming a bit too personal. She was flattered but she was also taken. She would give nothing but heartbreak for the young kid. She hit the dial button and placed the phone to her ear as she made her way further into the suite.

"Hello," he answered.

"Fly, we need to . . ." she halted her step and stopped mid-sentence when she looked out on the balcony. A shadowy figure stood, overlooking the strip. Alarm shot through her. If Fly Boogie was on her line . . . *who the hell is that?* She thought.

"Hello?" he asked again.

"There's someone in my suite," she whispered. She hung up the phone and tip toed to the couch where she kept a gun tucked under the cushions. She removed the small .22 and let the gun lead her to the balcony. It was dark. The only light that illuminated the space was the glitzy lights from the streets below.

"The only reason I'm talking first instead of plugging you with holes is because my suite is full of flowers. Who the fuck are you?" she asked.

"Ask questions last next time ma, never give a nigga a chance to catch you slipping."

The gun fell from Miamor's grasp as she cupped her mouth in complete shock. "Carter?" she whispered. He turned toward her, his hands tucked in his Gabbana slacks. "Oh my God," she whispered as tears filled her eyes. Suddenly Fly Boogie's boyish charm was the furthest thing from her mind. Carter Jones was a man . . . her man . . . and he was 100 percent all man. The way he hung the Italian cut suit made her heart swoon as she ran into his arms, their lips meeting while his hands roamed all over her body.

"I missed the shit out of you Miamor," he said, practically growling into her ear. She could hear his need and feel it too as he pulled her behind into him.

His kisses stopped her from speaking and his fingers ripped her panties to shreds as he lifted her leg, leaning her against the balcony door. When he filled her she gasped. It had been so long since she had felt him inside of her and she fit him like a glove. He grinded and she bucked hungrily, his face buried in her neck as lust took over them. His dick hadn't been wet in five years and it was too long for him to do any real damage. When he came, he didn't pull out. He spilled his seed inside of her. He would give her ten babies if it meant their souls could unite. Panting, he placed her on her feet and rested his forehead against Miamor's. Her hands touched his face, to make sure that this was real. She had dreamt of their reunion so many times that it felt like she was in a daze. "If you ever leave me again, I'll kill you," she cried, her tears burning her eyes as they slid down her cheeks. "Five years was too long. It felt like a lifetime." She wept. Finally, she was able to free the turmoil that she had concealed since the day he had been taken away. There was no better feeling than his embrace as he wrapped her in his arms.

"Shhh, I'm back Mia. I'm home and I'm never leaving again. The only thing that will ever take me away from you is death," he promised.

KNOCK! KNOCK! KNOCK!

"Who the fuck is that?" Carter asked as he adjusted his clothes. She pulled her skirt down and followed him inside as she wiped her eyes.

"It's probably Fly," she said. "I called him when I saw you standing on the balcony."

"My *murder mama* called Fly Boogie?" he asked. "He your body guard or something?" Carter asked.

"He's not the same kid he was five years ago," Miamor said. "He's put in a lot of work for me over the years. I trust him."

"Yo Miamor!" Fly Boogie's voice came through the door.

Carter pulled it open and Fly Boogie's eyes widened. He was caught off guard at Carter's presence. "Oh shit, my bad fam," he said. "I thought there was a problem up here. I didn't know you were home. When you touch down? Welcome back."

"Just now," Carter replied.

"You good?" Fly Boogie asked Miamor directly. She nodded, giving him a half smile. She could see that his feelings were slightly hurt by Carter's presence. They had spent a lot of time together over the years. Now that Carter was home that would surely cease. She was recognizing the signs of a crush from Fly Boogie, she hoped that Carter wasn't getting the same vibe.

"She's good," Carter confirmed, answering for her. "We can chop it up tomorrow li'l homie. I hear you've helped hold shit together in my absence. I'll get with you. Have a good night."

Carter closed the door dismissively and turned back to Miamor. "Where's my son?" he asked anxiously.

"He's at home with Magdalena and Aries," Miamor said.

"This ain't home?" Carter asked looking around.

"No, this is just a suite that I keep here at the casino. I'm usually here all day. I like to rest or switch clothes without having to leave the property," she revealed. She grabbed his hand and pulled him into her. "The home that we've built here is amazing Carter. It took so much work and so much time but we did it. I did it . . . for you. I'll show you everything tomorrow. We might as well spend the night here. C.J. is already asleep and you and I have a lot of catching up to do," she whispered seductively. She planted a kiss on his full lips and then dropped to her knees. Carter's head fell back in bliss as she went to work. She was determined to show her man just how much she had missed him. Tonight would be all about his pleasure.

Chapter 20

*"Sparkly diamonds and foreign cars
are some of the pros."*

—Leena

"I'm so proud of you Carter. Tonight belongs to you," Miamor said as she stood in the doorway, watching as the resort tailor hemmed Carter's pants to his Gucci suit. He looked exactly the same. The five years away had done nothing to age him. The only change she could see was the scar that ran along the side of his face. Even still he was the most handsome man she had ever seen. If anything, the scar added character. The years apart had almost made her forget how much his presence filled the room. Carter Jones didn't even have to speak. His aura was simply boss and Miamor felt a silky wetness building between her legs just from looking at him. Carter shook the Asian man off. "Thank you Xuan,"

Carter said, calling the man by name. He was making it a point to learn each one of his employees and considering that Xuan did excellent work, he used him every day. He adjusted his steel grey jacket and twisted his cufflinks as he stared at his reflection. Retrieving his money clip from his inside breast pocket, he removed a hundred dollar bill and handed it to the elderly man.

"Thank you, Mr. Jones."

Carter nodded and Xuan left the room. Miamor came up behind him, wrapping her arms around his shoulders as they stared at the perfect image of their reflection in the full-length mirror.

"I couldn't have come this far without you ma," he said.

"Neither could I," she replied. "Just because you missed the past few years doesn't mean that anyone has forgotten the work that you've put in. You are the king, Carter. It's time that Vegas witnessed your crowning."

"What's the status on Zyir and Monroe?" Carter asked.

"Everything's fine. They will be here. Tonight the Cartel will be whole again. There are no missing pieces. It will go perfectly . . . trust me," she said. She kissed the back of his neck and then walked out of the room, leaving him to his thoughts. She had an entire glam squad waiting for her at home.

Breeze could barely breathe as she waited for Zyir's plane to land on the private clear port. Loneliness didn't quite describe the despair that had fallen over her while he had been locked away. She had fallen into a state of depression . . . one that she had hidden well but depression all the same. She didn't have a child to look after or to substitute for the love that Zyir gave her daily. So without him, it was just her and it had been a struggle to get through every single day. Letters and phone calls did nothing for her soul. Over the past few years her heart had deflated but as she saw the lights from the incoming plane she knew that all of her pain was about to be erased.

She had driven herself. She didn't want anyone to witness their first moments together. It was intimate . . . private . . . and she wanted Zyir all to herself. She got out of the car . . . too anxious to wait inside the captivity of her BMW X5. *Why am I nervous?* She thought. Butterflies danced in her stomach. As the plane gently touched its wheels to the ground it brought a forceful wind with it. Her expensive dress and flawlessly silked hair blew all over the place, but she didn't care. She held her breath as the plane's door slowly opened and a staircase was attached to its side.

He emerged, suave like a model out of GQ magazine. He was already dressed to escort her to the grand opening. A man in a suit had never looked so good. He stood at the top of the steps, mesmerized at her beauty. It had been so long since he had laid eyes on her that the image had become fuzzy in his head. He had forgotten how truly radiant she was. His memories had done her no justice and when he saw her kick off her red bottom heels and start running to him full speed, he smiled. He walked down the steps and she jumped into his arms, practically tackling him to the ground. His usually prissy princess didn't seem to mind that her custom Alexander McQueen gown was covered in dirt from the un-paved landing strip. She cried a river as he fisted her hair, while kissing her passionately.

"Welcome home Zyir," she whispered. "Never ever do that me to me again."

"I won't B. That is my word," he replied. He stood to his feet, attempting to dust off his clothing. "I take it we're not going to the grand opening?" He reached down to help her up and then scooped her into his arms as if she were a new bride.

"The last place I want to be is around a bunch of people. I want to go home and I want you to put a baby in me tonight," she whispered. "I want a piece of you that I get to keep forever. It's time to plant seeds Zyir. It's time to grow our own family. I'm not comfortable in Las Vegas. The Cartel doesn't feel the same. Aries is here and as long as she's around I don't want to be." Breeze had held her tongue about Aries because she knew that her presence was necessary. Zyir was the only one she could speak openly with and she had no problem admitting, "she is not and will never be on my team. She scares me."

"You telling me you want to leave?" Zyir asked. "Did she threaten you B?" It took quite a bit to get Zyir angry, but the thought of malicious intent against Breeze was all it took.

"It's not what she says," Breeze replied. "It's what she doesn't say. She has a vendetta against The Cartel. She tries to hide it, but I will never fully trust her and I don't feel safe. She's too close for comfort."

"Don't worry about that tonight. As a matter of fact I'm home. Don't worry about that ever again B," Zyir said as he placed a hand around her shoulder and pulled her in for a kiss. "Consider it handled."

***

"Daddy! Daddy!" Monroe II was a replica of his father and as the eight year old came rushing to him with the speed of a young athlete, Monroe felt emotion burning his eyes. It wasn't until this very moment did he realize how much time had gone by. *Damn, I've missed too much,* he thought sadly. When he had been locked up his son was a toddler . . . three years old to be exact. Now he was a big kid and Monroe was feeling conflicted about how he hadn't been around to raise him. He remembered the lessons that Big Carter had drilled into him. There had never been a day that his father had not been there. He couldn't re-member one time that he had wondered, *Where is papa?*

As his son wrapped his hands around his waist Monroe held him tightly as he stared at Leena from across the room. She didn't see him but he admired her as he spoke to his son. "I missed you man," Monroe stated. "You been taking care of your mama, being the man of the house?"

"Uh huh," Monroe answered.

"You held it down like a G, I'm proud of you son," he said. "I know I've missed a lot, but I won't miss another day. That's my word and if a man don't have his word he . . ."

"Don't have nothing," Monroe II finished. Monroe nodded. His son had a roughness about him that reminded him of his brother Mecca and it took everything in him not to drop a tear. There were cameras all around him. The media had covered his release as if it were a red carpet event, but his goons kept them at bay. He didn't want anyone to get too close as he reunited with his family. This was a personal moment. "Ma will be glad that you're back. She was sad while you were away," Monroe II said.

Monroe frowned and looked his son in the eyes. "Why do you say that son?"

"She would cry every night when she thought I wasn't listening. After she put me to bed, she would go in her room. She said your name in her prayers all the time," his son informed.

Monroe pulled his son in for a hug and then straightened out the collar to his oxford shirt, making sure his son was put together well. "You will never hear your mother cry another tear over me."

"Your word?" Monroe II asked.

"My word son," Monroe responded.

He stood and watched as Leena talked to a group of people. The casino was impressive and he sat back admiring what their women had built as pride filled his chest. Leena had held up nicely under pressure. Ironically, the weakest link of them all had turned out to be a diamond after all. The grand opening was a success as the massive crowd slightly obstructed his view, but he maneuvered until he had come up on her from behind.

Leena smelled his signature perfume before she saw his face and she interrupted her conversation with the mayor to turn around to search for him. She was breathless when she spun and found him staring her directly in the eyes.

He caressed her face with both hands, cupping her cheeks as he gave her a single kiss on the forehead. "Hey you," he greeted as if no time had passed.

"Hey you," she responded.

He pulled her onto the dance floor.

She giggled slightly, feeling as if this were a dream. "Gangsters don't dance," she said.

"Yeah well this gangster has some making up to do, so dancing, holding hands, midnight strolls through the park, I'ma be doing all that sucker shit until I've made up for my absence," he said with a charming smile. Happiness melted all over her face. "You like that cornball shit huh?" he laughed.

She shook her head, "No, but I love that you know that you have some ass kissing to do. The new G-series Benz truck will do just fine," she replied.

"Oh really?" he asked, finding her incredibly sexy. She had changed . . . grown . . . come into her own during his time away. He loved this new version of her.

"Absolutely. A prison bid is one of the cons of being married to a kingpin. Sparkly diamonds and foreign cars are some of the pros," she replied. She planted a seductive kiss on his lips and whispered in his ear. The cameras from the paparazzi flashed all around them but the couple was in their own little world. "I missed you Monroe Diamond. Welcome home daddy." She pulled his hand and led him off of the dance floor. "Now let me show you around your new casino."

Chapter 21

"I get everything I want."

—Yasmine

Miamor smiled as she danced with her baby boy, holding his hand as she bent down to kiss him on the cheeks. He was clad in a Ralph Lauren suit and as she turned her head to see Carter watching them closely, she realized that life could not get any better. She held out her hand for him to join them and Carter shook his head to decline but gave her a wink instead.

Carter had never imagined that the fruit to their street labor would be so abundant, but Vegas seemed to be the reward. For all the loss . . . the blood shed . . . the misery that The Cartel had endured, they had finally reached the ultimate goal. Legitimacy. As the live band switched tunes he checked the presidential on his wrist. It was almost nine o'clock. It was time to send the children home with Magdalena so that a night of true celebration could begin. He motioned for Miamor to come off the dance floor. She was now grooving with CJ and her nephews Tre and Monroe Jr. She left the boys to entertain themselves as she went to her husband's side.

"Have Magdalena take the kids back to the condo," he said.

"Cool, you want me to send Aries?" Miamor asked.

"No, she needs to be here. She helped build this. The men, their families . . . the entire Cartel gets to enjoy this night," Carter said. Miamor kissed his cheek, recognizing his nostalgia before walking away to dismiss the kids.

He watched Miamor hustle out of the room but tensed when the feeling of soft hands covered his eyes.

"Guess who Mr. Jones?"

He turned, stepping back to create some distance. "Yasmine? What are you doing here?" he asked. He was cool under pressure as he rubbed his freshly lined goatee.

"You think my father would invest in a casino without protecting his investment. I'm his eyes and ears," she replied. "After hearing that you were out, I couldn't help but make the trip. We have unfinished business Mr. Jones."

Carter smirked at her persistence. Even after five years Yasmine didn't give up. She was a lioness on the prowl and she was looking for a king. She was prettier, more mature, and more glamorous. In another lifetime perhaps she would be his lady, but in this one the competition for his heart had already been won.

"What business is that?" he asked.

She stepped close, standing next to him as she leaned into his ear. Carter kept his eye on the crowd, not even looking down at her as she whispered, "No one has fucked me quite right since you and I know that little ghetto girl of yours can't suck your dick like I can. She's trash."

"Watch your mouth," Carter warned, still keeping his eyes straightforward.

She cut her eyes at him. "You know you don't love her Carter. If you did, you would have never slept with me. Silly man," she said with a mischievous grin. "If you think I came here to be turned away you're mistaken. We both know the connection we shared while you were in Saudi Arabia. If you like, I can refresh your memory."

She caressed Carter's hand but he quickly gripped her wrist tightly and pulled her across the room until he found a corner of slot machines that was practically empty. He cornered her against the wall. "Look ma, this is my life.

Shit was good in Saudi, I'm not gone play you like it wasn't but it isn't laying like that between us over here. I have a wife now . . . a family."

Yasmine reached down and massaged his print, feeling his thickness through the fabric of his pants. He shook her hard, slamming her back against one of the machines. "What the hell is wrong with you ma? I said it's not happening." He thumbed the center of her forehead. "Get that shit through your head."

She reached out to him, grabbing at his lapel but he dusted her off of him as if he were removing a piece of irritating lint. He was trying to save her. The way she was acting she would blow up her own spot and get herself whacked. *My bitch ain't bout them games,* he thought, shaking his head as he walked away briskly.

He didn't realize that his face was scrunched until he found Miamor. "What's wrong?"

He straightened his brow and took a deep breath as he replied, "Nothing ma. Everything's good."

"Good because it's time for the ribbon cutting ceremony and for you to make your speech," she said.

Monroe made his way to Carter's side and they hugged jovially. "We made it bro," Monroe said.

"We'll always make it," Carter replied. He looked around. He had his left hand, now he was only missing his right. Zyir was his hitter and it wouldn't be right to bust this cherry without him. The casino symbolized their rise into greatness. He had helped to achieve it. It was important that he be a part of this moment. "Where is Zyir?"

"Breeze isn't going to let that nigga come up for air anytime soon," Monroe replied. "We can get started without him."

Miamor walked up on the small stage where the live band was playing and signaled for them to stop playing as she took the microphone.

"Good evening everyone. First I would like to thank you all for coming to the official grand opening of The Davinci Resort and Casino. I would like to introduce you to the owners of The Davinci, my husband Carter Jones, and my brothers Monroe Diamond and Zyir Rich. Let's give them a round of applause ladies and gentlemen."

Miamor walked off stage as Carter and Monroe stole the spotlight. As she stepped off she was yanked into an empty broom closet. She protested, but her hands were held tightly at the wrists as a hand quickly covered her mouth to silence her scream.

"Chill Miamor, it's just me," Fly Boogie stated.

Miamor snatched away from him violently. "What the fuck is up with you?"

"I had to talk to you ma," Fly Boogie said. "You haven't fucked with me since Carter been home. It's been days Miamor. I've called you like a hunnid times ma."

Miamor shook her head. It was now confirmed that she had him lovesick. He was handsome, paid, hungry, and she had trained him to be a killer but he wasn't for her. He didn't have enough teeth in the game to even look her way. Her resume trumped his. Even if she wasn't in love with Carter she didn't have time to grow Fly Boogie up. They weren't in the same league. "Fly, my man is home. My husband," she said.

"I know and I respect big homie, but I'd be lying like shit if I told you that I haven't been thinking about you. I'm feeling you ma. I know it ain't supposed to happen like that but its true. Seeing you on this nigga arm is making me sick," Fly Boogie stated as he cornered her. He reached down and seconds before his lips touched hers she turned her face, causing him to kiss her cheek.

"Stop, just stop Fly," she protested. "Carter will murder you in this bitch. If you've never believed anything before please believe that. Just do your job Fly. Remain loyal. I'm not the girl for you and these are not the kind of problems you want."

"Look at this shit ma," he said, pulling up his sleeve to reveal a tattoo of her name on his wrist. "I'm riding with you Miamor. Everything I do is for you. I'm stacking my paper for you."

"Have you lost your mind? What if Carter sees that? What does that mean " she asked. "Fly, get a hold of yourself before you put yourself in a position you can't get out of."

"You didn't feel nothing. When Carter was away and it was just me and you? Tell me I'm imagining it," Fly Boogie challenged, wearing his heart on his sleeve. Over the years Fly Boogie had fallen for Miamor. She was the only type of woman he could see himself with. Carter coming home had thrown him off. He couldn't stand the sight of them together. It pained him greatly despite the fact that he knew what it was.

She looked into his handsome face and thought, *If Carter was any other nigga I would give you what you asking for little boy. But he holds the key to my heart.*

Miamor didn't respond, she simply walked out of the closet while shaking her head in disgrace. She wasn't a liar and she didn't want to insult Fly Boogie's intelligence. They had connected. She even enjoyed his company. Many nights they had stayed up until the sun came out, talking about the game . . . about life . . . his presence had made things a little less hard. She couldn't tell him that she hadn't felt anything, but she wouldn't confirm that she had either. Even thinking it made her feel like she was betraying Carter. With her thoughts running rampant in her head, she bumped straight into Yasmine.

"I love your dress. What is it? Yves Saint Laurent?" Yasmine asked, playing nice. "I had one just like it *last* season."

"I know one thing you didn't have last season," Miamor shot back. She wasn't even going to pretend to like this girl. She had no time for games. Not when Fly Boogie had her flustered and bothered.

Yasmine pursed her lips as she waited for the punch line. Miamor pointed her manicured finger up at the stage where Carter charmed the crowd. "That's all mine," she said. Yasmine rolled her eyes as Miamor joined her husband on stage. By the end of the speech and the ribbon cutting ceremony, Carter had made all of the attendees fall in love with him.

"What is Yasmine Baraka doing here?" Miamor asked, leaning into him so that no one could overhear her disdain.

"Her father sent her. She's here to stay so play nice ma . . . for me," Carter stated.

"I don't play at all. The sooner she learns that the better. I have no problem shipping her ass back to the middle-east in a box," she spat. Carter was already feeling the heat from the mistake he had made years ago. He only hoped that it didn't come back to haunt him. He had to make sure that Yasmine could keep a secret, because if his infidelity ever got out he could lose it all.

"Why exactly were the Italians brought in on the deal?" Carter asked. It was the first words out of his mouth as Miamor walked into their condo. She was carrying a sleeping CJ in her arms. It was the first day that she hadn't had to rely on Magdalena to play 'mommy'. She had spent the entire day with her four year old and she was exhausted. In so many ways being a regular wife and mother was more taxing than running an entire staff at the resort and casino. The last thing she wanted to do was come home and go over every single move she had made while Carter had been away.

"That's the first thing you say to me? I haven't seen you all day!" she said as she pouted playfully. She carried CJ into his room and laid him across his bed before rejoining Carter at the dining room table. He had requested that every contract that had been acquired during his absence be copied and sent to him. It was all laid out in front of him as he tried to wrap his brain around the entire operation. He couldn't be a boss without knowledge. He didn't want to have to go to Miamor every time someone asked him a question. He was playing catch up and it was overwhelming.

"Okay Mr. Jones . . . the Italians?" Miamor said rhetorically. "Well Jim Salerno runs this town. He's old school. Mafia. I could not get the gambling commission to approve my license application unless I cut a deal with him. He has a ten percent stake in The Davinci. I'll make the introduction if you like?"

Carter nodded and pulled her into his lap as he kissed her shoulder. "I'll set it up for the morning."

Carter and Miamor stayed up half the night as she filled him in on business. She was thorough and ran through it all, leaving no detail up in the air.

While she had him talking Miamor's thoughts drifted. She didn't like how Yasmine suddenly had a vested interest in The Davinci. *Where the hell was she when I was building it from the ground up?* "Can I ask you something?" she asked.

"Anything ma," he replied, distracted. Miamor used her forefinger to turn his chin toward her.

"I need you to·be honest with me Carter," she replied. "And I need to see your eyes when I ask you this."

Her tone worried him and he gave her his attention. "You ain't got to tip toe around anything Miamor. I'll tell you whatever you want to know," he said seriously.

"Have you ever fucked with Yasmine?" she asked.

The question caused his heart to stop but his face remained the same. He wasn't one to lie but he couldn't admit to that. To dig up skeletons from years ago would only bring trouble. He didn't want to upset Miamor or give her insecurity about Yasmine. He had told himself that it would never happen again and he had meant it. "No, I wouldn't have her here, around you everyday, if I had. I wouldn't disrespect you Miamor," he said. As he spoke he felt like scum because that's exactly what he was doing. Yasmine had an inside joke on Miamor and he knew how catty women could be. *I got to take care of that,* he thought. "You don't have to worry about that okay?"

Miamor wanted to believe him but her intuition was telling her otherwise. He had never lied to her before. It was she who had been the deceiver in their relationship. Even if she didn't want to she had to extend the benefit of the doubt. "Okay," she replied.

Carter saw the doubt in her eyes. The fact that she couldn't hide it told him that life was about to get real messy for him. Straightening out things with Yasmine would have to be the first thing on his agenda. *Fuck the Italians,* Carter thought as he shook his head. *They're the least of my worries. I've got to get this shit together before it blows up in my face.*

Carter, Zyir, and Monroe sat in the aficionado bar, sipping cognac and puffing the finest cigars as they absorbed all that had occurred.

"It took a lot to get here bro, but we made it my niggas," Monroe said as he raised his glass in the air.

"Indeed," Zyir agreed as they all touched glasses.

"There are a few things that can be fine tuned but over all the girls held it down. If it weren't for them . . ."

Monroe didn't even get to finish his statement before Carter interrupted. "We would have been stuck in Saudi Arabia."

"Saudia Arabia wasn't so bad though my nigga. The bitches over there . . ." Monroe replied, shaking his head.

"Speaking of," Carter said as he leaned forward and rested his elbows against his knees. He lowered his voice. "I need the two of you to run interference on Yasmine. Keep her away from Miamor. I don't know why she is here but the heat is hot at home. She thinks Miamor is some regular chick, but my li'l mama don't do the catty shit. She will set that trap and have Yasmine plugged. That would be bad business for everybody."

"I told you that one was bad news," Zyir said. "The smartest thing to do would be to send her ass back to Saudi Arabia."

"Baracka wants her here and we kind of need her. She has experience running a casino. If she can keep her head on straight it would be a good look," Carter said.

As if they had spoken her up Yasmine came waltzing into the bar. Her presence was like a magnet and the men in the building immediately turned their attention her way. She was a beautiful woman. That much couldn't be denied.

"Here you are," she said with a smile as she stood. "Hello gentlemen," she added, nodding at Zyir and Monroe. "Do you mind if I borrow him?"

Monroe nodded as he grinned, knowing the delicate position that his older brother was in. Carter gave him a stern look and then followed her up to her office.

He was glad that Miamor had played the back that day. Since his return he knew that she was trying to let him find his footing in the casino. Today her absence gave him the perfect opportunity to iron things out with Yasmine. As soon as they were inside the privacy of her office Yasmine was all over him.

"I missed you Carter and ever since I saw this desk, I've imagined you fucking me on top of it," she whispered.

Her seductive ways enticed him. He hated that she was so damn sexy. A lesser man would have taken her up on her offer, but he wasn't a dog. He wasn't in the business of lying. Cheating took too much effort. He grabbed her wrists as she tried to undo the buttons of his shirt while rubbing her body against his.

"Yasmine. Stop," he said sternly in a low no nonsense tone.

"Hmm," she moaned as if she couldn't help herself. "You know I'm never going to stop."

"I'm married ma. It was different when we were in Saudi Arabia. Things have changed," he said. "We can't do this."

"Oh we can," Yasmine stated. "And we will . . . as often as I want. Because if you don't, I'll ruin your marriage. You wouldn't want that little black bitch to find out about us now would you?"

Carter placed his hands in his pockets to stop himself from laying hands on Yasmine. His jaw tightened instinctively. He didn't take kindly to threats and she was testing him. Just for getting flip at the lip he wanted to wring her pretty little neck. She was too comfortable, too close, and he wasn't feeling the thin line she was dancing on. "Perhaps I'm not making myself clear," he stated his voice dangerously low. "I eliminate anything and anyone who poses a threat to my family. There is no way I'm leaving my wife or allowing you to embarrass her. So do your job, lets make this money together, and forget about the past."

Yasmine chuckled. Carter's threats only made her want him more. It was his gangster that she loved the most. "Forget about the past? You wish you could Carter. How many times did you think of me at night while you were locked up? The way I wrapped my lips around your dick? Or the way my body molded to it as I rode you? You probably see my face when you're fucking that average wife of yours."

"We're done," Carter insisted.

"We'll see about that now won't we?" she said as she licked her lips. "Because I'm just getting started." She reached down to stroke his manhood and it jumped. She was like a snake charmer, commanding it at her will. He gripped her hand but she was insistent as she massaged his rising manhood harder as she undid his slacks. He didn't even feel her slide his cell out of his pocket, he was too focused on the arousal she provided. "Maybe I'll just get rid of your bitch of a wife altogether and then I'll have you to myself." Everything in him wanted to bend her over and punish her. She was right . . . he had fantasized many times before just off her memory, but it was only a physical attraction for him. The more she played this game, the more she put his family at risk, the more she held their tryst over his head, the more his mental despised her. Carter pushed her off forcefully, causing her to stumble as she crashed into her desk. He glared at her as he adjusted his clothes. "You're biting off more than you can chew. Stay the fuck away from my wife."

"With pleasure, as long as I don't have to stay away from you," she replied. She hopped on her desk and spread her legs as she moved her panties aside, massaging her swollen clit. "Join me?"

It was a temptation that not many men could resist, but Carter knew that dipping into Yasmine was like sinking into quick sand. An affair with her would drown him. He fumed as he slipped out of her office, shaking his head in dismay because he knew that Yasmine was a problem. She was playing hard body and it seemed that the only way to control her would be to comply. Otherwise her slick talk would get him caught up. A part of Carter wanted to just come clean to Miamor. The secret keeping and covering his tracks was boggling his mind. He needed a clear head to take hold of the casino operations and to move the resort into a new direction. He couldn't focus on business when his personal life stood on rocky ground. If Miamor uncovered the truth on her own, her wrath would be severe. Yasmine thought she had control of this little game but what she didn't realize was that she was playing Russian roulette. There were only so many times she would be able to pull the trigger before Miamor popped off.

Miamor sighed in frustration as she was sent to voice-mail for the fourth time. "Where the hell is he?" she whispered as she slipped into her shoes. An impromptu meeting with the mayor of

Las Vegas had popped up and she needed Carter to be there. She was supposed to make the introduction. Right now all of the major players in the city were familiar with Miamor. They knew her as the owner . . . the face of the casino. Easing Carter into prominence was important. He couldn't officially be on the deed because of his prison history, but it was the unofficial business in a city like Las Vegas that made the world go round. She wanted to be the lady on his arm, but his presence was required in order to make that happen. She was beyond irritated.

"Relax, he will be here. I'm sure he's just busy. His phone is probably in his desk. When he gets to it, he'll be here," Breeze said. "In the meantime, Money and I will take C.J. for the night."

"Thanks Breeze," Miamor said. "You're a lifesaver. I already packed his bag." She walked into her son's room to find him sitting in the middle of the floor playing with his toys. She loved her son, more than life itself. She couldn't wait until things were settled. She just wanted to be a wife and a mom. She could hang her holster and her business hat up. She would be completely content with being Mrs. Jones forever and ever. "You ready to go with Auntie Breeze and Uncle Money?" she asked.

"Yeah!!!!" he shouted. He hopped up and ran to Breeze who was standing behind her.

"Can I get some love first?" Miamor said with a laugh. Her son ran back to her full speed and kissed her on the cheek repeatedly, inciting laughter. He knew exactly how to fill her with joy. He then rushed out of the door, following Breeze.

"Good luck tonight!" Breeze shouted as she eased out of the door.

Just as she made her exit the telephone rang. Miamor rushed to answer it. "Hello?"

"I'm downstairs, buzz me up ma," Fly Boogie said.

"What are you doing here?" she asked.

"You forget about the deposit? I was late going to the bank. Didn't want to keep that much paper on me," he said.

Miamor went to the door and buzzed him up.

He walked into the penthouse with a Gucci book bag slung over his shoulder. He held it out for her.

"I take it there is no need to count it?" she asked.

"I'm never short ma, you know that," he replied. "Where you going?"

"Carter and I are supposed to be meeting with the mayor but it looks like I'm being stood up. Carter has been unavailable all day. I can't get in touch with him. Did you run into him at the casino?" she asked.

"Nah, I ain't seen him," Fly replied. "The nigga slipping though. If he let you leave the house looking like that and you not on his arm, he's crazy."

Miamor laughed as she shook her head. "You need a girl Fly. I worry about you. You can't trap all day and night without someone to go home to," she said. She grabbed a bottle of wine and cracked it open as she poured two glasses.

"Before your boy got out you left me no room to get a girl. You took up all my time," he replied with a charming smile. "Had a nigga around twenty-four/seven. A bitch would have had a problem with that," he said.

"I needed you," she admitted. "I couldn't have held everything together while Carter was gone without you."

"I'ma always be here ma. No bird can get in the way of that," he said. "You're the priority. My loyalty is always with you," he said.

Miamor was speechless. She didn't know if Fly Boogie was loyal to her for business or in a more intimate sense. She knew that she should establish limits with him, but he was too good to her. He was good for her. She didn't mind having him around. Loyalty was hard to find. She handed him a glass.

"Have a drink with me while I wait?" she asked.

He took the glass and then downed the wine before handing it back to her. "I'ma get out of here. It's late," he replied. He stepped closely to her, dangerously close, making the temperature in the room increase. He smelled good, looked good, and his youth made him fear nothing, not even Carter. Miamor could feel his attraction. The more they interacted the more it grew. Fly had a thing for her. They both knew it, but they both were aware that it could never be. She would have to be very careful how she handled him. She didn't want to mismanage his young heart. Young boys were loyal but they were also reckless when wounded. He kissed her cheek. "Goodnight beautiful," he said. "If it were me, I'd never keep you waiting."

"I believe you," she replied. "But its not you Fly. Carter would kill you for even having the thought. He's out, things are getting back to normal. I need you to be okay with that . . . with my husband. You're loyal to The Cartel, not to me."

"Nah ma, just you," he answered.

He made his exit leaving Miamor's heart racing and she grabbed the entire bottle of wine, drinking straight from the bottle.

Where the hell is Carter? She thought, flustered and overwhelmed. While he had her wait-

ing he had no idea that there was somebody in
line just dying to snatch his lady.

"Mr. Jones, I have your messages," his secre-
tary said as he entered his office. His day had
been long and stressful. Thoughts of Yasmine
filled his head, distracting him, tormenting him
all day. He had never been one to tolerate blackmail, but she was Baraka's daughter. Baraka
owned half of The Davinci and on top of that his
power was unlimited. He couldn't handle Yasmine like he would any other chick, because she
was far from ordinary. He would have to handle
the situation with extreme delicacy. "Mrs. Jones
wants to meet for drinks. She's waiting for you in
your suite upstairs."

Carter nodded, deciding that he would handle the rest of his business later. He headed out.
The thought of seeing Miamor's face instantly
soothed his troubled soul. She was his safe haven, his peace, and his guilty conscience made
him feel like he could lose her at any moment.
He made his way upstairs, knowing exactly what
she had in store. He inserted his key card into
the lock and pushed the door open. He opened
it and walked inside, finding his favorite cognac
already prepared. A note accompanied it.

Have a drink and relax. Tonight is about us. Turn off your phone. I'll be up in five minutes.

After the day he had endured he could use a drink and he downed it in two large gulps before searching for the open bottle. He poured himself another, took it to the head and then finally slow sipped a third. Finally he felt the tension melt from his shoulders as he settled onto the couch. There was nothing like a good cognac to unwind but tonight he was feeling exceptionally loose. He licked his lips as he imagined the things he would do to Miamor. He wanted to taste her on his lips and the thought alone caused his manhood to brick. He lay his head against the couch as he adjusted his hard-on in his pants. The distress of his day had worn him out. He was more tired than he had realized. He hated that Yasmine had something over him. The pressure to live according to her terms was too much. *I'm not playing the blackmail game. I'm going to come clean to Miamor. If she has to hear it, it should come from me,* Carter thought. He heard the click of the lock and then the lights went out as the sound of stiletto heels click clacked against the tiled floor.

"I love that you set all of this up for me ma, but I need to talk to you about something important," he said.

"Shhh," was the only reply he got. The room was so dark that all he saw was the silhouette of her trench coat and when she lowered onto her knees and fumbled with his belt he knew what was next. He closed his eyes as she licked his length. He was throbbing and she could feel him pulsating in her mouth as she took him in. No gagging, no shallow throat, she was a pro as she worked his shaft with her hand while sucking the life out of him. It wasn't until she said, "I told you Carter. I get everything that I want."

When he heard her voice he jumped up, pushing her off of him. "What the fuck?" he exclaimed as he tripped all over himself while backpedaling away from Yasmine. He was stumbling all over the place. Suddenly he had turned into a clumsy oaf. He couldn't seem to gather his bearings as she advanced on him.

"Don't fight it Carter, just take me. Take me any way, every way, you want to," Yasmine said as she pushed him toward the bedroom. Either he was light as a feather or she had suddenly become he-man because he couldn't evade her as she aggressively pushed him onto the bed. His mind was screaming no, but his dick was clearly in the game as it stood to attention as she lowered her body onto his girth.

"You drugged me?" he asked in disbelief as he placed his hands on her hips. He didn't have the strength to lift her off of him. She hadn't meant for him to drink three glasses back to back. She had spiked the bottle with Ropyhnol, hoping to keep him submissive through the night. The amount he had drank had him completely sedated. He could feel everything, but even now remembering how he had gotten to this point with her was beginning to fade away. All he felt was the pleasure as she bounced on his dick.

"Damn," he whispered. The fact that he had fallen for her okie doke had him feeling like a sucker. She was in control, at least for the night and with him incapacitated there wasn't much that he could do. In his mind he knew that this would be the straw that broke the camel's back. In a situation where the truth sounded like lies, Miamor would never believe him. As he blacked out the last thing he heard was Yasmine whispering in his ear. "You should have just gone along with me Carter. You know you love it."

Chapter 22

"We all followed you out here. The Cartel of Miami belonged to Carter, but The Cartel of Las Vegas belongs to you."

—Fly Boogie

Miamor's heart instantly froze in her chest and then splintered like an icy windshield right down the middle. Blind rage. Unrivaled pain. Unending sickness. That's what she felt. The sex-capade in front of her was so intense that Carter didn't even realize that she had entered the room. Her first thought was to wreck havoc. She wanted to beat the breaks off of Yasmine. Throwing, swinging, biting, punching . . . it all would have felt so good at the moment but she couldn't. Her grief rendered her helpless. Suddenly the ring on her finger seemed so heavy. It weighed her down. She couldn't breathe, she couldn't think straight. She couldn't do anything but stand there . . . watching. She waited for him to come to his senses and push Yasmine off of him, but the look of pleasure on Carter's face confirmed that he had wanted this. He had betrayed her. After all that she had done to hold him down. After all that they had been through. All it took was a skinny, privileged bitch from Saudi Arabia to get him to switch up on her. She walked over to the bed, walking slowly as she clenched her stomach. The smell of another woman's sex filled her bedroom making her want to vomit. She took her wedding band off and when she was within eyesight she tossed it on Carter's bare chest. Before she could stop herself she grabbed Yasmine by her hair.

"Bitch!" Miamor shouted as she flung her to the floor, her rage giving her the strength of a madwoman.

"Oh shit!" Carter exclaimed as he stood to his feet. The room spun around him and he stumbled as he reached for Miamor. *What the fuck happened?* He thought. The paraphernalia that was strewn about the room told a story of a night of lust and he grimaced, cursing himself. He truly had a limited memory of what had gone down, but one thing was blatantly clear, he had fucked up. There was no stopping Miamor. She was locked on like a pit as she viciously delivered blows to Yasmine's face.

"I. . ."

PUNCH.

"TOLD . . ."

PUNCH.

"YOU . . ."

PUNCH.

"NOT . . ."

PUNCH. PUNCH. PUNCH.

"TO FUCK WITH ME."

Carter tried his hardest to get between the two women but his world was moving in slow motion. He could barely move. He was weak, legs wobbly, head unclear, stomach churning. He was incapacitated and could barely remember what had happened the night before. Images of what had occurred flashed in his mind. His body intertwined with Yasmine's, his fingers fisting her hair, her mouth kissing all over him. He saw it all. He had fucked up. No matter how unintentional his actions were, he had betrayed his woman. He could only imagine the sting that plagued her heart. "Mia chill!" he barked as he tried to pry Miamor off. He tried holding her back, but in his current state she shook him with ease. Miamor was relentless. "You're going to kill her!" Carter felt woozy and he didn't have all of his strength, which allowed Miamor to get the best of him. He was surprised she didn't turn on him with her blows. Miamor was going for broke.

What the fuck? He thought as he shook his head while pinching the bridge of his nose as he tried to steady himself. "Miamor!"

Hearing him scream her name with such aggression caused her to stop, fist raised in the air as she panted over Yasmine. The girl groaned beneath her, nose busted and crying. Yasmine covered her face as she rolled left to right in agony.

"You defending this bitch?" Miamor asked. She was so upset that she could barely catch her breath. It felt like she was hyperventilating as she leaned over, resting on her knees as complete agony took over her body. Carter saw the hurt in her face and it almost brought him to his knees.

Damn, I fucked up, he thought. His mind couldn't piece together the part of the night where Yasmine had drugged him. All he knew was that he had messed up and now the fall out was about to begin.

"Let me talk to you for a minute ma. Let me explain," he whispered. He went to touch her but she cringed as she slapped his hands away. He stumbled. *Get your shit together. Tell your wife something before you lose her,* Carter told himself. But what could he say? She had caught him . . . hand in the cookie jar. *How the fuck did*

I slip up this much? he wondered. *This shit is just sloppy. Hitting Yasmine in the suite that Miamor has complete access to.* There was no lying his way out of this and even if lies would get him off the hook, he wouldn't tell them. It wasn't in his character. He was tired of telling half-truths. He had done it. Why? He still couldn't make sense of it. How had he let himself take it this far when he had been so determined to keep her at arm's length? He had no recollection of the night's events and his head spun as he tried to piece it together. *Damn,* he thought, legs weak. Head clouded with confusion. He needed to sit.

"Mia," he said.

Yasmine rolled onto her knees then slowly climbed to her feet. "Fuck this Carter! Don't lie to her. We don't have to hide this anymore. Tell her! We've been together since you came to Saudi Arabia five years ago!" she shouted as she wiped the blood from her nose with the back of her hand.

"Yasmine chill!" Carter shouted.

"No! I'm not hiding it anymore! She should know!" Yasmine screamed, hysterically, filling the air with falsehoods and fanning Miamor's emotional flames.

Miamor shook her head in disbelief as tears fell down her cheeks. Her soul was heavy. It felt

like she was suffocating as shame fell over her.
She looked at him, wrapped in the bed sheet,
basking in the afterglow of his rendezvous with
another woman. *Damn why does this hurt so
bad?* She thought.

"Mia, I fucked up. Let me talk to you ma. Let
me . . ."

"Talk to her," Miamor said. It was like the sun
had fallen out of the sky and the world had come
to an end. "I'm done," she whispered. Carter
swiped his face with his hands. Her hurt was
hurting him. He wanted to say something to
make her stay, but even he was lost. How could
he defend what he didn't understand. He loved
her. He loved every single thing about her. How
had he fucked this up so badly?

Before he could respond she was gone and he
was across the room in a flash, knocking over the
lamp because he could barely keep his bearings.

"Carter I'm . . ."

Before Yasmine could even get the words out
of her mouth Carter wrapped his hand around
her throat, pressing her into the wall. It was like
his rage gave him strength as he held her thin
body in place. He wanted to choke the life out
of her, but he knew that this wasn't her fault. He
had done this. If he hadn't wanted to sleep with
her it never would have happened. No one had

forced him into this situation. Somewhere deep down he had allowed her to get into his head. His attraction, their flirtation, their deception was the gasoline that fed the fire. It had started years ago between them in Saudi. He should have stopped it then. He had made this bed, now he had to lay in it. He released her and then punched the wall beside her head. "Just get out," he whispered. He lowered his head in disgrace. He had been at a crossroads with Miamor before but never over another woman. He knew her well enough to realize that this was one transgression that she would never forget.

Miamor's tears blinded her to the point where she stumbled through the casino as she made her way to the front door. She was distraught and a snotty mess as people turned to look at her. She was a walking spectacle. No one had ever seen her so torn apart. Something had permanently broken inside of her as soon as she saw Carter inside of another woman. She had given him too much of herself, holding nothing back and trusting him to take care of her psyche. Now that he had dropped the ball she had nothing reserved for herself . . . no strength . . . no faith . . . no love. Carter had taken it all. *Selfish ass nigga!*

I hate him, I hate him. I will never forgive him for this, she thought.

Her heart was raw and she clenched her chest wishing that the pain would ease. It felt like someone was pouring alcohol over a bleeding wound.

"Miamor!"

She heard Breeze call her name. "Mia! Oh my God! What the hell happened? What's wrong?" she asked.

Miamor gasped as she tried to tell her but she couldn't even speak the words. She was weak and the trauma too great. She didn't even want to hear the words fall out of her mouth.

"Miamor!" When she heard Carter's voice she shook her head and broke away from Breeze. She rushed through the crowd and out of the door. Fly Boogie was the first person she saw. He was pulling up to the hotel and like always, he was right there whenever she needed him.

"What's wrong?" he asked in confusion as she rushed into his arms.

"I've got to get out of here," she said. "Get me away from him."

Fly Boogie nodded as he opened the passenger door for her and tucked her safely inside. Just as he got inside himself, Carter and Breeze emerged from the hotel.

"Miamor!" Carter roared. She didn't even look at him as Fly Boogie pulled away.

"Aries bring me my son!" Miamor screamed into the phone.

"I can't Mia," Aries replied. "Carter's here and he won't let me take him anywhere. He's afraid you're going to disappear on him again and take CJ with you. Are you okay?"

"Tell him I will murder him in his fucking sleep if he doesn't deliver my son to me!" Miamor's rage was real and all she wanted was to see her baby boy. She knew that his love would be like a dressing to a wound. He could stop the bleeding of her heart.

"Come home ma . . ."

Carter's voice filled the phone as he intervened on their conversation. She could hear his worry and regret in his tone. Miamor instantly hung up in his face. She knew that if she listened to him for too long she would become dumb to the truth. She wanted him to justify his actions and she would become one of those women who believed bullshit and accepted disrespect. No, she couldn't talk to him. Ever. Her legs gave out as she collapsed to the floor, sitting in her own misery with her head buried in her hands.

Fly Boogie swiped his face, unsure of what to do. She hadn't eaten or slept in two days. She just cried. She was the most official chick he had ever met and with the negligence of one man she was now broken. Carter had mishandled her. Fly Boogie walked over to her and scraped her off of the floor as he carried her across the hotel room. He had checked her into a room under his name because she knew that if she used her own, Carter would find her. Normally, Miamor would never let anyone see her so weak, but she couldn't help it. Life felt over. It would be less painful to put a bullet in her brain and call it a wrap. She was thankful for her son, because had it not been for his existence she was sure she would have done so by now. Murderous thoughts, suicidal thoughts . . . plagued her. She was a woman who had been hurt by a man. Fly Boogie laid her across the bed and turned to leave the room.

"Don't go," she whispered.

Fly Boogie nodded. "I'm right here. I'm not moving until you move ma. You can lay here and cry that shit out until your system is dry, but if you trust me and you take a ride with me . . . I think I know something that will make you feel better."

"I can't," she whispered as she lay, face stuck to the comforter while she squeezed her eyes shut.

"Well when you're ready, I'm here. Try to rest," he replied.

Miamor was grateful for his presence. Having him with her, so loyal, and accommodating didn't take the hurt away but it did help.

BANG!
BANG!
BANG! BANG!
BANG!

"I told you to trust me. Every time you're feeling a type of way you go to the range," Fly Boogie stated.

"How do you know that?" she asked, shocked.

"I've been with you for five years ma. A nigga notices you," he replied with a wink. She gave him a small smile as she re-aimed her gun.

BANG!
BANG!

His effort was sweet but not even the sound of Miamor's gun relieved her stress. This time her burden was too great. Shooting practice wasn't enough to make her forget her problems. She had a fetish for murder and right now she wanted to body something.

"You're like a surgeon with the burner ma," Fly Boogie stated as he leaned against his Range Rover, one foot propped up on the fender. There was no one around for miles. The only thing around them was mountains and desert air.

She flipped her hair out of her face and sighed. "This isn't helping," she replied. "I just feel like dying. How did this happen?" Her voice was a whisper. A rhetorical question that not even she could answer.

Fly Boogie was silent as she fisted both hands through her hair and closed her eyes as she fought back tears. Carter had blown up her phone all night, along with Breeze, Aries, and Leena. They all had been trying to reach her. Although she didn't want to be available for anyone, she knew that she couldn't hide forever. She had a child. It was only a matter of time before natural instincts would lure her home. She felt like she was losing her mind. Her mood was up and down. Her stomach was constantly queasy. She had to get her mind off of Carter. He was all that she could think about. She walked up to Fly Boogie and kissed him out of the blue, melting into him as she pushed him against the hood of his car. She had caught him off guard, but he didn't resist. He grabbed her ass roughly and then picked her up as she wrapped her legs around him. He was the perfect distraction. He was fly, young, and living the thug life. After doubting herself, wondering what she lacked, or what Yasmine had that she didn't, it felt good to have a man want only her. His kiss melted her as their tongues danced slowly, passionately. It surprised her when he pulled back. With her still in his arms he whispered, "Damn ma, I could love the shit out of you if you would just let me." He placed her back on her feet and brushed her hair out of her eyes. "You're only doing this to get back at your man. I think its time I took you home." He was so honorable, so thorough, and in that moment she knew that if it hadn't been for her fated romance with Carter, she probably would be Fly Boogie's girl.

"I would think that you would enjoy this," she said. "He fucked up. You're feeling me. Isn't this when most niggas make their move?"

"Lame niggas," Fly Boogie responded. Despite the fact that her body felt so good against him, he moved as he hit the unlock button on his keys. "Anything you do right now is out of character. This is all about him. I would be playing myself if I jumped on you. I can see the hurt in your eyes Miamor. I'm the last nigga you got to worry about taking advantage. I'ma get my shot at you ma, but this ain't it."

Miamor smiled, slightly embarrassed as she walked up to him once more. She kissed his cheek. "This kiss you earned." She blew out an exasperated breath and shook her head to try and gain some clarity. "I have to go home," she whispered. "I need to get my son and pack some things. I'm not beat for this Vegas shit. He wanted this life. I'm going back to Miami."

"Nah ma. I'll take you home but you pack up his shit. You built all of this out here. We all followed *you* out here. The Cartel of Miami belonged to Carter, but The Cartel of Las Vegas belongs to you. You got a gang of niggas that'll ride on your command," Fly said. He opened the passenger door for Miamor. He had given her something to think about and as she climbed inside the car, plots of revenge flooded her brain. Hurting the one who had hurt her sounded like poetic justice and she knew that the only way to get to Carter would be to take what he treasured most. She was going to hit his pockets, his empire, take his throne . . . she wanted it all . . . not because she needed it, but because he wanted it too much. He wasn't afraid of her gangster and she didn't know if she could ever hate him enough to handle him the 'murder mama' way.

She couldn't intimidate him with her reputation, but she could handle him like a wife scorned. She would divorce him and take everything, including the Cartel. He wouldn't be expecting her to play hardball and by the time he realized what was happening, it would already be done. She was going to take him to the cleaners and while she was at it, she would send Yasmine straight to hell.

Chapter 23

"I think I just started another war."
—Miamor

Three Months Later

"Dig deeper," Miamor stated coldly as she stood over the two burly men that were unearthing the desert soil. Their shovels clanged loudly against the earth as their grunts filled the air. "It can't be shallow. We don't want any mangy coyotes coming along and digging the body up." Miamor was livid and her heart pumped violently as her emotions went haywire. Her Cavalli sunglasses masked her watery eyes as she thought of the motivation behind her actions. She had murdered many times before. Fuck it. It was nothing for her to go boom on a nigga. She was in the business of extinction, but when business became personal it always played a tug of war with her mental.

Her judgment hadn't been this clouded since she had lost her sister at the hands of Mecca. She had promised herself that she would never let her emotions get so tangled again, but yet here she was . . . devastated . . . heartbroken . . . confused all over again. She should have been taking her aggression out on the root of the problem. Her man. Carter 'muthafuckin' Jones. He was the perpetrator to the crimes that had been committed against her heart. It was he who deserved to be buried in this shallow grave but instead it was his pretty little mistress who was in her crosshairs. Miamor saw red when the blacked out SUV pulled up a few yards away, because she knew who was hidden inside. They were in the middle of nowhere . . . Thirty miles into the Mojave on uncharted land. It was an unofficial graveyard. Many a mobster had held court in these deserted lands. There was no telling how many bones were buried beneath the hot sands. Miamor was about to host a funeral and the guest of honor was a Persian bitch named Yasmine.

The most dangerous thing in the world was a woman scorned, but a Miamor scorned was deadly. No one had seen the kind of damage that Miamor could do. She hadn't had to deal with groupies in Miami. Carter had always walked a straight line. Their love story had been so complicated that he hadn't found the time to entertain anyone but her. Even during her absence from his life he had remained true, but Yasmine . . . Yasmine had distracted him. She had seduced Miamor's man and there was a price to pay for that. *The bitch clearly doesn't know who she's fucking with,* Miamor thought, her temperature rising as she stalked across the desert. She was heated . . . not from the sun that blazed down on her, but from the hatred that burned in her heart. As an unsuspecting Yasmine climbed from the backseat of the car, Miamor approached.

"What the hell is the meaning of this?" Yasmine asked.

Miamor was feminine as ever in designer clothes and five-inch heels. She hadn't anticipated getting too dirty. She had men who followed orders at her discretion now. When she wanted someone to bleed, it never dripped on her shoes now. But this bitch Yasmine was a bit too pretty for her tastes. The smug, entitled, expression she wore irked Miamor to the point where she couldn't stop herself from slapping the taste out of her mouth. Before she could stop herself she struck her violently and muscled her to the ground. Miamor's vice grip on Yasmine's jet black hair caused the girl to scream in alarm as she tried to tear Miamor's hand from her scalp. Sweat started to form on Miamor's forehead as she spoke through gritted teeth. "There are plenty of men in Vegas. You should have chosen somebody else's," she said. She didn't even care about getting her hands dirty anymore. When her temper flared it took nothing less than murder to calm her down. She was on ten, it was too late to be rational now. She pulled Yasmine through the desert, destroying along the way, the all white dress that the girl wore.

"Agh!!" she screamed as she clawed at Miamor's wrist while kicking her legs violently as she tried to break free.

Miamor mustered strength that she didn't even know she had and she didn't stop until she had pulled her from the car to the hole that was now complete.

As soon as Yasmine laid eyes on the ditch, terror filled her. She turned to Miamor. "Do you know who I am? You can not get away with this!"

Miamor smirked as she shook her head incredulously. "I know exactly who you are. You're nobody. You live off of your daddy's name to get by. You think because you're a pampered little bitch from Saudi that you can do whatever you want, but you made one mistake. You didn't know who you were offending. You didn't check my resume. You see me in the casino in my fancy clothes, prancing around as Carter's arm accessory and you got me confused. You thought I was just a wife . . . just a mother perhaps? You didn't do your homework. Should have checked my resume."

"Please! You can have Carter . . ." the girl began to plead.

"Bitch I already have Carter. There ain't a woman alive that can take Carter away from me. I own that nigga. That's my dick, my houses, my cars, my everything."

"Okay, okay. I won't even look at him. I swear to you," Yasmine pleaded as she held her hands out in front of her. "Just let me go. This isn't necessary."

"You fucked my nigga. This is very necessary. I hope it was good," Miamor said. Suddenly she snatched one of the shovels from her bodyguard's hands and swung it full force, hitting Yasmine in the side of the face. She fell to the ground as blood poured from her ear. Miamor's rampage exploded as she hit her repeatedly, again and again and again and again. She showed no mercy as she took her frustrations out. Miamor knew that ultimately it was Carter's fault for sleeping with Yasmine. She wasn't married to Yasmine. Yasmine owed her nothing, but the fact that she was so smug about it had earned her this fate.

Miamor didn't care that she was literally beating the life out of the girl. Yasmine's efforts to block the blows were futile. There was no protecting herself from this ruthless assault and as the excruciating beating continued she could do nothing but pray. Miamor's chest heaved as she felt her clothes begin to stick to her skin. She held the shovel high above her head as she prepared to bring it down once more, but the sniffling, bloody, mess of a woman before her was no longer worth the effort. This beating wasn't making her feel any better. It didn't dull the pain that plagued her. She was still aching inside. The unbearable emotion haunted her, making it hard for her to breathe. Tears clouded her vision as she tossed the shovel to the ground. "Should have never crossed me," she said. She turned to her men. "Put the bitch in a box and bury her while she's still breathing. Leave a little air hole for her. I want it to be slow. Let her feel every single moment of what's left of her miserable life." Miamor left two of her men behind to clean up her mess as she headed back to the car with her driver. She had a meeting to attend. Yasmine was only the first to be punished. Carter would feel her wrath as well. As she climbed into the back of the car she knew that no matter what fate she delivered to him . . . she would always suffer behind his betrayal. Nothing she could do to him would ever make this right because even when she hated him . . . she loved him.

Carter was a man of little patience and as he checked the presidential that occupied his wrist he had to contain his anger. Tardiness was a sign of disrespect and Carter clenched his jaw as he folded his hands, placing them on the conference table in front of him. He was all business as he sat with a stern expression. The tailored Tom Ford suit he wore proved that he had graduated from the streets. He was no longer chasing hood fame; he was chasing them M's . . . the legal way. Owner of The Davinci, Las Vegas' newest resort and casino, he was a man with little free time. He had no hours in the day to waste. Miamor knew that. She had been by his side for so long that he already knew that her late arrival to their meeting was intentional. She was purposefully showing him that no matter how large he became, she would always run the show. He had given her the throne beside his. She was his queen and because of that he was on her time, like it or not. Carter leaned into the attorney that sat to his right. "We need to wrap this up."

Einstein looked across the table at the opposing counsel. "Mr. Levie, if your client doesn't show up in the next five minutes, we will have to reschedule this mediation session," he spoke. "Clearly she isn't taking this situation very seriously. Mr. Jones has asked her numerous times what she wants. We have yet to receive a response and today she doesn't even show up . . ."

Davison Levie drummed his fingers on the oak table as he leaned back in his chair with one hand placed underneath his chin. "She will be here . . ."

"I am here."

Miamor's voice caused all three men to turn their attention toward the door. Standing in a Carolina Herrera bodycon slip dress and five-inch heels, each of them were mesmerized by her beauty. Her hair fell in an asymmetrical bob around her face. Beautiful wasn't quite the right word to describe Miamor. She was dangerous, enticing, and alluring. Miamor was simply a bad bitch. The curves of her body were so sharp that they were deadly. Her face so pretty that it was deceptive. She was like a black widow. It was easy to get caught up in her web and very few escaped it. She took a seat beside her lawyer, sitting directly across from Carter. Her heart thundered in her chest. Seeing him made her blood boil, but oddly she loved him so much all at the same time. She could not believe that she was sitting across from him, when her place had been next to him for so long. Once lovers, they were now adversaries and it was still so hard for Miamor to believe. As she sat silently, soul bleeding, love dying, she wished that she could turn back the hands of time. Her eyes were cold, dark, and distant as she sat stiffly, trying to remain strong. There was no way she would give Carter the satisfaction of seeing her break, not over him, not over his infidelity and lies. She had thought he was so different. Carter had promised her a unique love, but in the end he had turned out to be just another nigga. He had broken her heart and now there was no turning back. They had survived many things, but his one mistake had brought their love to a screeching halt. Now they sat, at the divorce table, enemies as they each watched their love slip away.

"Glad you could make it," Carter said sarcastically.

Miamor nodded her head but didn't respond with words. She had nothing to say to him. She knew that if she opened her mouth to speak that nothing but tears and sobs would fall out. No, it was best if she remained composed and let her attorney do the speaking. She and Carter were beyond words at this point. She leaned into her lawyer and whispered, "Lay out my demands."

Levie cleared his throat. "Mrs. Jones wants everything. She wants to keep the fifty percent stake that they currently share in ownership of The Davinci Resort and Casino, she wants the house in Summerlin, and she wants the $10,000,000 that is in the joint savings. According to our records, Mr. Jones has another savings account that he opened last year. In that account is $50,000,000 that he had hidden from Mrs. Jones. She wants that as well. She wants to keep all vehicles that are currently parked at the home in Summerlin. She also wants all stocks and bonds that they have purchased since being married. The estate in Miami, he can have and the home in Flint, MI she has no interest in."

Carter scoffed as if he had just heard a joke.

"This should not be amusing Mr. Jones. Mrs. Jones is very serious about her demands. Considering that there was no prenuptial agreement . . ."

"She's not getting my casino," Carter interrupted coolly, with a calm but serious tone.

"That is my casino," Miamor said. "While your ass was hiding out from a Fed case in Saudi, I was here with Breeze, with Leena, establishing The Davinci."

Carter stood to his feet and Einstein followed his cue. "Let us know when you have a serious offer. Mr. Jones is willing to offer a generous settlement. He has no intention of putting Mrs. Jones out in the streets. He wants to ensure that she is comfortable. But these demands are ludicrous. No judge will grant them," Einstein stated.

"A judge won't have to," Miamor replied. "I've got more than enough dirt on you Carter. It's in your best interest to give me what I want."

"You're being ridiculous," Carter stated. He could see the hurt in her eyes. No matter how hard of a front Miamor put on, Carter knew her. He could feel the disappointment and resentment radiating from her heart. He turned to Einstein. "Take Levie and step out of the room."

Levie objected. "I don't advise my client to speak with you without me."

Carter's eyes turned dark as he turned his attention to Miamor's attorney. "Leave the room," he demanded, his shoulders squared in authority as his baritone banished both men from the room.

He turned toward Miamor when they were alone. It was the first time he had seen her in weeks. She had accepted no phone calls from him and hadn't been home since she had found him cheating. Carter had no idea where she was even staying. "Can we talk?" he asked.

"No," she replied, stubbornly.

"It's not what it looks like. If you let me explain . . ." Carter started.

"I caught a bitch half naked in your bed, it's exactly what it looks like. There's nothing more to say," Miamor spat. Her words were so sharp that they cut Carter to the core. He could hear the contempt lacing her words. She was scorned, dejected, and scarred by all of the promises that he had broken. So many apologies sat on the edge of his tongue, waiting to leap out of his mouth, but he held them back. She was too full of anger to hear anything that he had to say at the moment.

"I want it all," she continued. "Every dollar, every business, every asset."

"You're pushing me Miamor," Carter warned. "I'm trying to be patient with you because I know that I hurt you, but don't take that as weakness ma. You out of everybody know what it is. You know exactly what I'm capable of."

Miamor cut her eyes low in disgust. "Yes I do know Carter, but clearly you have forgotten what I'm capable of. You'll soon find out. There is a price to pay for breaking my heart. I'm going to ruin you nigga."

Miamor stormed out of the conference room, bypassing both Levie and Einstein as she made her exit. Heat pulsed through her as she made her way to her chauffeured vehicle. She was so full of emotion that it felt like she would combust. The history that she shared with Carter made it so hard to let him go. She had made him her everything and now that he had let her down, she was left with nothing but resentment. She looked at the world through bitter eyes as she slid into the plush interior of the Cadillac truck. The driver closed the door and Miamor leaned her elbow against the windowsill. Rest. Contentment. Peace of mind. She wondered if she would ever feel those things again. Turmoil had taken over her world and a sick knot was always present in her gut. She was sick from grief as she mourned the loss of the greatest love she had ever known. She let her head fall to the side as her chin rested against her balled fist. Tears came to her eyes. *How did I let another woman sneak into his bed?* she pondered, miserably. She tried to think of where she had gone wrong. What had she done to deserve the disloyalty that Carter had shown her? She hadn't even seen the signs or had she seen them and just ignored them? She had trusted Carter and he had burned her. Miamor was lost. She was once a woman

who needed no one until Carter had changed
that. He had convinced her to trust him, had
gotten her dependent on his affection. Now
that they were at odds all she felt was pain. Her
pain made her want to cause pain and she had
her cross hairs focused on the man whom had
wronged her. Killing his little jump off wasn't
enough. Miamor wanted Carter to pay for making her feel like just another lovesick girl. Taking
his empire was the only way to make him feel as
small as she did right now. Despite her hate for
Carter, she couldn't bury her love. It had been
too strong. It would take years for her to get over
Carter Jones. He was undoubtedly the great love
of her life. Miamor knew that the type of bond
that they had shared would never exist again. As
her mind drifted down memory lane she looked
for someone, something to blame.

She couldn't blame anyone but herself. She
had gotten lost in love and had trusted too much.
Miamor had broken her number one rule. She
had let her guards down.

"Where to boss?" the goon asked.

Before Miamor could respond a tap on her
window caused her to look up. Carter stood,
calmly with one hand tucked in his designer
slacks, impatiently waiting for her to roll down
her window. She did and for the first time she
allowed him to witness her tears.

The anger was peeled away like the layers of an onion and she reeked of hurt. Her story of heartbreak was written in her eyes.

"Mia," he whispered.

"You ruined me Carter," she sniffled. He opened the car door and leaned into her.

"I don't know what I was thinking ma, and I'll tell you I'm sorry everyday for the rest of my life if I have to. Just come back home Miamor. I don't want this. This ain't us. We've gotten through worse right?" he said, trying to get her to remember their history of overcoming the odds against them. He wasn't pleading. Carter wasn't the begging type but he could feel her slipping away. The way she looked at him . . . the glow in her eye that was strictly reserved for him was fading. He was losing her. Or had he lost her already? He didn't know, but he couldn't see himself letting his pride get in the way of saving his marriage. Miamor was the very best part of him.

"We got through worse because at the end of the day I knew you were mine. It was me and you against the fucked up world. I don't know that anymore. You broke your vow Carter and you pulled the switch that shut everything off for me. I'm not this girl. I should have never been this girl. Stupid in love over a nigga that will never give back the amount of loyalty I give to you. All you do is take Carter. Now I'm taking from you. Apparently I've been too nice. I've got to murder a bitch to make you remember who I am?" she asked.

Carter's face fell. "What are you talking about Miamor? What did you do?" he asked. The evil smirk on her face answered his question. "Where is Yasmine ma?" She slapped him swiftly.

"She's not dead yet," Miamor said with a condescending laugh. "A bullet to the head would have been too kind. I've been hurting for months behind the bullshit that you two pulled so I thought a slow death would be more appropriate."

"Where is she?" Carter asked.

"Don't ask me about your whore. Nigga if you wanted her alive you shouldn't have fucked her. You already knew what my reaction would be. Should have controlled your actions. Her death is on you," Miamor sneered.

"Miamor this isn't one of your Miami hits. You can't . . ."

"You want your whore alive . . . you take your ass out to the desert and dig her up," Miamor said passive aggressively as she thumbed through her phone, blatantly giving Carter no kick it. "I'm sure she's not out of air yet . . . better hurry though."

Carter grit his teeth, feeling as if he could snap Miamor's neck. "Do you know what you've done? Tell me you didn't bury that girl alive?" Miamor shot him a look that showed just how cunningly cruel she was. Carter hit the top of the car in frustration. "Do you know who the fuck her father is going to send our way when he finds out?" Carter exhaled sharply as a weight settled over his shoulder. "I'm talking terrorists Miamor. Fucking assassins. You just signed your death certificate. We have a son! You killed that man's daughter you think he won't take our son," Carter was so livid that he spit as he chastised her. "You should have checked that jealousy at the door and brought your hot headed ass home. You not ready for the type of consequences that Baraka is going to deliver." His tirade only pissed her off more and she pushed him back so that she could shut her door.

"You should have thought about that before you fucked the bitch," Miamor spat. She then stubbornly turned her head as the car rolled away. She couldn't stop herself from looking back at him but when she did, the red dot that illuminated in the center of his chest caused her mouth to drop in horror. Someone had a beam on him and regretfully she knew what was to follow. It all happened in a split second, their eyes met but before she could warn him . . .

BOOM!

"No!!!!!!!!"

The gunshot was so loud that it pierced her ears, causing a slight ring and interrupting the stillness of the day, mixing with the screams that erupted from her soul. Her driver hit the breaks in reaction to the blast. Miamor hopped out of the car and instinct caused her to run full speed to Carter's side. "Oh my God! Somebody help me!" her shrill cries were desperate . . . fear filled. Her love was leaking out of her, betraying her in this moment. She couldn't help but care. She hated him, but the line between love and hate was so vague that she loved him all the same. It was a double-edged sword and as she pressed her hands against his bleeding chest, adding pressure to his wound she wailed. Tears clouded her vision as they ran down her nose and dropped onto Carter's face.

He gripped her wrists as he gasped. "I'm . . . Mia . . . " Tears of excruciation filled his reddened eyes.

"Help me!!!" she screamed. She felt hands pulling her off of him as she struggled to stay near him. "No!! No! I have to be with him! Get the fuck off of me! I need to be with him!" Sirens were heard in the distance and curious bystanders filtered out of the casino. She heard Zyir and Monroe fighting their way through the crowd.

Carter motioned for Zyir as he opened his mouth, attempting to speak. Zyir kneeled by his man. "Don't talk bro, just hold on," Zyir coached. Carter was persistent however and used the little strength he had to pull Zyir.

"Leave . . . town . . . go back . . ." he grimaced as he grit his teeth as blood filled his mouth. "home. Live . . . through . . . this."

Zyir nodded, but Carter seemed to be talking in circles. Live through what? Hadn't they already survived the worst. Carter was speaking as if he knew that today was his day of reckoning; as if this was only the beginning. "Where's the fucking ambulance?!!!" Zyir screamed, fearing the worst.

Pure horror crossed their faces as Monroe sprang to action. "We not waiting on the fucking ambulance. Help me get him in the car!"

Leena rushed out and hurried to Miamor's side, but Breeze paused as she looked at Miamor in doubt. "Did you do this?"

Miamor squinted her eyes in confusion and shook her head in denial. *How could she ask me this? Why would she . . .* "Did you shoot him?!"

The question came out like an accusation, smacking her in the face and suddenly all eyes were on her. Leena placed her hands over her mouth in shock as everyone waited for her to answer. Miamor had no response. She was stunned into silence as she shook uncontrollably. *Did Baraka do this? How did word get back to him so fast?* Miamor had known that there would be repercussions for killing Yasmine. Her rage had prevented her from caring, but now that she was covered in Carter's blood, fear seized her. Zyir helped her from the ground. He didn't know what had gone down, but Miamor was Carter's wife . . . his everything. He knew Carter well and if today was his day to die, Miamor's face would be the last one he would want to see. "Let's go. Figure this shit out later. Carter needs you."

Miamor stood shakily to her feet as she was escorted to his car. She looked up at him with terrified eyes. "Zyir, I fucked up," she whispered with tears in her eyes. "I think I just started another war."

"What did you do?" he asked.

"I killed Yasmine," she replied.

Zyir's eyes widened at the revelation and his jaw clenched as he grit his teeth. He put the car in drive and sped away. Now he knew why Carter had told him to shake town and he knew that his days in Las Vegas were numbered. As soon as he got the chance he and Breeze would kiss sin city good-bye and start their lives over somewhere else. Zyir didn't know how to clean up this mess but he was sure of one thing. There was a storm coming and he didn't know if The Cartel could weather another disaster.

Fly Boogie quickly dismantled the M-24 sniper rifle with speed and placed it in a large duffel. Not wanting to draw attention to himself he strolled casually to his Range, tossing the duffel in the backseat before getting in and driving away.

Fuck that nigga, Fly Boogie thought. *She better off without him anyway.* Fly Boogie had just risked it all for Miamor and she didn't even know it. Carter had crossed her and broken her heart but that wasn't enough. Fly Boogie knew that a man like Carter never lost. Miamor loved him too much and as long as he was breathing she would have taken him back. Fly wasn't standing for it. He wanted to throw his hat in the ring and in order to do that he had to get rid of the competition. He only wished he had a better shot. His nerves had caused him to aim low. One to the head would have put a tag on Carter's toe for sure. Now he would have to wait and see how Carter fared before making his move. Malice hadn't been his intention when he first followed the Cartel. In fact, he had nothing but respect

for Carter but five years of being next to Miamor
had him fiending to make it forever. She would
never admit her feelings for him as long as Carter was breathing. All was fair in love and war.
When it came to Miamor he would do whatever
to ensure that he won her heart . . . if it meant
going against the grain and biting the hand that
fed him . . . than so be it.

Chapter 24

"Today just might be the day I die."
—Carter Jones

One Week Later

Beep! Beep! Beep!

The steady pace of the heart monitor was the only cryptic sound that filled the room. Monroe sat silently, head bowed, forehead resting on his steepled fingers as he prayed for a miracle. Gangsters weren't at the top of the blessings list. The life style they led made them undeserving of one, but Monroe prayed all the same. Shit was in disarray. Everyone was on edge. Miamor had sparked a flame that was about to burn their entire empire down. Monroe had goons at Carter's door 24 hours a day. Even when visiting hours ended, a skilled gun waited in the lobby for the clock to spin until they began again. Carter was too vulnerable to go unprotected. With a bullet to the chest, he was lucky to even be alive. He hadn't opened his eyes yet, but after days of being on a ventilator he was finally breathing on his own. That was one step in the right direction. The grim reaper was at Carter's door and there was nothing that anyone could do to save him. Carter had to fight it. "Just open your eyes bro," Monroe stated.

The weight of the world seemed to fall on Monroe's shoulders. Carter's wishes were to send Zyir away and although Zyir had fought it, Monroe sent him away. Baraka had been silent but Monroe knew that enemies unseen were the worst kind. He needed Breeze safe. He didn't want her in the middle of another war and although they needed the manpower, Zyir had to leave. Zyir was the only person on Earth that Monroe was sure loved Breeze fully. Zyir would die before he let anything happen to Breeze. It had been imperative that they leave. Monroe had wanted to lead the Cartel for so long. He had wanted to fill his father's shoes, to be the boss . . . but now that Carter's life hung in the balance it no longer mattered. They were blood brothers; the only two men left to carry on their father's legacy. There was a time when their bond hadn't been so strong but now they were each other's keeper. If Carter's death is what it took for Monroe to step into his father's shoes, than he no longer wanted to. It was family over everything, including ambition. Monroe's phone rang and he knew exactly who it was before he answered.

Miamor. She had been calling on the hour for a week to see if Carter had awakened. She too had been sent away. Monroe had sent her to Aries' place in Idaho. No one, including Baraka would look for her there. The last thing he needed was for her to die on his watch. Until Carter awakened Miamor would remain in hiding. No matter how gangster she thought she was, Monroe could see the fear in her eyes. She had crossed a dangerous line, and until Carter woke up, it was Monroe's job to keep her safe.

"Money, how is he?" she asked without saying hello.

"He's the same. Not good, not bad. There is no change in his status," Monroe informed.

"I need to see him," she whispered. He could hear her strife in her tone. "I need to see my son. Maybe if I just come . . . if he knows I'm there . . ."

"It's not safe Miamor. Everyone is ducked off somewhere. C.J. is safe with Leena and my son. She will keep them safe. They have protection. Baraka is going to come for you and when he does, C.J. can't be anywhere near you."

"I know . . . I know," Miamor whispered with regret. "I was upset with Carter, but I didn't do this Money. I never meant for any of this to happen. I was so mad. I wasn't thinking straight."

"I know Miamor. Look, I'll keep you posted. I've got to go. Try to rest and don't get restless. Just stay put," he instructed.

"Hmm."

The sound of Carter's groggy moans were music to Monroe's ears. He looked left to see his brother opening his eyes, slowly as if his lids were weighted down. Monroe raced to the bedside. "Wake up bro. Come back to this side my G," Monroe coerced as he leaned over him, anxiously. Carter woke up, struggling, fear filled as he attempted to rise. "Nah man, you can't Carter. You got to relax. You've been shot."

Carter laid back, exhausted, weak, and in extreme pain. Monroe rushed out into the hall and grabbed the first doctor that he saw. "He's awake. He's finally awake," he said.

The woman rushed in behind Monroe and immediately went to Carter's aid. "Welcome back Mr. Jones," she said, speaking calmly.

"What happened?" he asked.

"You were shot, a bullet pierced your lung and you lost a lot of blood. I would say that you're lucky, but you had a pretty skilled surgeon on your side," the doctor said with a wink. She had skin the color of coffee beans and her hair was cut short. With majestically dark eyes and a smile as white as pearls, Carter felt like he was staring into the eyes of an angel. She was beautiful, not only because she had saved him, but because she was uniquely crafted. God broke the mold when he made her.

"I believe you," he replied in a low tone. "Can you work that same magic and take some of this pain away?"

He grimaced as he spoke and the way he slurred his words made it obvious that he still wasn't clear headed.

"We had you on a mild sedative to allow your body to heal without much effort. I'll run something stronger through the I.V. and be back to check on you in a few hours. The most important thing for you to do is to rest up. You have a good team of doctors. We'll make sure that you make a full recovery," she assured.

Monroe spoke. "That won't be necessary. I'll need his discharge papers immediately. He will heal at home. I'll hire the best doctors . . . you if I have to."

The woman shook her head and frowned in confusion. "I can not issue discharge papers for him. He is in the best care here. Anything could happen. He is in ICU. Once his healing progresses that may be an option but for now, he's not going anywhere," she responded.

Monroe nodded and waited until she left the room before turning to Carter. "I've got the entire floor guarded. There are two at the door and one in the lobby. Nobody's getting to you bro. You're safe. Zyir and Breeze are back in Flint. Leena and the kids are safe . . ."

"Miamor?" Carter asked.

"She's safe. Off the grid. Baraka will never find her as long as she stays put," Monroe said. "She's hard headed than a mu'fucka though bro. You've got your hands full with that one."

Carter couldn't help but give a lazy chuckle. He grimaced as the laughter sent pain quaking through his entire body. "Tell me about it," he replied.

Monroe picked up his cell. "I'll call her. She'll be glad to hear you're awake," Monroe said. He attempted to dial, then frowned when the call failed. "No service," he said. He went to the land-line and picked up the hospital phone. "Damn this mu'fucka dead too." A knock at the door interrupted them as Fly Boogie slowly entered.

"Come in li'l nigga, you look like you've seen a ghost," Monroe stated.

Carter spoke up. "Go make that call G. Tell her to stay put and that I love her. Fly can hold it down until you get back, plus there are two on the door. I'm good."

Fly Boogie eased into the room as Monroe made his exit.

"Glad to see you're up big homie," Fly Boogie stated as he stood at the foot of the bed, staring down at Carter. His heart beat rapidly. He felt see through, as if Carter could sense the snake in him. He knew better however. He had been careful. He had covered his tracks. No one, not even Miamor knew that he was the trigger man behind the gun. His only regret was that he had been unable to get a head shot. One between the eyes would have ensured Miamor's widow status and given Fly Boogie nothing but opportunity to move in on her. He would become her shoulder to cry on and once her mourning was over, he would eventually become her man. He wanted to be Carter. He wanted to stand in his shoes. Little did he know, they were too big to fill.

"Glad to be seen my G," Carter responded. "I want to talk to you."

"About what?" Fly asked, nervously.

"Have a seat next to me. I just woke up. I'm weak. Even speaking too loudly hurts," Carter stated.

Fly Boogie slowly walked to the chair next to the bed and sat.

"Zyir is taking a little vacation and shit is about to get real. I'ma need someone to take his spot . . . someone I can trust. Monroe and I can't hold shit down by ourselves. While we were away you held my family down. You were loyal to Miamor and to the Cartel. I want to pull you closer, put some money in your pocket, show you the game."

"I'm good. I'm eating," Fly Boogie stated.

Carter smirked. "That's mediocre money. You're hood rich. You're on the distribution side of the game Fly. I'm talking corporate. Private jets, hundreds of kilos, all that. We ain't on no corner shit. I'm asking you to stand beside me, not behind me," Carter explained. "But there's a war to get through first. Lines have been crossed and if we're going to come out on top I need killers around me; loyal niggas that I can trust. Can I trust you li'l homie?"

Monroe stepped out of the elevator and walked across the marble hospital floor, his red bottom designer shoes hitting hard against the tile. "Fuck is up with the service in this bitch?" he mumbled to himself as he tried to get his phone to work. He stopped over at the reception desk. "Is there a phone I can use?" he asked.

The nurse shook her head and replied, "The phone lines are down in the entire hospital."

He nodded and turned away, "Of course they are," he mumbled sarcastically. "How hard is it to find a working phone?" It was important for him to get the word out that Carter was now awake. It would keep Miamor in place and stop her from doing anything drastic. He stepped outside the hospital doors and held his phone up trying to catch reception. When his eyes caught sight of the red beam that was traveling through the air and aimed at his chest he panicked. "Oh shit!" he said as he backpedaled, rushing back inside the glass doors of the hospital. He looked outside and his eyes widened in shock. Five SUV's sat in front of the entrance. The windows were blacked out, but when one of them rolled down he recognized them instantly. They were Arab. Baraka's men and they had the entire entrance covered. "Fuck!" he uttered. He rushed to the back entrance and opened the door slightly to find that another Caravan of trucks waited there as well. They were surrounded and although he was strapped, and he had guards at Carter's door, they were outnumbered. He rushed back to Carter's room. They had to get out of there one way or another.

"Can I trust you?" Carter asked again.

"Of course, yeah fam, I got you," Fly Boogie replied. Carter held up his hand and Fly Boogie gave him a gangster's shake, but when Carter looked at his wrist he frowned. Carter tightened his grip, using all of his strength as he pulled Fly Boogie near in hostility. "The fuck is this?"

Fly Boogie's eyes went to the tattoo that adorned his wrist. MIAMOR. It read. He had completely forgotten that it was visible. He snatched his arm back, shaking loose from Carter's vice grip as he stuttered. "That's . . . nothing . . . big . . ."

Before he could get the explanation out of his mouth Monroe rushed in. "We've got a problem.

The whole fucking hospital is surrounded by
Baraka's men. They got this bitch locked down.
I stepped one foot outside and almost got my
fucking head blown off. Fly you strapped?"

Grateful for the interruption, Fly Boogie
averted Carter's deadly stare and lifted his shirt
exposing his pistol. "Always my nigga," he replied.

Carter saw red. He wanted to body Fly Boogie, but he kept his cool and placed the issue at
the back of his mind. Right now they had bigger
fish to fry. "We've got to get you out of here,"
Monroe said, directing his attention to Carter.
"I couldn't get word to Miamor. My phone ain't
working, neither are the hospital lines. Hand me
your phone," he said to Fly Boogie. Fly immediately tensed because if Monroe went through
his phone he would find dirt on him. Fly Boogie
had all types of pictures of Miamor in his phone.
Pictures that he had taken of her when nobody
was even paying attention. Her number was also
in his call log too frequently but if he refused he
would arouse further suspicion. He could feel
Carter eyeing him. The spotlight was on him,
he pulled out his phone and looked at it, quickly
switching his screen saver from Miamor's face
to default. He erased her contact information
as well. "The fuck? Li'l nigga hurry up," Monroe
said impatiently. Fly passed it to Monroe, appre-

hensively. Monroe slid the bar across the screen but before he could even dial one number he saw that the bars were low. "Your signal is blocked too."

"Its Baraka," Carter informed matter of factly. "Every phone in this building is probably useless. That's the oldest trick in the book."

"I'll go out and see if I can find a working line," Fly Boogie stated. Just as he was about to slide out of the room Carter stopped him.

"We gone finish that conversation," he stated, his bark fierce . . . territorial.

Fly Boogie didn't respond, but his eyes widened in reaction. He slipped out of the room and Monroe turned to Carter.

"We're sitting ducks in this bitch," Monroe stated.

"One way or another Baraka is coming through them doors. Miamor put Yasmine in the dirt. I love her bro. She's my rib. She sinned. Somebody has to pay for that. It won't be her though. It won't be my son. It doesn't have to be you either Money. You should have left with Zyir. This is my debt. I'll pay it on behalf of Miamor. Get out of here Money. Today just might be the day I die."

Monroe pulled up a chair and sat beside his brother's bed. He pulled the gun from his waist and put it in his lap and then pulled the gun from his ankle and passed it to Carter. "We're brothers. We live through this together or we go out in a blaze of glory together. Either way I ain't running."

He held out his hand and Carter gripped it while grimacing. "That's real shit. I love you bro," Carter said.

"I love you too man." Monroe replied.

Silence filled the room as they waited for the storm that was waiting outside the hospital doors. There was no resolution. Death was about to rain down upon them and all they could do was embrace it.

"I don't even know why we're here Mia. Monroe told you to stay hidden. The Arabs are serious. Dis isn't a hood war. Dis shit is international. Dey will . . ."

Miamor cut Aries off. "I don't care Aries! We've gone up against plenty of mu'fuckas. Baraka and his turbans don't scare me. Not enough to stay away from Carter. He's shot. He needs me," she argued as Aries pulled into the parking lot of the hospital.

As soon as she pulled up she noticed the caravan posted at the entrance. She ducked down in her seat. As they drove by she watched a security guard approach one of the tinted vehicles. The window of one of the SUV's rolled down slightly

and Miamor watched in horror as a silenced bullet slumped the security guard. Two men climbed out of the back seat and picked up the body, stuffing it into the back of the truck without anyone even noticing. Miamor and Aries' were the only witnesses.

"Its him, Baraka's here," Miamor whispered.

"I won't die for Carter, Miamor. I have a child, you have a child," Aries replied.

"Than let's make sure we live to see another day," Miamor replied sadly. Aries drove past the parking lot and back onto the street as their taillights disappeared into the night. Miamor couldn't go up against a force so deadly without a plan. She would have to think first if she wanted to survive. She only prayed that Baraka didn't get to Carter in the meantime. As much as she wanted to be by his side there would be no getting to his room tonight. Baraka knew her face and the army of Arabs waiting beyond the hospital doors were too dangerous to fight off alone. Anyone going up against them, would lose. *What the hell have I done?* She thought.

Fly Boogie rushed into his apartment in a frenzy but halted as soon as he smelled the pungent aroma of weed wafting from his living

room. He came off his hip with his pistol and silently followed the path where the smoke was leading him.

"Put that shit down li'l nigga before I lay you out in this mu'fucka."

Murder sat comfortably in Fly Boogie's Lay-Z-Boy chair while smoking a blunt with one hand and holding a pistol in Fly's direction with the other. "You're a hard one to keep up with Fly. I hired you five years ago to get in with the Cartel. Paid you good money too my nigga. Twenty grand. To infiltrate and murk that nigga Carter. Imagine my surprise when I found out you skipped town. You just disappeared out of Miami. In fact, the entire fucking Cartel disappeared from Miami and came here. Only reason I even knew where to find you is because the news reported Carter Jones' shooting outside a popular Vegas casino."

"It ain't like that Murder. I was just putting in work. It took time to get close. I was going to reach out. I finally hit the nigga Carter but he didn't die. The nigga down bad though. He in ICU and everything. I slipped in to finish the job tonight but some shit popped off. I had to sneak out that bitch in hospital scrubs like I'm a nurse or some shit. Money was there and . . ."

"You keep insulting my intelligence and I'ma pop your melon," Murder said, silencing Fly Boo-

gie. Fly Boogie thought about shooting first but Murder read his mind. "By the time you get your aim right I'll have one off already. I'm the better shot, believe that young."

It was true, Murder had hired Fly. Just like Fly Boogie, Murder had a thing for Miamor. They both had a common goal to get Carter out of the way. At first, Fly Boogie was all about business. He had worked his way in. Miamor trusted him. Carter trusted him. Zyir had vouched for him. Monroe never doubted him. By the time he got down fully with the Cartel he was making way more than the measly twenty grand that Murder had paid. So he moved west and said fuck Murder's hit, but by the time Carter got out of jail Fly Boogie had become completely smitten with Miamor. He wanted her for himself and he was determined to knock Carter off so that he could get close to her. Murder's reemergence was another problem he would have to solve. Now not only was Carter in the way, so was Murder.

"I can still finish the job," Fly Boogie said.

"Thing is why? Why would you shoot Carter five years later?" Murder asked rhetorically. He snapped his fingers as if a bright idea had just hit him. "Unless you're in it for self. I recognize that look in your eye homeboy. That's a murder mama spell li'l nigga. You fell in love with my bitch, that's why you cut me out. Once Carter was dead you was going to move in on her yourself."

"Nah, it ain't like that," Fly Boogie lied.

"It's exactly like that," Murder answered. He hit his blunt and chuckled as the smoke blew from his lips. "That's a baaad bitch. She does something to a nigga," he said. "She almost killed me and I'm still running back to that pussy. She's like a drug."

"Now what? You gone kill me?" Fly Boogie asked. "Might as well quit playing games and get this shit over with." He was fearless. He had heart. Despite the treachery, Murder still liked him.

"Nah, you gon' finish what you started. Murder Carter. Then I'ma get my bitch back you gon' shake this school boy crush you got going and we gon' take over The Cartel and the casino," Murder said. "From what I understand it all belongs to Miamor now anyway. It's her kingdom now and once I get her from under the nigga Carter she will come back to daddy. I'm her beginning. I taught her everything she knows. I'm home. A bitch always comes back home . . ."

To be continued . . .